PRAISE FOR

"Chiavaroli delights with this homage to Louisa May Alcott's *Little Women*, featuring a time-slip narrative of two women connected across centuries."

PUBLISHERS WEEKLY on *The Orchard House*

"Beautifully written, this God honoring and compelling story is Heidi Chiavaroli's best yet."

CATHY GOHLKE, Bestselling, Christy Hall of Fame and Carol Award-winning author on *Hope Beyond the Waves*

"*Hope Beyond the Waves* tugged at my heart from page one, and I was totally immersed in the seemingly insurmountable challenges of both the past and present day characters. Kudos to Heidi Chiavaroli for pouring out this beautifully raw and moving story about finding love and hope in the most unexpected of places."

MELANIE DOBSON, Carol Award-winning author of *Catching the Wind*

"*The Hidden Side* is a beautiful tale that captures the timeless struggles of the human heart."

JULIE CANTRELL, *New York Times* Bestselling author of *Perennials*

"First novelist Chiavaroli's historical tapestry will provide a satisfying summer read for fans of Kristy Cambron and Lisa Wingate."

LIBRARY JOURNAL on *Freedom's Ring*

"*The Edge of Mercy* is most definitely one for the keeper shelf. "

LINDSAY HARREL, author of *The Secrets of Paper and Ink*

To Elizabeth,

WHERE FAITH BELONGS

HEIDI CHIAVAROLI

With Hope,

Heidi Chiavaroli

Visit Heidi Chiavaroli at heidichiavaroli.com

Hope Creek Publishers LLC

Cover Design by Carpe Librum Book Design

Edited by Melissa Jagears

Scripture quotations are taken from the New International Version.

Where Faith Belongs is a work of fiction. Where real people, events, establishments, organizations, or locales appear, they are used fictitiously. All other elements of the novel are drawn from the author's imagination.

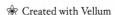 Created with Vellum

ALSO BY HEIDI CHIAVAROLI

The Orchard House

The Tea Chest

The Hidden Side

Freedom's Ring

The Edge of Mercy

Hope Beyond the Waves

The Orchard House Bed and Breakfast Series

Where Grace Appears

Where Hope Begins

Where Love Grows

Where Memories Await

Where Dreams Reside

Where Faith Belongs

Where Promises Remain (Spring, 2023)

To Aunt Dianne,
Thank you for your never-ending encouragement!

Despite what my family says, I am, in fact, an understanding person.

Yes, I have opinions. But I like to think that simply means I have good taste.

That's it. That's what I am. A person with good taste.

A person who tries to understand why my older sister insists on wearing open-toed shoes without first polishing her toenails. A person who tries to understand how anyone could watch *The Notebook* without bawling their eyes out. How my brother can sleep at night knowing he didn't floss that day. How *anyone* could dismiss yoga without even trying it.

All these things and more, I try to understand.

But I will never—ever—understand what I've just seen on this crisp, sunny first day of May. I grappled with it. I abhorred it.

I am *appalled* by it.

I blinked, staring out the window of my old Jeep Wrangler. Surely, this would not take place in Camden, in broad daylight, in the Hannaford parking lot.

But no, I wasn't mistaken—the evidence lay on the ground in all of its coffee-stained, Styrofoam glory.

The driver of the black Ford truck, parked haphazardly between two yellow lines, had committed an inexcusable offense, punishable by at least a five-hundred dollar fine.

Littering.

And this wasn't any kind of littering. This was so much more than casual, throw-your-paper-napkin-out-your-window-in-the-dead-of-night littering. This was blatant, daylight *Styrofoam* littering.

I pushed open my car door, nearly forgetting my keys in the ignition. No doubt he thought no one noticed his blatant disregard of nature and civilization. Little did he know, Amie Martin was on the prowl. Amie Martin—short in stature, perhaps having a bit of a bad hair day, but powerful in all things that involved the betterment of humanity.

I threw my shoulders back, the beaded earrings I'd made the night before jangling lightly in my ears. I pushed up the sleeves of my army-green jacket and strode across the parking lot to the black truck.

"Excuse me!" I called as I approached.

Nothing.

I continued toward him.

Don't pretend you can't hear me with your window fully down.

By the time I reached the driver's side of the truck, I fumed. Men. Men, and their callousness toward people and relationships and innocent animals and the environment.

"I said, excuse me!"

A head of dark blond hair turned toward me.

My steps faltered and my mouth grew dry, the fury in my chest changing to shock and, to my horror, a tiny bit of longing.

August Colton grinned at me with twinkling cerulean blue eyes. "Amie."

My name hung in the air between us as his gaze tangled with mine. I waited for something more. A "You look good," or "It's been too long," or "I missed seeing you at Christmas."

All the things I wanted to say to him.

I shook my head, scolding myself for faltering in my mission. Surfer-boy good looks tended to do that to me.

He shoved a box of chicken wings toward me. "Want one?"

I gritted my teeth. "I'm fasting."

His eyebrows rose. "Oh, is that part of your new . . . spiritual explorations?"

I blew out a breath, fanning the hair from my face. "No, it's not part of my *spiritual* explorations." I didn't mean for the words to come out so snappy. It wasn't August's fault my idea to create a group for those seeking spiritual truth had flopped. Sure, I could have given it more effort last summer. Could have been less *flighty* about it, as Bronson said. But a little support from August wouldn't have killed him.

Who knows, maybe it would have made all the difference.

"Whoa, sorry. So, is everything okay? Are you having a medical procedure done or something?"

A medical procedure? Oh. My face heated as I remembered Mom having to fast and drink some horrible-tasting fluid before having a colonoscopy last year. "I'm fine. Great, really." Great. "Fasting periodically is actually a great way to increase autophagy in your cells."

Autophagy . . . that was the word, right? Or was it autophony? I was forever mixing up words.

"Autophagy?"

"It's your body's way of cleaning out damaged cells to regenerate healthy ones. It's fascinating. You should google it."

"I will."

No, he wouldn't. Since when did he care about anything I thought important?

"You want to sit in my truck?"

It was a pretty truck. Several steps up from the beat-up Chevy he'd driven around in high school.

But no. I hadn't stalked over to play nice.

"You littered."

"What?"

I pointed at the Styrofoam cup, clear as day, on the patch of grass by the curb of his truck. "I saw you. You threw it right out the window without any regard for the birds who might chew it up and choke on it or the people who have to pick it up for you—"

"Amie—"

"You always were selfish though, weren't you, August? Never giving a care about what's humane and right. Sauntering through life, worried about your hair and your stupid surfboard and—"

"Amie." My name came out in a near growl, his jaw firm and eyes smoldering as he said it. Without warning, I remembered those smoldering eyes fixed upon me in an entirely different way. I remembered the feel of his hands brushing along my sides, the scent of him all musky and sweet, the taste of his lips on my own.

I blinked, forcing the unbidden—and unwanted—thoughts away. "What?"

"I didn't litter."

I jabbed both hands at the coffee cup on the ground. "Oh, really? What would you call this, then?"

"My worst fear."

I cocked my head to the side, my head spinning. August's worst fear. Shouldn't I know what that is?

"An *empty* coffee cup?" I guessed.

"Come on, Ame, we dated for six months and you don't remember my worst fear?"

I swallowed. Maybe August hadn't been the only one less than invested in our relationship.

I shook my head. "I got nothing."

"Spiders."

My insides twitched. I wasn't much a fan of the eight-legged creatures myself. I crouched down, cautiously, peering into the cup. Inside, perched at the very bottom, was a hairy black-and-yellow spider with a body the size of a quarter.

I shot up. "Ew!"

"If he didn't crawl out by the time I finished my lunch, I was going to dump him out. Figured it would be the most"—he cleared his throat—"humane thing to do."

My chest deflated. "You weren't littering?"

What did it say about me that I almost wished he had been littering simply so I didn't look so foolish?

"Nope. After I escorted our hairy friend onto bigger and better things than the inside of an old coffee cup, I was going to pick up my trash and be on my way."

I blew out a gust of air, fanning my long blonde bangs out of my face. "Guess I owe you an apology, huh?"

"No worries. I know saying you're sorry has never been your strong suit."

Something tiny but sharp pinched my insides. I racked my brain for what apology I might owe August. If anything, he owed *me* an apology for that horrible day we broke things off a little less than a year ago. He'd accused me of being selfish, inward-focused, and spoiled. He couldn't see I only wanted the best for my family, the best for him, the best for my community, the best for the world even. At the time, I accused him of being selfish, too, of refusing to see how his actions affected others.

But apparently, he still believed me to be in the wrong. Well, I'd show him I could give an apology.

"August, for what it's worth—I *am* sorry. I shouldn't have stormed over here like the litter brigade."

He raised an eyebrow. "Litter brigade, huh? Is that a thing, because I'd nominate you as president."

I rolled my eyes. "Thanks." Another silent moment passed between us. "I guess I should get to my shopping. Mom sent me with a list a mile-long."

"How's things going at the good ol' B&B, anyway? Tripp said you all barely got a rest this past winter and things are in full swing again."

I don't know why—or maybe I do—but my gaze can't hold August's at the mention of his older brother. My sister's husband. True, I spent most of my teenage years mooning over the oldest Colton. But that ship had sailed the moment he'd chosen Josie. I was happy for them. *Of course*, I was happy for them. I was not the spoiled, can't-handle-not-getting-my-way youngest Martin child I'd been in elementary school. I loved Tripp like a brother now, and that was that.

"We're busy. How about you? Congratulations on graduating, by the way. You going to be some big-shot architect, now?"

"No danger of that while working for Grandpop and big brother."

Oh. "You're working for Colton Contractors? I didn't realize." For some reason, the news niggled at me. I suppose, deep down, I'd wanted bigger things for August. A big city where he would build skyscrapers and bridges, make his mark on the world. Not boring little Camden, where each day looked almost identical to the next. Where one relegated themselves to the good ol' family business.

I swallowed. There was nothing wrong with small towns if that's what one wanted. If that's what *August* wanted. But I didn't have to hunker down and accept the same fate. My life could be different.

I could break free.

"Yeah, I'm happy about it. Grandpop isn't getting any younger and the company needs a good architect."

He'd grown up in the last year. He exuded a confidence and stability he hadn't possessed when we were dating. Something about that drew me at the same time my brain screamed for me to turn and run, fast.

Talk about spiders. I refused to fall back into August's web.

"That's good, August. Real good. I'm happy for you."

"What about you? How's your art selling?"

"It's selling."

Not a lie. My enviro-friendly lampshades sold in the Camden shops faster than I could make them. The problem was, I couldn't make them all that fast. My profit often ended up being less than an hourly minimum wage. While I'd experimented with a price increase, sales had suffered drastically. Until I could figure out how to make my lamps faster, my profit margin would suffer.

"I actually got accepted to Parsons School of Design."

If I could save up enough money for living expenses, I'd go. I pushed my hair over my shoulder. While I'd qualified for some financial aid, Mom had offered to help with the rest, but I had refused. Mom wasn't getting any younger. Not that she was *old*, but she'd started the bed and breakfast only a few years ago. She needed to save for her own future, for the unexpected. I was a fully functioning woman who could provide for myself.

And once I found the perfect summer job, I'd do just that.

"Where's that?" Was I imagining the flash of disappointment in August's eyes?

"New York City. I'll be moving there in the fall."

Nope. Hadn't imagined it. Perhaps I was vain to relish the fact that August obviously still had feelings for me. Perhaps it was selfish and spoiled—all the things he'd accused me of the day we'd broken up—but in that moment, I didn't care. I savored the twinge of satisfaction that I meant something to August Colton after all.

We bid goodbye shortly after, and once I entered the foyer of the grocery store, I peered back for a last look. My heart swelled at the sight of him crouched low to the ground, gently dumping our eight-legged friend out of his coffee cup.

Then, he picked up the Styrofoam and climbed back into his

truck. I might have imagined the last look he gave as he surveyed the Hannaford foyer, but I don't think I did.

August had always held a flame for me.

Too bad, in the end, he simply wasn't the man I thought he was.

August Colton pulled out of the Hannaford parking lot with a whole lot more on his mind than lunch.

After nearly a year of living life Amie Martin-free, he couldn't deny how this latest encounter shook him up.

Shook him up good.

He'd never been able to resist her—the classic American beauty—that long blonde hair and those blue eyes the color of a clear sky, her feistiness, her honesty, the way she challenged and provoked him. He even missed the way they'd argued. More so, how they'd made up.

He kept his window down, allowing the cool air to rush over his face. No denying he'd come home with hopes they could start things up again. But was it wise to pursue a girl who'd dumped him once, who was probably still secretly hung up on his big brother, even if she would never admit it?

Amie Martin didn't admit weakness, after all.

His phone rang out on his Bluetooth, and he answered. "Hey, big brother."

"August, where are you? Grandpop is having one of his conniptions, and now that you're on board, I expect you to be here when the ball drops."

August rolled his eyes. "Chill, man. I went to grab some lunch. Isn't that allowed?"

"Not when the secretary's having her first grandchild and my wife is going to birth my own child any minute now."

He groaned. That's right, Eileen had called out that morning, saying her daughter was in labor. Since August had been out visiting customers this morning, he'd forgotten the office was short-handed.

"I'm on my way."

Tripp allowed a burst of air to escape through the phone lines. "Good. I have a couple estimates I need to get to this afternoon, and between you and me, Grandpop either needs a nap or some Priscilla Martin time. Maybe you can help me convince him to give it a rest when you get here."

August chuckled. "Sure thing." He didn't understand why Grandpop and Priscilla Martin, his high school sweetheart who just happened to be Amie's great-aunt, didn't up and get married already. They could take naps together. Much more fun than going solo if anyone asked August's opinion. "I'll be there in five. Maybe you can take a nap, too." No denying his brother had been on edge lately, what with the upcoming arrival of his baby.

"No time for naps. Thanks, August."

August.

Not "little brother" or "surfer boy" or "colossal screw-up"—all names Tripp had called him at one time or another. His ship had finally come in.

Sure, he may have had some rough teenage years. He may have had a little too much fun—maybe *way* too much fun—his first year of college, but he'd managed to straighten himself out. Thirteen months ago, he'd even thought he was on the road to settling down. With one woman. With Amie Martin.

But it had all gone wrong. His confession had thrown her over the edge. She'd whipped out her holier-than-thou card and flashed it in his face when what he needed most was understanding, not condemnation.

He pressed the gas pedal harder, gaining speed up Route 1. Yes, best to forget those bottomless eyes, legs as long as California and curves more enticing than thundering waves on a beach. He needed to focus on his new job, on serving the family business, and on proving himself to Grandpop and Tripp.

That was a full-time job in itself. No sense adding a firebrand like Amie Martin to the mix.

❦

I SCANNED THE LIST OF JOB SEARCH RESULTS ON MY LAPTOP AND sighed, taking a potato chip and munching it thoughtfully from where I sat at the dining room table of our living quarters in the Orchard House Bed and Breakfast. I had planned to break my fast with a protein shake and some trail mix, but the thought of job hunting called for something a little more comforting than nuts and raisins.

Truck driver, no.

Pharmacy Technician . . . that could work if I was certified, but no doubt such a certification would take at least a couple of months. A couple of months I didn't have.

A local burger joint position. Ugh. If I had to witness the behind-the-scenes of fast food I might keel over and die from disgust.

Cashier at a home improvement store. A possibility. If I got really desperate, that is. I suppose I could keep it in mind.

Marine technician, no.

Speech pathologist, no.

Pizza delivery driver . . . they made good tips, didn't they? As long as I didn't have to deliver to one of my peers from high school. I imagined myself donning a ballcap and shapeless polo t-shirt as I walked a Hawaiian pizza up to Jenny Simcock's house. I cringed as I imagined Jenny's conniving smile. Jenny, the girl all the high school guys had called "easy." The girl who couldn't name one element on the Periodic Table and who thought Macbeth wrote Romeo and Juliet.

The girl who had apparently pulled herself together and was now a practicing CPA in downtown Camden, handling other people's money while growing her own.

Oh, good grief. It wouldn't do any good wallowing in jealousy. I may have floundered through the last few years with a handful of college classes, a couple of boyfriends, and fits and starts with selling my art, but I had to help Mom with the bed and breakfast, right? And now, *now*, I was really going to do something with my life. Sure, it'd taken me a few years to figure out what that was, but I'd done it. I was going to art school. And not just any art school. *Parsons*. In New York City.

I could be proud of that.

If I could just scrape up enough cash to afford a few months in the big city . . .

Maybe my friend Lacy would hire me at the yoga studio. I tapped my fingers on the table. No, Lacy handled everything at the studio swimmingly on her own. She'd even complained her bottom line veered dangerously close to red after a bumpy start the year before.

I didn't want to burden my friend.

A loud knock on the back door made me jump and I knocked a few potato chips off my plate. I peered out the window, my heart skipping a beat at the sight of Tripp.

I swallowed, ordering it into submission. Enough was enough. Tripp was simply a silly schoolgirl crush I couldn't quite shake. Josie would positively die if she knew I still battled such ungodly feelings for her husband. It was wrong. Immoral. And certainly not Christian. Each of my angelic family members would be mortified.

I was mortified.

It wasn't as if I dwelled on him, or even dreamed of him. It was just my body's reaction to seeing him. Like now, when I opened the door and took in his easy smile and steady stance. After Dad died, he'd stepped in to help us in so many ways. He'd let me cry on his shoulder more than once.

Was that what was wrong with me? Was I mixed up in some weird crush due to the loss of Dad? I'd have to google that later. *Dad-loss crush?* Or *Romantic feelings and vulnerability*, or more appropriately, *How do I stop crushing on my sister's husband?*

"Hey, Tripp." I attempted a breezy air. "Josie's not here."

His face fell, reminding me how much Tripp was completely and unabashedly in love with my sister.

When they started dating, Josie told me she would stop seeing him if I wanted her to. She said sisters were more important. Of course, I'd rejected her offer.

And August thought I was selfish . . . selfish would have been denying my sister happiness. Denying Tripp happiness. I had not done that!

"She's not answering her cell. Why wouldn't she answer her cell when she's nine months pregnant?"

"Why don't I get you a drink of water? Come on in."

He obeyed, looking at his phone for what I guessed to be the fifth time in the last two minutes. I pressed a clean glass to the water dispenser in the refrigerator and held it out to him.

"Thanks." He took a long swig.

"Tripp, Josie's fine. If she went into labor, you'd be the first one she'd call. Why don't you track her?"

His eyes lit up and he slapped his head. "Amie, you're a genius."

I shrugged. "That's what I keep trying to tell everyone around here."

He shook his head, tapping on the "Find My Phone" app. "Why didn't I think of that before?"

But before he finished, his phone jingled an upbeat tone and he swiped to answer. "Josie?"

I returned to my computer and the mess of job offerings on my screen to give him some privacy.

"You've been at the house all this time?" A long pause. "Yes, yes, I understand, but it'd be nice if you'd answer your phone, honey . . . okay, see you later. Love you, too. Bye." He hung up the phone and shoved it in the pocket of his jeans. "Your sister is going to be the death of me."

"Let me guess. She was deep into the writing of her latest book and didn't even hear the phone ring."

"You got it." He shook his head, but the gesture held more fondness than frustration. His gaze landed on my computer. "What's that? You looking for a job?"

"Just something for the summer to help me get to the city."

"You think you could handle secretarial work?"

I perked up. "Yes . . ."

"Eileen asked for some time off to help her daughter get settled with the new baby. I've been running around like a chicken with its head cut off trying to keep up with scheduling and phones. You interested in filling in?"

I popped up out of my chair. "Yes!" I flung my arms around his neck, then, realizing the awkwardness this incurred, at least on my end, snatched my arms back. "Thank you, Tripp. I won't let you down, I promise."

It meant so much to me that he trusted me. A real job. Not cleaning at a bed and breakfast or serving fries at McDonald's or even putting my art on consignment at one of the shops down the street. This was a legit job. I scrunched up my shoulders and squealed. "I'm so excited!"

"Okay, why don't you stop by the office tomorrow morning, say eight o'clock?"

"Perfect."

He placed his glass in the sink. "I better run. I have to meet up with August and Grandpop."

"Thanks again, Tripp."

I closed the door behind him, excitement bubbling up within my chest as I watched him climb into his truck. Only after he'd pulled out of the drive did I realize that in accepting this job, I'd be seeing on a daily basis, the two men who'd caused me the most romantic grief I'd ever known. My girlhood crush, Tripp. And his brother, August, the one man who'd truly crumpled my heart.

❧ 3 ☙

A ugust threw his keys on his desk and looked around, surveying the office.

His office.

A simple space, with a window that overlooked a hedge of lilacs and a white picket fence that bordered Colton Contractors, as well as a desk and two chairs for clients. Now, early morning sunlight splashed a patch of light on the hardwood floor.

Eileen had ordered a name plate for his door.

August Colton, Company Architect.

Looking at that sign, he couldn't deny the surge of pride that rushed through him. He'd made it. Despite all his screw-ups and mistakes, that was *his* name on the door.

Now, it was time to get to work.

He sat at his desk, turned to his computer, and clicked the file for the plans he'd worked on for the Hills. New construction. Nothing like starting from scratch. Mrs. Hill wanted a kitchen the size of Georgia and August sought to give it to her. Two islands, one with a sink and abundant counterspace, the other with seating and plenty of light, a large window overlooking the sink, a refrigerator behind paneled doors, a commercial oven and gas range, and a kitchen nook with plentiful seating.

A bit too much in his opinion, but he wasn't getting paid for his opinion. He was getting paid to make his customer happy.

A knock on his open door pulled him from his work. Tripp stood at the threshold. "Morning. You're here early."

"What's the matter? Miss the days when you had to wrestle me out of bed?"

Tripp grinned. "Not in the least. Grandpop just called. He's not going to be able to make it in today."

August straightened. "He okay? Want me to go check up on him?" Though August lived with the older man in his massive house, they stayed out of one another's hair. Sometimes they'd pass on the stairs or eat dinner at the same time, but more and more, Grandpop spent his time with Priscilla Martin. Either that, or his grandfather holed himself up in his room.

Tripp shook his head. "This hasn't been unusual for him lately." He hesitated, seemed to want to say more. "I think we have to face facts that Grandpop isn't getting any younger. I think it's natural that, more and more, he'll be handing the reins of the company over to us."

"To you, you mean."

It used to bother August that Tripp was Grandpop's favorite, but he'd made peace with it a while back, when he'd decided to take responsibility for his decisions, his mess-ups, and his life. Being bitter never got anyone anywhere. Besides, with what Grandpop and Tripp knew about him and his past handling of money, he didn't blame them for keeping the checkbook and credit cards far from him.

"To us," Tripp said, a bit more firmly.

Leave it to Tripp to try to make him feel better. But a bit of wounded pride wasn't going to cause him to fall anymore. He'd made mistakes. Colossal mistakes. And he was prepared to take steps to make them better.

"It's okay, big bro. I'm just glad to have a job where I get to work with people I like—most of the time, anyway." He winked at his brother, but Tripp didn't smile.

"About that . . . Eileen called me yesterday. Her daughter had some complications during delivery. She's asked for a few weeks off so she can help with the new baby. I didn't realize it, but her son-in-law is in the Marines. He won't be home until the end of the month."

"Oh, man. Okay, so, what do you need? I can juggle playing secretary in between drawing and meeting with customers." Not what he had in mind his first month on the job, but he'd do it. He'd do about anything to let Grandpop and Tripp know they hadn't made a mistake in hiring him.

"Actually, I found us a fill-in for Eileen."

Was August imagining it, or had Tripp's face turned a slight shade of pink?

"What—is she here? I'll go out and introduce myself."

Tripp glanced at his watch. "She'll be here any minute. Look, August, I honestly didn't even think about how this might affect you—"

"Don't get your panties in a bunch, man. I can handle an inexperienced secretary. I'm just glad I don't have to juggle answering the phones and pulling permits on top of this massive pile of work."

"It's Amie, August. I hired Amie."

His blood seemed to stop flowing, and then, in a rush, surged through him, warming him all too quickly. He couldn't have heard right. "Amie . . . Amie Martin?"

"The one and only. I saw her looking for jobs on the computer yesterday and I didn't think. It seemed like a logical answer to our need. Not until I mentioned it to Josie last night did I—"

August gritted his teeth. This would not affect his personal life. He was professional enough to work in the same building as Amie Martin, to see her day in and day out, to smell her Victoria's

Secret perfume and hear that bubbly laugh of hers. He'd be able to work fine with her on the other side of this wall, answering phones with her legs crossed, one foot swinging.

Absolutely fine.

August leaned back in his chair, forcing himself to relax. He simply needed to man-up. "It's cool, Tripp. Amie and I are fine. I saw her yesterday. We talked things over."

And they had, hadn't they? They'd talked over his fear of spiders, her passion for keeping the environment and her cells clean, how she intended to leave him forever in September to attend some fancy-pants art school. No matter if, in the smallest corner of the back of his mind—okay, maybe more towards the front—he hoped against hope they might start things back up again.

The thing they hadn't talked over—the thing they needed to talk over more than anything—was that horrible day they'd broken up. That horrible day they'd bared their souls to one another and found they couldn't move forward knowing each others' secrets. Couldn't accept the other's baggage and short-comings.

No, that wasn't true. He could accept her, quirks and all. The way she threw a fit if he tried to eat non-organic produce off the dirty dozen list (he hadn't known what the dirty dozen list was until he'd met Amie). The way she scrunched up her face whenever he used the microwave. How she'd thrown herself into forming her new church—spiritual group, whatever it was—but had sobbed when only two people showed up the first time.

He thought she would have been able to handle his baggage, but he'd been wrong. Dead wrong. He should have known a girl who demanded nothing less than perfection from her mail carrier, manicurist, and chiropractor wouldn't put up with a past like his.

He sighed. Maybe it was his fault for not telling her sooner. You didn't keep stuff like that from a girl you loved as long as he'd loved Amie.

"Good. Glad to hear that."

Tripp's words jolted him into the present. His brother leaned against the threshold. "I'm proud of you, August. You've really done some growing up these past couple of years."

August's neck heated. Not without a little guilt, he thought of the contents sitting in his glove box at this very moment. But that wasn't something to be ashamed of—was it? He was no different than half of America. No different at all.

But Tripp wouldn't see it like that.

Good thing Tripp wasn't in charge. Not anymore.

"I appreciate that." And he did. He'd made a lot of progress these last few years, *had* done some growing up. He split with one of his closest friends, Liam, because he hadn't been able to keep his nose clean when around his old college roommate. It was nice Tripp recognized his hard work.

August had been six when their parents died in a train crash on a business trip in France. Tripp had taken it upon himself to step up as subsidiary father to August after that. And although August resented it, he could see now he was probably better off. Grandpop had been great for supplying them a home and their physical needs—but some needs had been harder to meet.

August raked a hand through his hair. Tripp had tried, anyway. It wasn't fair his brother had found himself in such a predicament. But neither was it fair to August. He'd never figure out why God had allowed their parents to be taken from them—or why Tripp simply accepted the fact without any hit to his faith.

"Hello?" A familiar feminine voice called from the main entrance of the building.

"Ready to give our new secretary a big ol' Colton Contractors welcome?" Tripp asked.

"You are so lame."

Tripp pounded his chest with a fist. "You hurt me, man." He turned and walked toward the main foyer of the office. "Be right there, Amie."

August pushed off his chair and followed his brother, glancing at the name plate on the door one more time.

August Colton, Company Architect

He'd earned this position. And so he would find a way to work with the woman who'd strewn the pieces of his heart along the wharf for the seagulls. He was a professional. And a small slip of a woman like Amie Martin didn't scare him.

At least he'd keep telling himself that until he believed it.

⚜

I SWALLOWED DOWN MY APPREHENSION AS I ENTERED COLTON Contractors. I placed my Coach bag on the carpeted floor beside the large desk in the office foyer and smoothed my flared, mid-length skirt that I'd paired with a striped dress shirt, heels, and some simple macrame earrings.

I squared my shoulders and dragged in a deep breath. Tripp would not regret his decision.

Where was Mr. Colton, anyway? I always did have a soft spot for the old man.

"Morning."

I lifted my head at the sound of Tripp's voice, my breath catching at the sight of both Colton brothers standing side-by-side a few paces from the foyer desk. Tripp smiled. He stood a couple inches taller than his brother. Beside him, August stood freshly shaven and a bit cocky, one arm leaning against the wall of the hallway they'd come from. In khakis and a polo, his hair curling at his neck and falling partly in front of one eye, I questioned the wisdom of putting myself so directly in his path each and every day.

I cleared my throat and gave them the brightest smile I could manage at eight o'clock in the morning.

"Morning!" My voice came out loud, forcedly excited. "I'm so ready to do this!"

So ready to do this? Was I revving myself up to climb Mount Washington or answer phones at a construction company?

I didn't miss the twitch of August's lips or the twinkle in Trip's eyes.

I shooed them both away. "Oh, go on with your day, boys. I can handle things here. I don't need a welcoming committee."

Tripp stepped forward. "There's just a few things we should—"

The office phone jangled out a merry ring. I held up my hand as I answered, lowering my voice to my most professional. "Colton Contractors. This is Amie. How can I help you?"

Note to self: *professional*, not sultry. I didn't want Colton customers to think they dialed some sort of raunchy phone line instead of a construction business. My face heated and my neck grew scratchy as I caught August holding in a laugh. No doubt he was thinking the same thing. I fought down the urge to throw the stapler at him. Couldn't they leave already and let me do my job?

"Hello, my name is Ted Hill. You all are working on some plans for me and my wife. We met with August last night, but we're hoping to make a few changes to the house plans before it's too late. I don't mean to be a bother."

I grabbed a small legal notepad and pen, jotting down Ted Hill's name.

"Oh, you're not a bother at all, Mr. Hill. We here at Colton Contractors pride ourselves on going above and beyond for our customers. Your home is where you'll spend most of your time. We don't take that lightly."

I cast a confident smile in Tripp and August's direction. Tripp stared at me with a bemused smile on his face. August rubbed his nose, an attempt to hide his laughter.

Seriously, what was wrong with that man? Was everything I did so terribly funny?

In my ear, Mr. Hill cleared his throat. "Um, yes, thank you. I agree. I appreciate your willingness to reach out to August for us."

"Of course! I'm sure Mr. Colton has your number, but why don't I take it just to be sure?"

Mr. Hill rattled off his number as I wrote. "August really had some amazing ideas. We appreciate his insight."

I imagined August with a clipboard, jotting down notes, perhaps offering suggestions, as Mr. and Mrs. Hill spoke of the dreams they held for their renovation, or perhaps their new home. August bit the inside of his cheek when he concentrated—I'd forgotten about that until now. Forgot how endearing I'd found that simple action, didn't realize how much I missed it.

In a rush, a memory of him staring out at a wave-tossed ocean, wetsuit on and surfboard under his arm, came to me. He'd worn the same expression I just imagined as he studied the surf.

I'd frozen my limbs off watching him that day, trying to support him, to show him I cared about what *he* cared about. But all I'd gotten in return were frostbitten fingers and a cold.

I dragged in a deep breath, forcing my focus on the task in front of me. "I'll be certain to get this message to Mr. Colton as soon as possible."

"I appreciate that, miss. Thank you." A moment later, Mr. Hill hung up.

I did the same, ripping off the notepad paper and handing it to August. "Mr. Hill would like to discuss some changes in the plans you discussed with him and his wife. I assured him you'd be happy to accommodate." I gave him my sweetest smile.

One corner of August's mouth hitched up in a faraway smile as he held my gaze. There, in a flash, it seemed all our history swirled around and through us, causing a shiver to chase down my spine where it settled deep in the pit of my stomach. It was as if something within me came alive. Something I thought long dead. Something that *should* be dead.

Tripp slapped August on the back, snapping us out of whatever we shared. "I think it's safe to say the front desk is in good hands, wouldn't you, little brother?"

August's gaze seared my own. "I'd say so."

Was it hot in here? I'd have to check the thermostat later. I swallowed, peeling my gaze away from the younger Colton's. I turned to sit back at my desk, feeling the weight of those blue eyes still on me.

Tripp came around to my side of the desk. "Let me show you around the computer." He opened up the scheduling application on the desktop and August headed toward his office. I forced my focus away from the broad expanse of August's retreating back.

Well, I guess I didn't have to worry so much about that schoolgirl crush I had on Tripp. Because even though he was leaning over me and I could smell the faint musky scent of his cologne, it wasn't the older Colton brother that occupied my thoughts in the least.

I hummed softly to myself as I closed the door of the Alcott guest room and entered the Thoreau room of the bed and breakfast. For years, Mom had dreamed of a book-inspired bed and breakfast, and four years ago, when Josie showed up without a college degree and a surprise pregnancy a year after Dad died, my second-oldest sister had convinced our great-aunt to open up her Victorian home for the task. Living with Aunt Pris had been an adjustment. I'll admit, I took leaving the home we'd grown up in harder than my sisters and brother. But now, I can see it was the right decision.

Mom loved the newfound purpose she discovered in running a successful business. Josie loved managing the renovated book-shop. Maggie found her business-degree came in handy while managing the promotion and bookings. Lizzie was happy to play chambermaid and tend the gardens and Bronson had opened up the orchards for apple-picking last fall and managed a summer camp for youth. Even Aunt Pris, who'd fallen into a second-chance romance with Ed Colton and busied herself helping Bron-son's camp financially, seemed to have found her niche. Yes, everyone knew their place.

Almost everyone, that is.

With soft steps, I walked into the Thoreau bathroom with a basket of travel-sized toiletries. I placed shampoo, conditioner, lotions, and soaps on the counter, arranging them to be pleasing to the eye. When I finished, I stepped back, surveying my work.

There, I could contribute something worthwhile to the family business, after all.

Lace and Bath, one of the downtown Camden shops, offered us a steep discount on their organic, locally-sourced products. In exchange, we tucked coupons for the store in guest folders. The advertisement of the travel-sized products didn't hurt, either.

I arranged a small bar of soap beside a man's razor and a can of Barbasol shaving cream, thinking it odd there was no sign of a woman staying in the room. Though it happened before, a solo male guest was not our norm. More often than not, a male guest traveling alone was on business and had either heard about Mom's gourmet five-course breakfast, or hadn't wanted to book one of the more economical hotels farther outside of town.

I continued humming as I moved the small basket of face towels beside the products I'd arranged. My thoughts fell to my first week at Colton Contractors, and with not a little satisfaction, I recalled Mr. Colton's words as I left the office on Friday.

"You're doing a fine job, Miss Amie. We appreciate your help." His soft gray eyes were the closest thing I knew to a grandfather, and I'd beamed beneath his praise.

"Thank you, Mr. Colton. I'm grateful for the chance."

I'd left the office, floating with the compliment. Not that my life goal was to be a secretary at Colton Contractors, but it meant a lot to be told I was good at something that involved concentration and dependability. Sure, I had a gift for the creative and the arts, but my family always left the important and practical matters —matters like figuring the budget or ordering product—to Maggie or Josie or Bronson or Mom. Even Lizzie would be a better choice.

But here I was, doing a *fine job* at Colton Contractors. Making a difference with my work.

And, getting paid for it.

August had avoided me the last few days, and while I tried to remind myself he was busy adjusting too, I couldn't help thinking how nice it would be if he stopped at my desk to talk every now and then, as Tripp did.

Although Tripp's stops at my desk consisted mostly of out-loud-wondering why his baby hadn't made an appearance yet, I appreciated the visits.

I walked out of the Thoreau bathroom and took in our smallest guest room. Our most rustic room, it had a log-cabin feel to it. Josie told me this Thoreau fellow was all about nature, so I supposed that made sense. Lizzie had finished cleaning a half-hour earlier and the bed was made without a wrinkle, throw-pillows arranged artfully on the coverlet. My gaze moved to the two comfy chairs by the cozy fireplace. I stopped. An easel sat in the far corner of the room, in front of the window.

My breath hitched as my brain caught up with what my eyes took in.

Some wall art is beautiful simply because it imitates the splendor of the natural world. Some art is beautiful for the abstract—for colors and shapes, some for the fantastical appeal or pop art or surrealism it created. And some art is in a class all its own.

And that's what this painting was.

It drew me in and wound around me in an entirely unique and mystical way. It pulled me like the moon pulled the tides. An impressionist piece with a refreshing contemporary feel. I couldn't help but be drawn to the history and romance of the Impressionists, a group of Parisian artists that include Monet, Renoir, Degas, and Pissarro. Though I'd tried my hand at it a number of times, I could never create a piece that quite satisfied.

Mom and Josie looked to books to tell stories. I looked to art. And here was a story of an entire world, all on a single canvas.

My gaze roamed over the painting, drinking it in. The loose brushstrokes, the vivid light and luscious color combinations, the unfinished beauty of it all. It was a scene from the harbor, looking onto land. A striking sunset peered out around clouds behind the steeple of the church on the green, casting the sky in breathtaking purples, pinks and oranges. The lights of the Grand Harbor Inn twinkled in a quaint, magical way, an old schooner in the foreground on the water reflecting the shining sunset. Distant shops and a backdrop of trees completed the picture. I could only stare at the beauty and magic of it, the shade and light, the texture and color. All of it washed over me until I momentarily lived in the meditative state of being *inside* the painting.

To think someone this talented was in Camden, staying at our bed and breakfast, was unfathomable. Who was he? I'd never even set eyes on him, and yet it felt like love at first sight. This painting was a message, a piece of its creator, and I was captivated, enthralled.

I heard voices on the stairs, and though I knew it was wrong, though I knew it went against everything I stood for as an artist, not to mention the rules of privacy we kept at the bed and breakfast, I whipped my phone out and snapped a picture. I'd fall asleep looking at it. I'd dream about it. I'd study it and give it all the attention it deserved.

I backed away almost reverently, and once the door of the Thoreau room was closed, I nodded my head to a couple in their forties entering the Dickinson room. As soon as they closed their door, I flew down the winding staircase of the old Victorian to the foyer, where my oldest sister could usually be found at her desk.

"Maggie?"

No Maggie. I walked through the butler's pantry to our living quarters, also empty.

Where was everyone?

I glanced out the back window and caught Maggie's profile at the bookshop. I headed out the door, waving to Bronson and Morgan, who walked down from the orchards holding hands. Seriously, they were too cute. My annoying older brother had finally found his person. I couldn't wait for Bronson to go ahead and pop the question already.

I opened the door of the bookshop, the bell above ringing its merry chime. Rows of books greeted me, the gentle scents of soy candles for sale mixed with that of paper and ink. Four-sevenths of my family sat or stood around the cheery fireplace in the far corner.

"Just the person we need to weigh in on this conversation!" Josie sang out when she saw me. As the official manager of the Orchard House Bookshop, Josie, with her belly like a large balloon ready to burst, looked as if she had all the energy in the world despite the extra human she carried.

"Oh, yes! Tell us what you think of this idea, Amie." My sister Lizzie, who stood in front of a large stand stocked with my eco-friendly *Leaf and Lamp* nightlights, looked at me expectantly.

I glanced from Josie to Lizzie to Maggie to Mom, trying to hide my hurt. "You guys having a pow-wow without me again?"

They didn't do it on purpose. At least, I didn't think they did. It just seemed I was always late getting in on the important things. It didn't help that, although I'd never doubt the love of my family, they deemed me a curiosity. The only one to favor art over books. The only one to put incredible effort into her looks. The only one not to fully embrace the faith passed down to us.

Josie waved her hand through the air. "This was entirely spur of the moment. We're asking your opinion now."

Josie always accused me of being overly dramatic. But was it my fault I was always the last one my family consulted when it came to the bed and breakfast? When it came to family?

I flopped down on an overstuffed chair on the right side of the fireplace. I guess my sleuthing about the Thoreau guest would have to wait. "Okay, what's up?"

"We think Mom should take a vacation this summer. She deserves some time away." Maggie pushed aside her dark hair. My oldest sister looked good. Maybe she'd tried out that new eye cream I'd given her.

"I think that's up to Mom . . ." I looked to my mother, who perched on the edge of the chair beside me.

Hmm, maybe I should have given the extra eye cream to her instead. "Is everything okay, Mom?"

"You girls are super sweet, but I'm perfectly fine. And, perfectly capable of planning my own vacation, if needed." Our mother pushed back a strand of her graying hair. Up until recently, the grays had looked like highlights, but not so much anymore. When had she stopped getting it highlighted? She was still beautiful, regardless. I could only hope to look like her when I was fifty-one.

Josie paced in front of the fireplace. "It's been four years since we opened this place, Mom, and you haven't once taken a vacation."

"That's not true. I went skiing last winter." Mom beamed.

"To babysit Grace so Josh and I could ski with the boys!" Maggie said. "You should have a real vacation, Mom. Not just from the bed and breakfast, from the mission too."

Mom helped at Dad's mission as much as she could, serving meals to the homeless or helping the jobless put together resumes. Seriously, I didn't know how she did it all.

Lizzie tapped her fingers on the floor where she sat. "We can handle everything at the bed and breakfast. Oh, Asher knows a great place in Malibu. Imagine, time on the beach to read, soaking up the sun, fancy restaurants at night, maybe you'll even meet someone."

Josie's mouth fell open. "Meeting someone is *not* the goal of this vacation."

I stifled a laugh. "Oh, come on, Josie. Dad's been gone four years. Would it really be so horrible if Mom found someone to share her life with?"

Lizzie shrugged. "I'm with Amie."

"Me too," Maggie piped up.

Mom cleared her throat. "Thank you, girls, for your intense interest in my love life, but—"

I almost choked on my laugh. "Love life? Seriously, Mom. What love life? Aside from this bed and breakfast and our family, you barely have a *life*."

"Golly, sweet daughter, and here I thought I was living out all my dreams."

Josie rubbed her round belly. "We just think you could use a break is all. No pressure to find romance. Just some relaxation."

"Girls, thank you. I love you all so much, but I have everything I could possibly want right here. My beautiful daughters, my ambitious son, my amazing grandchildren. I'm happy at the bed and breakfast. We closed for two weeks in January, so I'm well-rested. I don't need Malibu or California or romance. I only need this." She glanced around, her gaze settling on each of us one by one. "My family."

I used to think Mom less-than-interesting for always wanting the simple things, but something about the way she spoke now made me almost envy her. What would it be like to be that content, right where I was? To not be longing after the future, New York, Paris, or art and experiences around the world? And yet, was it wrong to long for those things? I wasn't settled like Mom, with a business and a family and grandchildren. I was still finding myself.

"Are you sure we can't convince you?" Maggie asked.

"Tell you what. While I don't need fancy or extravagant, it would be lovely to get up to see Charlotte for a few days. Would that satisfy you all?"

Josie bounced on her feet. I wanted to tell her to stop all that jumping—she was apt to dislodge the baby, but when she was excited, her entire body showed it. "That's a phenomenal idea! Acadia's the perfect place for a summer trip. Only two hours away. And it's been ages since you've seen Charlotte."

Charlotte Zurly and Mom had been close friends since Charlotte had hired Mom as a chambermaid at the Bar Harbor Inn years before she'd met our father. While Mom had gone on to grow a family, Charlotte and her husband had opened the Beacon Bed and Breakfast, a beautiful inn on the Acadia coast featuring a historic lighthouse. Mom's dream of owning a bed and breakfast spurred to life as she watched Charlotte accomplish her own dream. While we'd camped on Mount Desert Island annually when I was little, visiting Charlotte just as often, it had been a long while since any of us visited.

I had no doubt that Charlotte would do Mom some good.

"It's a perfect idea. As long as you don't go overworking yourself helping Charlotte with *her* inn," I said.

Mom winked. "It's not work if it's fun."

A twinge of longing pierced me at the words, a favorite saying of Dad's. I hadn't dwelled on him in a while, and the sudden need for his big arms around me came swift and sure. I could still hear the soft timbre of his voice as I indulged in one of my introspection sessions.

"Come here, Amie girl, and tell me what's bothering you."

I'd always been his baby girl. While he'd held Maggie, Josie, and even Bronson to incredibly high standards, he'd simply seemed to enjoy my company.

Did he not think me capable of being smart like Josie, or kind like Maggie, or even brave like Lizzie? I was simply Amie. Seeking and curious and fun-loving and creative.

I hoped that had been enough for him.

Maggie tossed up her hands. "It's a plan." She glanced at her watch. "Yikes, I better get back to the desk. Guests will be checking in any minute."

I tapped my phone, scrolling to my most recent picture.

"Before you go, please tell me everything you know about Mr. Thoreau."

Maggie scrunched up her face. "Mr. Thoreau?"

"Henry David Thoreau was a naturalist, a philosopher, a writer, an abolitionist, a—"

I shook my head, cutting Josie off. "Not *that* Thoreau. The guest staying in the Thoreau room."

The corners of Mom's mouth turned downward. "His name is Luke Beckham. He prefers eggs instead of pancakes, and that's about all we have a need to know about our guests, Amie Martin."

I winced at the use of my full name, something she hadn't used in quite some time. "Come on, Mom. Most of our guests talk to you or Maggie and aren't terribly private about their affairs, anyway."

Josie's eyes narrowed. "Why the interest?"

I huffed and tapped my phone. "This. This is why."

They all leaned in, squinting. Mom's eyes grew wide. Josie's lips pursed, and Maggie murmured a "wow."

"I saw that when I cleaned his room," Lizzie admitted.

"But you didn't take a *picture* of it." Josie crossed her arms over her chest. "That's an invasion of privacy, Amie."

She sounded like she wanted to add my last name, too.

"Not to mention it goes against everything we represent here at Orchard House." Mom didn't look angry, she looked disappointed. It had been a while since I'd earned that look.

Still . . .

I turned the phone back to myself. No. No, I hadn't made a mistake. Were they seeing what I saw? That amazing, beautiful, breathtaking painting? I flipped it back in the direction of my family and shoved it closer to them. "But do you *see* this? Normally, I'd agree with your privacy stance, but this is an extenuating circumstance. This is a *masterpiece*."

Josie flung her arm up in the air. "That's not the point. It doesn't matter if DaVinci himself was up there creating his next great work, you're not supposed to take pictures. You need to think without being so impulsive all the time. Delete it."

In a reactionary manner, I brought the phone to my chest, as if to protect it from my sister, the purveyor of all things anti-beauty. The girl who got knocked up by her college professor was going to tell *me* not to be impulsive? "I will not."

"Isn't that stealing art that's not yours?" Maggie asked. "I'd think you, of all people, would understand."

I cradled the phone in my hand, falling more and more in love with the painting as I looked at it. "I'm not replicating it or selling it. I simply want to find out more about it." To stare at it tonight until I fell asleep.

Okay, I admit, I might have problems.

Mom rubbed her head. "Why don't you help me serve breakfast tomorrow morning? Perhaps, in making authentic, *nonintrusive* conversation with Luke you can find out more about him and his art."

Sunday morning breakfast. Though I usually enjoyed my beauty sleep before dragging myself out of bed for church, I'd sacrifice my beauty for this cause. "Done," I said.

Josie raised her eyebrows. "Wow, she must be serious about this."

I rolled my eyes. "I've served breakfast before."

"About as often as you clean the guest rooms."

I wagged a finger at her. "I'm going to let that slide because you're very pregnant and likely very hormonal."

Josie stuck out her tongue at me and I blew her a kiss as I slipped out of the bookshop.

I could hardly wait for tomorrow morning.

༝ 5 ༝

With his chest against his surfboard, August paddled hard toward the oncoming wave, calculating its timing, feeling it with his entire body. He popped up on the board, grounding himself to it, allowing the water to take him speeding along its surface. Adrenaline surged through his core as the wind hit his face and the wave rolled beneath him, breaking behind him as he skimmed along. When he raced too far ahead of it, he twisted his body sharply, putting his board back in the thrust of the water.

He could never get enough of this. The saltiness of the ocean, the high of being one with the wave. Another wave exactly like it would never come, and for just a slice of time, August shared in its power, its unique majesty.

Moments like this, he understood the God his grandfather and brother worshipped. Moments like this, he respected a higher power, an ultimate being. Even wanted to know more about Him.

As the wave finally fizzled, August paddled out once more, his heart racing from the ride. This time, he didn't seek a wave but paddled beyond the breaking point and simply let the swell and fall of the surf move beneath his board, lulling him into a state of peace.

He'd taken the hour drive south to Pemaquid Beach in hopes of catching some great waves on this Saturday morning. With a storm coming in later tonight, he hadn't been disappointed. The sound of the surf, the rush of adrenaline, the power of the mighty water, was enough to clear his head and his senses.

A perfect end to his first week back in Camden.

His time at the office had been a success overall. He'd completed the Hill plans, along with their changes, and had earned the stamp of approval from not only Grandpop and Tripp, but from the Hills. The project could move forward.

As he lay on his board, listening to the distant call of seagulls, the woman who never seemed far from his mind wheedled her way into his thoughts. He pictured her sitting at the front desk of Colton Contractors, intent on the computer in front of her, surrounded by the earthy scents coming from the essential oil diffusor she'd placed at the corner of her desk. She'd worn her hair up yesterday, baring that delicate, creamy neck. The urge to come behind her and kiss the spot where her golden hair met unblemished skin had nearly overtaken him. To dispel it, he'd simply muttered a greeting to her and practically dove into his office.

Five days of seeing her proved it—he was far from over Amie Martin.

And it wasn't only the physical attraction he held for her, although that most definitely played a role. It was the memories that pummeled him with the ferocity of a thundering wave—the time she'd dragged him to the Camden Opera House to see a folk band and he'd fallen asleep, how she'd kept elbowing him to keep him from snoring. The time she'd playfully shoved her ice cream cone in his face at the library amphitheater, the time she'd sneaked out of the house and they'd gone skinny dipping at Lake Megunticook . . . the time he'd told her he loved her on the front porch of her home. The time they'd both lost their virginity on a blanket beneath a canopy of moonlit trees in a private space in Camden Hills State Park.

He'd thought that meant something. Thought they'd be together forever. Sure, he'd made mistakes in his past—mistakes he was still paying for—but not now or ever could he make himself believe that Amie Martin had been a mistake.

Too bad she seemed to think differently.

Now though, being back in Camden, breathing the same air as the first and only girl he loved, he couldn't help but think this might be a second chance for them.

He closed his eyes, letting the sun beat down on his wetsuit-clad body.

She planned to leave. Now, when he'd finally finished school and earned himself an honest-to-goodness job, when he was beginning to prove himself, she would leave. In less than four short months, she'd go to New York. Make a new life for herself, find some hippie art guy to have ice cream fights with. And she'd be happy in the city, he knew she would.

What right did he have to take that happiness from her?

And yet, Amie was a big girl. She could make her own decisions. He wouldn't be stealing anything from her by letting her know there were other options. Maybe a year apart had been enough' time for things to cool off between them. Enough time for both of them to realize what they really wanted.

With sudden decision, August paddled back, catching one more wave before bringing his board onto shore and walking to his truck in bare feet. After peeling off his wetsuit, toweling off, and pulling on jeans, he hopped in the driver's seat and aimed his truck north for Camden.

North, for Amie Martin.

"I'll get it!" I called from the butler's pantry, where I may or may not have been spying on the guest staircase.

On the counter below the staircase, Mom put out a baked dessert every afternoon—anything from extra-large chocolate chip cookies to hummingbird cake to chocolaty oatmeal chews. Guests rarely missed the daily treat, and so I'd busied myself on starting a macrame hammock swing, stationing myself in the kitchen where I could hear them on the staircase, or coming in from their day. Whenever I did, I sneaked a peak to see if I could catch Luke Beckham.

So far though, only three couples. No artist.

When the back doorbell—our living quarters doorbell—rang, I tore myself away from my spying game.

Probably better off. Tomorrow morning would come soon enough. No doubt Luke Beckham wouldn't miss an Orchard House breakfast.

I walked through the kitchen, relishing the afternoon quiet. Mom had gone to the market, Bronson was working in the orchards, and Josie manned the bookshop. Maggie had gone home and Lizzie had gone to Paramount, her husband's large-chain sports store, to bring him a late lunch after she finished cleaning the rooms. Only Aunt Pris was in the house, in her room resting.

My heart picked up speed at the sight of August through the back window. What was he doing here? Unless he was looking for Tripp. Or perhaps . . .

But no. August had no reason to come and see me.

I pushed my hair out of my eyes and pinched my cheeks before opening the door. "August. Hey." His hair was tussled and slightly wet. He wore a light blue t-shirt that pulled at the muscles on his chest. Impressive muscles. Muscles that had gotten bigger since the last time I'd seen him in a t-shirt.

I tore my gaze away to see him staring at me, a half-smile on his face telling me he didn't miss the direction of my gaze. Great. Not exactly the humble pie he needed.

"Amie."

The way he said my name, deep and slow, filled with meaning, made something bloom beneath my breastbone. A longing that made me doubt the breakup of a year ago. Could we have worked things out between us? If I had been able to see past his secrets, if he had been able to see past my faults, could we have made something lasting?

I shook my head, trying to jiggle off the effect August had on me. "What can I do for you?"

He stepped forward, seeming unsure where to put his hands—the first uncertain movement I'd seen from him since we'd met in the parking lot earlier that week. "I was surfing."

"Uh huh." I swear, if he came all the way over here to brag about a big wave he caught, I was going to scream. How many times had I sacrificed a date for a big storm coming in? Seemed there was always a storm, always waves to catch. Seemed I was always second on August's list.

His throat bobbed. "I mean, I was thinking about you. When I was surfing."

Had he been remembering all the times he'd ditched me for his surfboard?

"Okay . . ." I wasn't making this easy on him, but that was the guard I'd erected around my heart when it came to August Colton. Our history caused me to err on the side of caution. Either that, or suffer the consequences of a broken heart.

He raked a hand through his uncharacteristically tangled hair. It looked dry from the salty water, and I wanted to run my fingers through it. Comb out the tangles, feel him lean into my palms.

He inhaled deep. "I miss you, Amie. That's what I was thinking."

My body hummed beneath his words, all the old feelings surging through me, all the memories we'd shared—how he'd save the last bit of his ice cream cone for me because it was my favorite part. How he'd throw rocks at my window, his wordless way of begging me to sneak out of the house in the middle of the night. How, even though we'd gone with a group of friends, he held me close as we danced to Ed Sheeran's *Perfect* the night of my senior prom.

August still wanted me. Despite that horrible last argument, despite all we'd been through—or maybe because of it—he still wanted me.

I tried to stand straight, but instead I wilted against the door frame. This was not the plan. I refused to risk my heart again. "I —I don't understand."

I did understand. I was stalling. Stalling for time, for space to convince myself this was not a good idea.

"I mean, I miss you. I keep wondering if maybe we made a mistake last year. If—"

"August, I can't. It's been a year. I don't want . . ." *To get close to you again.* I knew from experience that once we crossed the line, there'd be no turning back. If I went out with August—if I crossed that line, I'd be sucked in swift and sure before I even had a chance to evaluate if the relationship was wise to continue. And hadn't I deemed it doomed already?

He stepped closer. My brain told me to back away, but my body didn't obey.

"Can you honestly say you don't think about us being together again, Ame? Don't we deserve another chance? Don't you miss me, even a little?"

Those probing blue eyes sucked me in, leaving me unable to squeeze out a denial.

I released a breath, powerless to stand firm against his persistence. "Maybe."

He broke into a grin. Oh, those dimples. They always were my undoing.

But I must be cautious. "Don't think this means anything. You were my"—I lowered my voice—"my first." First love. First kiss. First everything. "It's only natural I've thought about you."

A wickedly devilish grin carved his features. "What kind of thoughts?" He wiggled his eyebrows.

I stepped into the house, prepared to close the door on him. "Forget it. I can't do this."

He put a hand out, stopping me from closing the door. "Wait. Amie, wait. I'm sorry. Please, give me another chance. Can I see you tonight? Let me take you to dinner? Please?"

I swallowed, sensing I was about to walk through a door that would be hard to find my way back out of. "I'm leaving in September. You just got back. I don't—we don't want the same things. I can't . . . trust you." We'd established this, hadn't we? In the end, we'd be back in the same place as before.

"One date, Amie. One night. That's all I'm asking."

"I am not sleeping with you," I hissed. Though sex before marriage might be the social norm in America, it was not the social norm in the Martin home. It was one rule I'd broken with August. The reasons to not have sex simply hadn't seemed to stand up to the reasons *to* have sex with him. And while we'd had our share of fun, I sometimes wondered if we'd made a mistake. If giving ourselves over so fully to one another without a mature commitment had been one notch in the many that had caused our failure.

His face turned pink. "That's not what I'm asking for. Just a date."

If that were true . . .

"You promise? Just us hanging out?"

"Scout's honor." He *looked* sincere. He wanted to earn my trust.

What would one little date hurt?

"Okay. Dinner, then back home." I scrunched up my nose. "And do you plan on washing off that seaweed cologne you got going on before then?"

"You don't like it? I bought a bottle with you in mind."

I smiled. "I think you wasted your money."

He winked, sending a tingling sensation straight down to my toes. "Can I pick you up at five?"

I nodded.

He gave me a grin that held the power to melt me into hot wax. "See you soon."

I watched him saunter with his easy stride back toward his truck. I shut the door and sighed, closing my eyes. No denying I wanted to be with August. No denying every bone in my body ached for him.

But there was also no denying that what my body wanted may not be the best thing for my soul.

6

August turned off the steamy shower and reached for a
towel, drying off before wrapping the towel around his
waist and making his way to his bedroom. The large
room on the second floor of Grandpop's veritable mansion used
to be Tripp's before he'd married Josie. When August had moved
back home from college, he'd taken it for himself.

Not that he planned to stay beneath Grandpop's roof longer
than he had to. As soon as he paid off the last of his debts—
which, at this rate, might be several years—he'd find a place of his
own. Or maybe he'd talk Grandpop into letting him stay in the
apartment above the garage. Ever since Finn, the biological father
of Josie's first son, had moved out, it sat empty. Maybe he'd
broach that subject after he proved his worth at Colton for a few
months.

He pulled on a fresh pair of jeans and a button-down shirt.
After calling Hartstone Inn and ordering two of their gourmet
curbside cuisines along with a bottle of wine, he brushed his hair
and set out downstairs to find picnic essentials. He hoped Amie
would approve. Though not especially an outdoorsy girl, he took a

chance that a romantic picnic at Lighthouse Lookout could possibly sway her.

He found a clean blanket in the laundry room and rummaged up an old picnic basket from the pantry. He stared out the kitchen window to the harbor in the distance, drumming his fingers on the counter.

"You gathering wool, boy?"

He moved to stand at attention at the sound of his grandfather's words. "Hello, sir. I didn't hear you."

"Apparently not." Grandpop shuffled into the kitchen, opening the refrigerator and grabbing a bottle of Pellegrino. It fizzed when he twisted the cap off. "Looks like you have big plans." He gestured to the basket sitting half open on the counter.

"I'm taking Amie on a picnic."

Grandpop's mouth twitched. "Little Amie Martin. Oh, boy."

August's throat tightened. "Something wrong with that, sir?" He patted himself on the back for keeping his tone pleasant and respectful.

Grandpop shook his head. "Not at all. In fact, I'd love to see you two end up together. I just don't want to see you kill one another on your way there."

His grandfather's words poked a tender spot in his heart. For isn't that how he'd always felt about Amie? That he couldn't live without her almost as much as he couldn't live with her. She called to him like a siren, soaking him in her spell. When he was in her presence, it was ecstasy. Perfect. Until they disagreed. Until they couldn't stand to be in the same room as one another.

He'd told himself that's what passion was. Times of immense love colliding with occasional disagreement. Deep down, he hoped that the last year had changed them both. Had helped them grow. Was it too much to hope they might be able to grow together?

"We're taking it slow." Well, maybe those words weren't

entirely accurate. August opened the utensil drawer, taking out two forks, two spoons, and two butter knives. He'd only confessed to Amie that afternoon that he missed her. So at the moment, they weren't taking anything either fast or slow—it only just started. Whatever it was or would be.

Grandpop cleared his throat. "Actually, there's something I've been wanting to talk to you about, August."

August straightened. He and Grandpop weren't in the habit of sharing a lot of heart-to-hearts. "Okay." He placed the utensils into the basket alongside a pile of napkins and leaned against the counter, giving his full attention to his grandfather.

Grandpop swigged his sparkling water, then placed it on the large counter of the island, sliding into a bar chair with some effort. Was it August's imagination, or was the older man's movements less fluid and more rigid? "I know you could have gone to another company. Somewhere in New York, even. With your talent, you would have made out well, too."

August soaked in the words. They were rare, these compliments from his grandfather. And it wasn't because Grandpop was stingy, it was because August had done so little to earn them.

"Thank you, sir. But I'm happy to be at Colton. It's a fine company, and I wanted to be home."

With his family. Grandpop, Tripp. The only family he had. And, of course, with the Martins. They'd been his stand-in brother and sisters growing up. All except Amie. He'd never been able to hold sisterly thoughts toward the youngest Martin, even when he'd wanted to.

Grandpop drummed his gnarled fingers on the counter of the island and dragged in a deep breath. "Still, it's not lost on me that you may have felt obligated. Not because we're family, but because of your past."

August winced. He really didn't want to talk about this now, and especially not with Grandpop.

"I'm paying off my debts as best I can." What he owed his grandfather was so much more than what the older man had given him growing up. Even now, it stung to think of the foggy haze of shiftlessness that had caused him to steal from his grandfather.

"I know you are, son. And I know you're sorry. I don't wish to make it harder on you than it has to be. That's why, as of this afternoon, I paid off the remainder of your student loans. I also want you to consider your debt—the one you owe me—paid."

August's knees grew weak. "What?"

"You've proven yourself these last few years, and I want to help you succeed, which I'm confident you'll do."

August shook his head, foreign emotion squeezing his throat. "I can't accept that, Grandpop. I don't deserve a cent of your money."

"That's grace, young man. It's what God's given me and it's what He offers you every day. It's what I'm giving you now."

As the full implication of Grandpop's words coursed through him, August's throat tightened and he swallowed hard, trying to keep himself together. But as his grandfather's words replayed in his head, the fight withered inside of him. He slid against the kitchen cabinet until he sat on the cool tiled floor, covering his head, unbidden sobs choking him as he burrowed them into his knees.

Sixty thousand dollars in student loans. The twenty thousand he'd stolen during his first year of college when he'd been in the throes of a gambling addiction. Money he *should* pay back.

He heard his grandfather's footsteps approaching, but he couldn't look up, couldn't face the older man with his shame.

"Son."

August shook his head. He wanted to tell his grandfather to go away, to not look at him while he was overcome by unmanly tears.

"Son," Grandpop repeated.

August drew in a shaky breath, swiped at his eyes, and lifted his head. Not enough to meet his grandfather's gaze, but enough for the man to see his face.

"I can't accept this, Grandpop. It's too much. I deserve to pay—"

"Young man, please don't tell me you grew up in my home without having a concept of what grace is."

August swallowed. "I know what it is, I just always thought it was for people like you and Tripp." People who were naturally good. Who deserved it.

"It's for anyone. And today, it's for you. There's no other option, August. Your debt is paid, you owe me nothing. I want you to live your life without your past hanging over your head."

August stood, slow, then clutched at his grandfather, the old man's body feeling so much frailer than it used to when he'd given Tripp and August rare piggyback rides on Christmas day. "Thank you, sir. Thank you so, so much. I won't let you down."

And he wouldn't. He was free. This gift from his grandfather had opened his eyes to a whole new world. It made him want to be a better person. A person his grandfather could be proud of. A person his grandfather would never regret helping.

"I love you, Grandpop."

The older man cleared his throat, apparently uncomfortable with the words.

August pulled back to look into his gray eyes. "Thank you isn't enough."

Grandpop squeezed his arm. "It is more than enough, August. You turned your life around, and I'm so proud to call you my grandson."

August sniffed. "You're going to start the waterworks again, Grandpop."

"We better finish packing your picnic basket, then. Get those paper napkins out of there, I'll show you where my cloth ones are. If Amie's anything like her great-aunt, you'll have to show her some class if you want to impress her. And paper napkins are not classy."

August chuckled as he obeyed his grandfather, packing dishes and wine glasses and even a couple of peppermints the housekeeper had tucked in a drawer. As August drove away for his date, he sensed a new beginning upon him.

Hopefully, Amie Martin would be a part of that fresh start.

7

"**W**hat? Mom, please don't look at me like that." I placed my hands on my hips, feigning ignorance over what my mother was about to say.

I gave her credit, though. She didn't speak right away. Instead, she continued rolling up her flattened, raw chicken around Swiss cheese and ham, then dipped it in egg and breadcrumbs before placing it on a baking sheet. "I don't want you getting hurt again, Amie. That's all."

"I know what I'm getting into."

The corners of Mom's mouth turned downward. "That's what worries me."

"What's that supposed to mean?" I tried to keep the defensive tone from hitting the high notes of my voice, but it was too late. Good grief. I was twenty-three years old, and I could date whoever I wanted to date.

"You seem to have forgotten who comforted you last year after your breakup. I'm trying not to judge, honey. I am. But no one else in this family knows how hard you took it. I don't want to see my little girl hurt again."

I sniffed. She was right. I'd been too ashamed to tell even

Maggie about August's revelation. Ashamed for him as well. A gambling addiction was a big deal. And though he'd said he'd given up the habit, he confessed that he'd stolen twenty thousand dollars from his grandfather his first year of college. Confessed to not fully trusting himself not to gamble away a paycheck.

I'd spent hours online reading real-life stories of how gambling addictions ruined relationships. Was I a fool to entertain a date with August now after deciding against staying with him a year ago?

No. People *could* change. I had to believe that.

"I appreciate your concern, Mom, but I think August has changed. He has a real job now. Mr. Colton and Tripp trust him enough to hire him on. That's saying something, isn't it?"

Mom looked thoughtfully at the breaded chicken. "I suppose . . ."

"And I'm not going into this with blinders on. It's one date. We both had some growing up to do. Maybe now that we have, it's time to give us another try."

"Or maybe a little more growing wouldn't hurt." Mom raised her eyebrows, but she fought a smile.

Out of the corner of my eye, I glimpsed August's truck pull into a parking spot in front of the bookshop. I wagged my fingers at my mother. "Have a good night. Don't wait up."

She rolled her eyes heavenward. "Lord, help me."

I giggled, smoothing my Boho-style summer dress that I'd paired with a jean jacket, chunky bracelets, and sandals, and walked out the door to August's truck.

He jumped down from the driver's seat. "Gee, Ame, you don't even let me be a gentleman and come fetch you at the door."

"Fetch? What am I, a dog's ball? I'm perfectly capable of walking out the door on my own."

"I know, I know." He walked me around to the passenger's seat and opened the door, but not before I caught his red-rimmed eyes.

"Hey, you okay, August? If tonight doesn't work for you—"

He shook his head, a sheepish grin on his face. "Thought I'd wiped all my emotions away by now."

Warning flags waved inside my head. I didn't want volatile August. Unstable August. I'd convinced myself he was dependable this time around. Had that been a lie? His bloodshot eyes scared me. Had he been drinking?

"We can reschedule. I—"

"No, Amie. I really want to spend time with you tonight." His voice was low, husky, stirring my insides like sweet cream. "I'll tell you why I'm a bit of a wreck—a good wreck—while we have our picnic."

I raised an eyebrow. "A picnic, huh? You cheapin' out on me, Colton?" I teased, realizing how much I missed this, how easy it was with him. It may be a first date of sorts, but it wasn't our first date. Being with him was familiar and comforting, and at the same time new and exciting.

He closed the passenger door, leaning in slightly through the open window. "Does Herb-Seared Cod, Fennel Tiger Shrimp, and Chocolate Espresso Mousse Cake with a bottle of Ferrari Carano Chardonnay sound like cheapin' out to you?"

I fanned myself. The man was speaking my love language. "Hartstone Curbside Cuisine. I'm flattered." He'd taken me to the inn's restaurant once on the Saturday before he'd gone back to college, and I couldn't stop raving about the food. It was pricey and way out of our budget, but we'd splurged. And he'd remembered, right down to what I'd ordered that night.

He winked at me before walking around to the driver's seat. "I thought a picnic would give us some extra time to talk. We just have to pick up the food."

"Let's not delay, then. Tiger Shrimp is waiting."

We drove the short distance up the street to get the bag of food, which August placed in his back seat. The scents of seafood and spices wound around us as he drove down Bayview Street and parked on the side of the road.

"Lighthouse Lookout, huh? Very romantic. But did you make a reservation?"

"God did the reserving tonight. The stars are aligning for me today, Amie. No one will be there. I just know it."

Something inside me froze at August's mention of God. It was a small thing. Something anyone might say in an offhand manner. Why then, did it put me on edge?

I climbed out of the truck. "Okay, we'll see then, Mr. Stars. If we have to go too far and my cod gets cold, I'm not going to be a happy camper."

He handed me an adorable woven picnic basket and grabbed a blanket and the food, leading the way down the short path to a bench with the best—and only—view of Curtis Island Lighthouse on land.

"See? What'd I tell you? All ours."

"It's gorgeous," I breathed. From the bench, the lighthouse sat white-washed and picturesque on the hunk of land across the harbor. Green leaves bloomed on the island as well as around and above us, the waters of the harbor gentle. The scent of the sea mingled with that of pine. By the time August had finished spreading out the blanket and our place settings, complete with a candle, I wanted to paint it all in order to capture the beauty of the moment.

"Since when did you get so romantic?" I asked, settling myself on one side of the blanket.

He shrugged. "Maybe I don't want to screw things up this time." He uncorked the chardonnay, a slight fizz erupting from the bottle. I held my glass out to him as he poured for me, and then for himself.

"To new beginnings," he said, holding my gaze.

A quivering breath surged through my lungs, but I didn't move my gaze from his own probing one. He was serious about this.

Serious about starting over.

Serious about me.

I gulped down a cleansing chill of air. "To new beginnings." We clinked our glasses together and sipped our chardonnay—notes of citrus, pear, and buttercream alongside baked apple and cinnamon. A perfect wine for a spring evening.

Over our shrimp and cod, we chatted amiably about our work week. August asked me about my art, and he listened more intently than he ever had in the past. He was trying, but more than that, he seemed genuinely interested.

In the middle of talking, I shook my head. "What is it? Stop looking at me like that."

"Like what?"

"All goofy, like you can't stop staring at me." I raised my eyebrows. "August Colton, I know you're not interested in art, so stop pretending you are."

He shifted in his seat, moving an inch closer. "I may not know all the art terms or even appreciate it like the guys at your New York school will, but I know I love watching you talk about art. You light up. You're even more beautiful, if possible."

I tilted my wine glass toward him. "I already told you I'm not sleeping with you. So, stop trying to get me drunk on this most delightful chardonnay while you sweet-talk me."

He sat up, crossing his fingers at his side. "Scout's honor. Nothing I said tonight has been untrue. I'm realizing what I lost when I lost you, and I'm trying like the dickens to get it back."

Despite the cooling temperatures, heat burst inside my chest. I cleared my throat. "Tell me why you looked like you'd been crying when you came to pick me up."

"Because I was." His answer came fast, too fast for me to think it anything but honest.

"How come?"

He placed his clean plate on the blanket, leaning back on his hands and looking out to the lighthouse. "Grandpop told me this afternoon he paid off all my student loans."

"Oh, my goodness. August, that's great."

His mouth tightened as he nodded. "That's not all. He's cancelling my debt." His jaw trembled, but he sniffed hard, seeming to get himself under control.

My mind raced. "Your debt. You mean . . ."

"The money I stole from him."

I breathed deep. "Wow." The last time we spoke about this was on the horrible day we broke up. August had finally told me what he'd done his freshman year of college—taken cash from his grandfather's vault to gamble at a local casino—and how he still struggled every so often with the urge to gamble.

I shouldn't have taken it as hard as I did. I mean, I wasn't naïve, I'd known August wasn't perfect. He flirted too much with other girls, he was cockier than the King of Spades. But allowing himself to fall so far into an addiction that he stole from the man who'd given him everything?

I'd already been frustrated with August at that point. He hadn't supported me in the spiritual group I wanted to start, hadn't shown interest in my art. Seemed he'd only been interested in one thing when it came to me, and the more he showed his true colors, the less I was interested in the act.

We'd yelled, we'd screamed. I'd told him he was selfish and irresponsible; he told me I was haughty and a know-it-all. He'd tried to kiss me in the middle of our argument, as if we could transfer all that anger and heat into sexual energy—as if our bodies could be used as a means of making up without working through our problems.

I'd slapped him after that, and he'd left. The next time I saw him was in the Hannaford parking lot earlier this week.

And now this.

His grandfather had cancelled his debts. Did Mr. Colton

believe August had conquered his addiction? He must have if he hired him to be the company architect . . .

August stared out at the harbor. "He said it was grace, Amie. And for the first time, I think I really understood it, you know? Getting what you don't deserve."

My skin prickled. I sipped my chardonnay. "I almost feel like I'm talking to Tripp now instead of August." I laughed nervously.

He squinted up at me. "That's what you used to want."

Ouch.

"That was a long time ago, August. Now, I want . . ."

"What? What do you want?"

I shook my head. "I want to be loved how Tripp loves Josie, how Asher loves Lizzie, how Josh loves Maggie. Wanted, just because I'm . . . me."

What was I saying? This was crazy. This was the wine talking. But it was true. And here, with the sun setting fast, the chardonnay and food warm in my belly, things finally open between me and August, it almost felt safe to bare my soul.

He moved the dishes aside, slid closer to me. "I want you, Amie. Just because you're you."

I smiled, dipped my head. "We're getting a little ahead of ourselves, don't you think? You haven't even told me how you're handling your . . . addiction."

"I haven't gambled in nineteen months. I've thought about it, but haven't bet one penny."

I smiled. "That's good, August. That's real good."

He grinned, the light from the candle flickering across his face. "Dessert?"

"Oh, yes."

He dug out the mousse cake from the last of the takeout containers and served me one of the slices on a small white porcelain plate.

"I could have reused my plate to save you the trouble."

"You see, that's where I waffled. Because reusing the plate

would have earned me recycling points, but I know how you hate it when your foods touch. And chocolate expresso mousse cake on top of fish and shrimp juice just didn't strike me as classy."

I giggled. "Good call." I slid the edge of my fork into the mousse and lifted it to my lips, savoring the velvety chocolate richness. I let out a groan. "That is divine."

He shifted on the blanket. "I'm enjoying watching you eat it more than I probably should."

I pointed my fork at him. "Okay, you've now convinced me Tripp hasn't taken over your body. You're definitely August."

He pouted. "Hey, you're not the only one who wants to be loved for who they are."

He joked, but I glimpsed the truth in his words. A rush of affection came over me and I leaned in, kissing him softly on the cheek. "I know. Thank you, for all of this, August."

We finished our dessert and laid down on the blanket, staring at the spattering of stars in the sky.

"You know," I said. "I'm not usually a nature-lover, but I think I might not be giving enough credit to Whoever put together those stars."

August turned his head so he looked at me. "God, huh?"

I threw up my hands. "The Creator, whoever organized this beautiful mess of nature and humanity, I don't know. You think we're here by more than chance?"

"I do." They grew quiet before he spoke again. "I'm sorry I didn't give your church more of a chance. It meant a lot to you, and I never showed any interest. I think I even made fun of you a couple of times."

I swallowed. "You did." The memory still hurt. "And I never called it a church. It was a spiritual group."

"So, how did it go? Are you guys still meeting, because I'd love to come one day."

Now, he showed interest. Now, when it was too late.

"It never really got off the ground, actually. We had one good discussion, but honestly, people are into some weird stuff. It scared me, you know? I wanted to talk about differing beliefs, about seeking a higher power and light, but one person was outright into worshiping demons." She shivered. "I guess that's when I gave up. Not that I put my all into it, either. Just decided I'd be a misfit forever, you know?"

"You're not a misfit any more than I am."

I turned my head so my cheek was flat on the blanket to face him. The candle had grown low, but it illuminated his handsome profile—that strong Roman nose, that chiseled jaw. "I didn't know you ever felt like a misfit."

"I think you're forgetting I grew up with Ed and Tripp Colton. Perfect specimens of humanity."

I giggled. "At least there were only two of them. Try growing up with the Martins—the modern-day March family. Talk about expectations."

"You were always my favorite Martin."

I knew I was. And I think that's what drew me to August in the first place. He didn't compare me to smart Josie or pretty, sophisticated Maggie or even sweet Lizzie. To him, I was Amie, and that was enough.

I inched over, snuggling into the crook of his arm.

"Whoa, whoa, whoa, Amie Martin. I'm fully aware of how strong the August Colton charm is, but I feel the need to remind you that I will *not* be sleeping with you tonight."

I slapped his chest. "You bet your surfer-dude butt you're not." I cuddled closer. "But this is . . . nice."

His arm came around me, warm and strong, his bicep hard against the back of my head.

"You've changed, August. You're still you, but you're also different. I like it."

He kissed the top of my head. "I want to be worthy of you, Amie Martin. I hope to God I don't let you down."

8

After they packed up the remains of their picnic and August drove Amie home on the darkened Camden roads, he was already missing her, despite the fact she sat relaxed in the passenger seat of his truck.

"Will I see you at church tomorrow?" he asked.

"If you'll be there, I'll be—oh, wait. I told Mom I'd help serve breakfast."

"Wow, I'm not the only one who's changed."

She laughed. "There's a guest I want to meet. I saw this amazing painting of his when I was stocking the rooms with toiletries. Mom told me I couldn't hound him, but I could talk to him over breakfast."

He swallowed down a twinge of jealousy. "Him, huh?"

"You can't see it in the dark, but I'm rolling my eyes over here. No competition, I'm sure. He's probably some sixty-year-old recluse who hides away at remote inns to accomplish his great works." She shook her head. "Seriously, though. This painting belongs in a museum." She lifted a water bottle to her lips. "I think I drank too much wine. I better dilute it before I stumble up the stairs and wake Mom."

"Just like our teenage years, huh?"

"I hope not. I hope we've grown up a bit since then. In fact, I'm counting on it."

"Me too." They drove through downtown, and when August drove a bit too fast over a speed bump while Amie was swigging her water, she yelped.

"Oh, that's cold!"

"You spilled?"

"Only because you don't know how to drive over speed bumps properly."

"It's the truck. It has awesome shocks. Check the glove box, there should be some napkins."

She reached forward, clicking open the compartment. A small light inside the box lit up the contents—two napkins, his registration, the car manual, and . . . oh no. He fought the urge to dive across the console, grab the napkin, and slam the glove box shut before Amie noticed.

The napkin, frozen in her hand, the water on her dress forgotten. "August . . . what's this?" She grabbed the two slim tickets from the box.

He made a quick decision to play it cool. "Just a couple scratch tickets. I picked them up a few weeks ago. Completely forgot about them."

He hated himself. Hated himself for playing like the purchase of the scratch tickets wasn't a big deal.

She grew silent as he turned into the Orchard House drive. Finally, she spoke. "Nineteen months, August. You told me you haven't gambled for nineteen months. That you haven't bet one penny."

"I haven't. Amie, those aren't even scratched. And who counts scratch tickets as gambling?" He despised his defensive tone while at the same time he couldn't keep himself from it.

"That's like an alcoholic saying a sip of beer doesn't count, and you know it. I can't believe you. I can't believe I thought you'd changed. I should have known better, should have known this would follow you forever. One penny my behind."

He parked the car. Lights from inside the Orchard House spilled onto the back patio, lighting Mrs. Martin's herb garden and the grass beyond.

"I have changed, Amie. Please believe me."

She tossed the tickets at him and opened the passenger door, hopping out of the truck. "I can't believe I even thought about trusting you again."

He grabbed for her hand. "Please, don't leave. Let's talk this out."

She wrenched her arm from his grasp. Panic erupted in his chest as he realized he had found her and was losing her again, all in one night.

Words tunneled from his lips. "I was scared."

That made her pause. She stood outside the truck, the door still open, her knuckles tight on her bag beneath the harsh interior lights of the truck.

"I was scared I'd screw up coming back home. With the company. With proving myself to Grandpop and Tripp. It was a moment of weakness, I swear it. I stopped at a convenience store on my way into town, stupidly thought there was a chance I could win enough to pay Grandpop back and be done with my debt. But I couldn't do it, Amie. I sat in this seat for fifteen minutes wrestling with myself, fighting the urge to scratch those tickets and see if I could change my future. In the end, I shoved them into the glove box. For me, scratching those tickets would have been like selling my soul to the devil. It would never be enough. I had changed my future, already. I didn't need a couple of scratch tickets to help me along."

She stared at him, listening, studying him with those endless blue eyes.

He continued. "They don't let you return them. Maybe I should have given them to the guy pumping gas next to me.

Maybe I should have thrown them away. But I kept them. I guess, if I'm being honest, something about having them there, just within reach . . ."

He swallowed. That might have been too much information. How vulnerable must he make himself?

Still, she didn't say anything. But neither did she go.

He tore up the scratch tickets, the silver pieces falling in his lap. "There. I should have done that all along." It was easy to do, here with Amie watching him. A flicker of wondering if he'd just torn up ten thousand dollars passed through his mind, but he refused to latch onto it. Grandpop had set him free from his debt. He had everything. *Had*, everything, until he'd gone and messed things up tonight. "Please, Ame, don't leave. Can we go for another ride? I don't want to leave you like this."

Her pretty face shown pale beneath the truck light. "I want to believe you, but a part of me is saying I'm a fool for entertaining the thought."

He reached for her hand again. "You're not. I promise, I'll prove it to you. Please, come back in the truck."

She shook her head. "Not tonight. I can't be with you right now. I need to think."

He wanted to continue begging, continue speaking words that might convince her. But he had a feeling that, right now, they'd only push her away. "Can I call you tomorrow?"

"I don't think so. I'll see you Monday." She closed the truck door and he felt like his very life—his very hope—was walking away from him.

He stumbled out of the truck, meeting her around the front, blocking her from going into the Victorian. "Can I say one thing?"

She didn't answer, but neither did she make a move toward the lighted path.

He grasped her hands, kneading them with his thumbs, willing her to see his heart, to hear his words. "I love you, Amie Martin. I have always loved you and I will always love you. And I will do whatever it takes. I will move heaven and earth in order to prove myself to you. I'm sorry for breaking your trust already. Believe me, I am kicking myself from here to kingdom come. But you will never, ever have to question me again. I swear it, Amie. I swear it."

She pressed her lips together before speaking. "That's the thing, August. I'm not asking you to move heaven and earth. I'm only asking for your honesty." She shrugged, let out a sad snort. "So much for hoping to God you wouldn't let me down, huh?"

She released his hands and walked away.

He didn't move until she disappeared inside the house. When he finally climbed into his truck, he hit the back of his head against the headrest several times, resisting the urge to scream, to punch his steering wheel.

This was not who he was, not who he wanted to be, not how he vowed to live only a few hours ago after breaking down in front of Grandpop. If only he'd torn those tickets up sooner, or better yet, not even bought them.

He was a better man than this. A better man than one who depended on those scratch tickets.

He just needed to prove it to Amie. First though, maybe he needed to prove it to himself.

❧ 9 ❧

I woke to the blare of my alarm clock radio, being the only
one in the family besides Mom who didn't use their phone
alarm or a Fitbit. I was a firm believer in a cell-phone free
sleeping area. Bad energy and all that, not to mention that WiFi
signals and cell phone radiation contribute to cancer. No one else
in my family had quite bought into that, mind you, but I was
convinced.

I smacked the sleep button and turned away from the light of
the window as I hovered at the edge of consciousness, trying to
tamp down the events of the night before.

My head ached—probably from drinking too much wine.

I groaned at the thought of the beautiful picnic, the decadent
food, the sweet chardonnay . . . August. I squeezed my eyes
together to keep my emotions at bay.

Why had he come back to Camden at all? Okay, that wasn't
fair. He had a right to return to his hometown. But he didn't have
to show up at my doorstep, saying he *missed* me. He didn't have to
be all romantic, creating the perfect evening, saying all the perfect
things, getting my hopes up that this could be it, that now was
our time. Yes, I was leaving in the fall, but we could work things

out, couldn't we? Maybe he'd even find a job in New York after working with Colton Contractors and gaining some experience. I could practically see us romping about the city, trying out new restaurants, walking over the Brooklyn Bridge, going to art museums.

But the contents of August's glove box had brought my imaginings crashing to a halt. I was a fool to believe an addiction as deep as August's, one that had caused him to steal thousands of dollars from his own grandfather, could be kicked so easily. Sure, it was possible, and sure, part of me wanted to believe August. But the fact remained: if his gambling problem was a thing of the past, he wouldn't have bought the tickets in the first place.

I turned on my phone, a twinge of disappointment niggling my insides at the lack of notifications. Of course August hadn't texted. What would he say that would change things?

I threw the covers off and headed down the hall to the shower. As I prepared for the day, I breathed deep, in through my nose and out through my mouth, attempting to dispel the poisonous memories before they seeped into my psyche.

One, two, three, four, breath in . . . this was no great loss. Twenty-four hours ago I had been August-less, and I'd been perfectly fine. Great, even. I squeezed the water from my hair, grabbed the towel, and stepped into my slippers. One, two, three, four, five, six, seven, eight, breath out. A few hours shouldn't have the power to change my emotional state. I'd simply transport myself back to yesterday morning. I was happy. Carefree. Appreciative of my new job but looking forward to the possibilities of art school in the fall. I slid in my earrings, shaking my head a little to watch them sparkle. My biggest problem had been figuring out how to meet Luke Beckham.

That's right. Luke Beckham! Things were looking up already. I brushed on some eyeshadow, pulled my hair back so it wouldn't end up in the guests' food, and studied my reflection, deciding at the last minute to change out my maxi skirt for a dark pair of jeans and ballet flats. I wrapped a light burgundy scarf around my neck to add some color to my black shirt, gave one last critical look to the overall effect in my full-length mirror, and started down the stairs.

"Morning." I forced a peppy pitch to my voice as I entered the kitchen. Mom stood at the counter, apron on, and Aunt Pris sat at the breakfast nook, coffee and crossword before her.

"Morning, honey." Mom split open English muffins. "Did you have a nice time last night?"

I felt the weight of both of their gazes, almost as if they held their breath for my answer. "It was fine."

Aunt Pris grunted as she placed her coffee cup down. "You surely weren't swept off your feet with *fine*."

I straightened. It was on my lips to tell them that August and I had simply grown apart. We gave it another try for old time's sake, but it simply wasn't going to work.

But then his words from the night before stopped me.

I love you, Amie Martin. I have always loved you and I will always love you. And I will do whatever it takes—I will move heaven and earth in order to prove myself to you.

I shook my head. How many chances would I give August? How would we survive a long-distance relationship without trust? How would we survive *any* relationship without trust?

"August and I have a lot of history we need to work through. I'm being cautious about being swept off my feet."

There. Honest without closing any doors, either.

Mom shot me an approving grin. "That sounds wise. I'm impressed."

Impressed that I was wise? Would she be impressed if it were Josie or Maggie? I had a feeling she wouldn't be. But her youngest making a wise decision—now, that was impressive.

I sniffed away the hurt. Being overly sensitive didn't serve me. I breathed deep, allowing Mom's words to roll off me instead of soaking through me.

HEIDI CHIAVAROLI

I exhaled long and slow, then clapped my hands together. "Should I go out and check on the guests?" The sooner I met Luke Beckham, the sooner I could get my mind off other things.

"Guests don't come down until eight, at the earliest. Would you slice these strawberries?" She handed me a pack of the red fruit. "It's topping for the coconut almond granola."

My stomach growled. "Yum." I began slicing the stems off the berries and cutting them in a fan shape.

Mom eyed the effect. "I never thought of that. Beautiful."

I smiled. "I might not be useless in the kitchen after all, huh?"

"I never said you were useless." Mom's mouth turned downward.

I shrugged. "I know. But I'm pretty sure Josie has."

Mom laughed. "I don't think Josie's one to talk about skills in the kitchen."

True. My sister was lucky if she knew the difference between a lemon squeezer and a can opener. "Touché."

I busied myself with arranging Mom's homemade granola into fancy glass dishes, setting the berries aside so they would stay fresh until presentation time. Mom checked the thick-cut bacon and the roasted tomatoes she'd use for a spinach and goat cheese omelet, and prepared the whole-grain pancake batter.

I watched her work as I rinsed the blueberries she'd add into the batter. Her every movement was a beautiful thing. A dance in the kitchen with her food. There was a rhythm and grace to it I'd never noticed before as she moved from adding flour into a mixing bowl at the counter, to the oven to check on the bacon, to the refrigerator to grab milk and juice, to the bar to arrange the plates in artistic fashion.

She must have caught me staring, for she stopped mid-step. "What?"

"You're good at this, Mom."

She laughed. "You sound surprised."

My face heated. "I know I shouldn't be. Of course, you're

good at this. You're running a booming business. I just forget how much work it is, sometimes, you know? You make it look easy."

"Well, I love it. I think that helps."

That word, *love*, made me remember August's words from the night before. I wondered if love shouldn't be so hard. Maybe if we'd taken things slower when we first started dating, the idea of love wouldn't be so hard for us now.

"I'm proud of you, Mom," I said, the idea a new one to me.

She smiled, the gesture settling into the fine lines around her mouth. She really was a pretty lady. Maybe *she* should serve breakfast. Luke Beckham might be a great catch for her. "Thank you, honey. That means a lot to me."

I turned back to the granola. "Mom, do you think you'll ever get married again?"

Her hand fell to the counter. "Where in the world did that come from?"

I shrugged. "I don't know. I guess I'm just noticing all you have going for you, and I was wondering . . ."

Aunt Pris cleared her throat. "I think she's saying it'd be a shame to let all your talent and beauty go to waste without a man," Aunt Pris said dryly.

"Glad those new hearing aids are working out for you, Aunt Pris," I muttered. "And that's not what I meant." I leaned one hip on the counter, facing my mother. "I just wondered if you ever get lonely."

Mom slid the tomatoes out of the oven. They smelled heavenly with bits of spices on their sliced tops. "I'm afraid there's not much opportunity for loneliness around here. Grab the cooling rack, will you, honey?"

I opened a bottom cabinet. "But if the right guy came along?"

She placed the tomatoes on the rack and slid her hands out of the potholders Aunt Pris had quilted for her as a Christmas gift last year. "We need to concentrate on breakfast, not romance. Both of us. But to answer your question—yes, I suppose anything's possible. But I'm not going out of my way to look."

I grinned, already imagining how I might set her up with the perfect man. I glanced at the door of the butler's pantry. Maybe even a man waiting for breakfast this very minute. I could already picture them together—him, creating his masterpieces (he'd give me pointers, of course), and her—checking on his latest progress while going about the business of the bed and breakfast.

Mom glanced at her watch. "Why don't you go and take drink orders?"

I tied an apron around my waist and grabbed a notepad and pen, checking my hair in the reflection of the oven before heading into the guest area.

"Oh, Amie! I almost forgot."

I stopped short, turning to her.

"Yes?"

"It appears we have a duchess among the common folk."

I cocked my head. "A duchess? You can't be serious."

"I'm not entirely certain I am. But she's quite insulted if we don't bow to her upon entering a room."

"Duchess of where?"

"She claims she's the Duchess of Tonga, but when I searched it last night, something seemed a little off. I would just play along."

"Are you saying she's lying, and I'm obligated to feed into her delusions?"

"I'm saying we can't prove she isn't who she says she is, and so if you don't want to meet the wrath of the people of Tonga, I would bow upon meeting her."

"What does she look like? How will I know it's her?"

The corner of Mom's mouth lifted. "You'll know."

I threw my shoulders back, questioning whether Luke Beckham was worth the trouble this morning. But with the simple remembrance of the majestic beauty of his painting, I plowed forward out of the pantry and into the dining room.

"Good morning!" I sang to a middle-aged couple who had already served themselves coffee from the bar beneath the stairs.

They tore their gazes away from one another to greet me. This must be the Miulers. Mom said there was a couple on their honeymoon. I hadn't realized they were older, a shining example of second-chance happiness right beneath Mom's nose. Good.

I took their drink orders and greeted the couple coming down the stairs. Then a woman in a sequined gown and a gorgeously elaborate headdress more appropriate for a costume ball than a Maine bed and breakfast descended the stairs.

I froze, then remembering Mom's warning, I bowed. Only it was more of a Namaste yoga pose than an actual bow. Realizing my mistake, I rushed to curtsy instead, feeling completely foolish as I dipped one leg and put the other behind me, holding out the ends of my apron as I would a dress. "Duchess." I looked beyond her to the man beside her. I gave another small curtsy. "Mr. Duchess."

Mr. Duchess? Seriously? This was the *last* time I was volunteering to serve breakfast.

The woman gazed down her nose at me, then at the dining room. Though I was conscious of another person on the steps behind them, I didn't dare move my attention from the presence of royalty.

Or pretend royalty. Who knew? We were here to show our guests a good time, and if acquiescing to their whims about being of a royal family line was what mom wanted, so be it.

"I prefer to eat on the veranda." The duchess lifted her chin. Her English was perfect. Not a hint of Tongan. If Tongan was a real language. I sure didn't know.

"Certainly, your majesty." I scooped two place settings from a nearby table and led the couple out onto the veranda. They chose a corner table, and after they were seated, I asked them what they'd like to drink.

"Mint tea. No juice, the acid does a number on my stomach."

"Yes, ma'am."

She raised a thin eyebrow at me.

"Your duchessness," I corrected.

She rolled her eyes, waving me away.

I gritted my teeth as I walked back through the dining room. A man in his late twenties or early thirties with dark hair and a leather necklace poured himself coffee at the bar. My breath caught. Was this him? Luke Beckham? If so, he was definitely too young for my mom.

I cleared my throat. "Good morning."

He smiled at me and it was warm and inviting and easy. Unique. I imagined him at his easel, painting that amazing piece of artwork, and my stomach lurched.

"Morning."

"Can I get you something to drink?"

His eyes sparkled and his voice slid up a notch. "Nothing acidic. It does a number on my stomach."

A giggle slipped out of my mouth, and I chanced a look at the other guests, hoping no one heard us.

"I'm joking. That was rude, sorry."

I shook my head. "I needed that. She has me on edge."

"I couldn't tell with your curtsy. You looked like such a natural."

He'd *seen* that? I stopped myself from fanning my face, attempting a quick recovery. "I'm not sure it's wise to poke fun at the person in charge of your food." The moment the words were out, I kicked myself for allowing their escape. *Not professional, Amie.*

Mom would kill me. Not only was I flirting with our guest, but I hardly knew him. Maybe he couldn't take a joke when it came to his food. Some people were *serious* about their food. Good grief, who was I kidding? *I* was serious about *my* food.

He bowed to me, a perfect Namaste pose. "You're right. Forgive me. And if it's not too late, I'll take some good ol' OJ."

OJ. Somehow, I didn't picture the painter of gorgeousness to "take some good ol' OJ."

"And you are . . . ? I need to know what breakfast to bring you."

Nice save. And I really did need to know. Mom gave the guests a choice of two main dishes. Lizzie left the small forms in their rooms after she cleaned and they dropped them off in a box on the coffee counter beneath the stairs the night before breakfast.

"Luke. I'm in the Thoreau Room."

Score.

I jotted down his drink order on my notepad, a jagged beat thrumming through my body. "Great. Sit anywhere you'd like."

"Thanks . . . I didn't catch your name."

I shoved the notepad in the pocket of my apron. "Amie. I'm your waitress."

He smiled, and it was a nice smile, though a bit unassuming. Somehow, I expected more from the man behind the painting upstairs. He placed a hand over his chest and bowed. "Amie My Waitress."

The way he said my name sent a breath of wind chasing down my spine. I smiled at his theatrics and managed to make my way back into the kitchen, where I wilted against the refrigerator. "I met him," I said.

Aunt Pris raised an eyebrow at me. "Oh, no. Hannah, she has that look to her."

I blinked, opening the fridge to get the juices. "I don't have a look."

Mom smiled. "She's swept off her feet, all right, Aunt Pris. But maybe not with our guest. With his art."

I couldn't be sure. One of my faults—a fault I didn't pride

myself on—was the fact that I'd always been a bit guy-crazy. I didn't want to be wishy-washy, moping after August one minute while swooning over Luke Beckham the next. But just the memory of Luke's painting alongside the memory of those glistening scratch tickets in August's glove box was enough to push the younger Colton brother from my mind.

I finished pouring the juices, grabbed the elegant wooden serving dish Mom used, and wrestled in a deep breath.

"Now, remind me. Am I supposed to bow every time I walk in the same room as the duchess, or is once a day upon first meeting sufficient?"

❧ 10 ❧

I considered it a victory when I successfully finished serving breakfast without 1) earning any more looks of disapproval from the Duchess of Tonga and 2) pouncing on Luke about his painting while he enjoyed his omelet.

But as soon as he took his last bite, for fear he'd return upstairs and disappear forever when I slipped into the kitchen, I lingered at his table. It sat in a private windowed nook of the dining room, and I busied myself by arranging his empty coffee cake plate on my serving platter with extra care.

Finally, I couldn't take it any longer.

"I saw your painting," I blurted, unable to come up with something more appropriate.

He raised an eyebrow, his mouth turning thin and serious.

I squeezed my eyes shut, giving myself a mental thrashing. I should have approached this differently. Asked what he did for a living, asked what brought him to Camden. Now that it was too late, I could see the million other, more tactful ways to broach the subject.

"I was stocking the bathrooms. I usually try not to look, but—"

"Amie." He said my name with a smooth cadence, like the mixing of white into red—a blending of soft and bold. "Don't sweat it. I have nothing to hide."

I allowed the serving tray I'd been holding, which had tilted precariously toward his table, to rest beside his now empty glass of orange juice. "It's amazing," I gushed. "Mesmerizing. Beyond engaging. Stimulating."

He studied me, and my face heated as I wondered once again, if I'd said too much.

"What do you like about it?"

"Everything. The color combinations, the vivid light. It was unfinished, and yet . . . perfect. Radiant."

His eyes didn't leave my face for a moment. Finally, he pushed his plate away and rested crossed arms on the table. "I struggled with it for a long time before it came together."

I pulled out the chair opposite him and sat. "Maybe that's what I loved about it. Maybe I sensed the struggle. It created a depth, an authentic beauty that resonated."

"Are you a student of art, then, Amie My Waitress?"

"I will be in the fall. I'm going to Parsons," I said, quite proud that I could say so.

"I tried to do art school, but it didn't work with my spirit. I found I could express myself better without a teacher telling me how to reveal that expression. Turns out the best teacher was my own soul."

His words both inspired and discouraged. "I think my soul could use some help."

"You want my advice, Amie My Waitress?"

I licked my lips, nodded.

"Take the money you've set aside for Parsons and take yourself to Paris. Drink in the City of Light, study the masters, paint your heart out if it's art you choose to study, and let it shape and form and inspire you."

I sat back in my chair, allowed his words to carry me away.

"My family would never approve of me taking off to Paris to be inspired."

"And you need your family's approval?" Luke asked.

I straightened, trying to imagine planning a trip to Paris instead of a move to New York. My breaths came fast, ragged. "But what if it didn't work? What if I spent all that money to go there and nothing great came from it?"

"Art's not about being great. It's about expressing what's in here." He placed two fingers ever so lightly at my sternum, and I swayed where I sat. Then, his fingers were gone and his eyes were alight with talk of art. "Besides, who's to say art school will make you great?"

"True," I mused, then smiled and stood, figuring I'd taken enough of Luke's time. "Thank you. I'd love to see more of your work. Do you have a website or something?"

He dug in his back pocket for his wallet and handed me a business card done in natural shades of grassy green, brown earth, and blue sky. It read simply, *Luke Beckham Art*.

"Thanks. I can't wait to see more. I hope you enjoy the rest of your stay." I gave him a smile and turned to leave him in peace.

"Wait."

I stopped.

"I saw some lamps in the giftshop. *Leaf something*. I think it had your name on it."

"*Leaf and Lamp*. That's me." My creations seemed piddly beside the remembrance of Luke's masterpiece.

"Those lamps were awesome. What's your process?"

I explained the materials I used, the process of gathering the leaves and dying them with a natural colorant, piecing it all together with varnish and tissue paper.

"You do have a creative soul, then."

I smiled. "Nothing like you." It was on the tip of my tongue to ask if he could give me some pointers, or if I could simply watch him work for a half-hour or so, but it was too forward, too unpro-fessional. "Maybe I'll see you around?"

"Actually, I was going to spend the afternoon visiting some art galleries around town, see if they were interested in selling my work. Is that something you'd—"

"Yes! I'd love to come." I pushed my hair behind my ear. "I mean, I'd love to help you convince them to take a chance on your work."

He grinned. "Okay, then. Would one o'clock work for you?"

"Absolutely."

"Let's meet near the front desk?"

"Perfect."

I floated back into the kitchen, contemplating not only Luke, but his words about art school. As I cleaned up the breakfast dishes, my thoughts turned to August. Not once had he offered to visit an art gallery with me. The one time he'd gone it was because I'd begged him, and he'd acted as if it were the chore of the century.

How refreshing to find a guy who enjoyed the things I did. An amazingly talented guy. A handsome guy. A guy who assured me straight off that he had nothing to hide.

Augustus walked out of church alongside Tripp, who carried two-year-old Amos on his shoulders.

"Daddy, touch trees!" Amos shouted as his chubby hand skimmed a maple leaf, and August smiled at the wonder in his voice. The innocence. To his little nephew, nothing was more marvelous than time with his father, sitting on the shoulders of the biggest man in the world.

For a minute, August envied his brother, but not before remembering that his older brother's seemingly perfect life hadn't been without hardship. The boy on his shoulders—the boy who called him Daddy—wasn't completely his. In fact, Tripp didn't share an ounce of blood with Amos.

Not that you could tell at times like this, with Josie smiling at her husband as if she'd married him yesterday. Not with Tripp's sure fingers on Amos's little body, protective, caring, watchful.

August swallowed. Would he ever have that? Funny, but until recently, he never thought he *wanted* that.

Tripp buckled Amos into his car seat and spoke softly to Josie, who nodded, and shimmied her large belly behind the driver's seat of her SUV.

"Really? The lady's nine months pregnant and you're making her drive?"

Tripp grinned. "She can handle herself, believe me. I thought we could use a little time to talk."

"You don't see enough of me at the office?"

Grandpop pulled his truck up alongside them, Aunt Pris in the passenger's seat, her gray hair in tight curls. "You guys want a lift?" Grandpop asked.

Tripp shook his head. "We're going to walk over to Orchard House. I'll give August a ride home later."

"Maybe we'll see you there."

Aunt Pris waved out the window. "Bye, boys."

August waved. "Bye, Aunt Pris." He wanted to ask her if she'd talked to Amie that morning, if her great niece had hinted at anything that had happened the night before. If he had completely blown any chance there was for them.

He sighed. He was going nuts. Absolutely crazy.

They walked toward a bench on the green, cars bustling by as traffic began to pick up.

"Spill your guts, little bro."

He didn't even have the strength to argue as they sat on the bench. "I blew it, man. Completely blew it."

"What happened?"

"I went out with Amie last night. Everything was perfect. Except for the royal screw-up you call a brother."

"Uh-oh. What'd you do?"

August tried not to let the lack of surprise in Tripp's voice offend him. *Typical August, always screwing up.*

Then again, he didn't have anyone else to talk to, and his brother cared enough to notice he wasn't himself this morning. Cared enough to pull him aside and get in his business.

But telling Tripp what happened last night would mean confessing to the scratch tickets. Man, he wished he'd never bought them, that's for sure. Two lousy scratch tickets. Something

Grandpop used to put in his stocking as a kid. And yet now, those who knew him best knew he couldn't handle something most eight-year-olds could.

And they weren't wrong. August knew himself. Knew if he'd scratched those tickets, it would have been hard not to buy more. If he'd won a little bit of cash on them, it would have been all the harder. It was never enough. Soon, he'd be contemplating a drive to Oxford or Hollywood Casino.

"I had a weak moment when I was coming back home. Started getting anxious about if I was good enough for Colton Contractors." He raked a hand through his hair, knowing how these next words would take him down several notches in Tripp's eyes. "I thought if I could just pay Grandpop back for good, I'd be free. It was stupid, I see that now, but I stopped at the variety store and bought a couple scratch tickets. When I got in the car though, I couldn't do it. I knew if I scratched those tickets, all I'd worked for would be ruined. I shoved them in the glove box and forgot about them. Until Amie opened it last night, looking for a napkin."

Tripp closed his eyes, breathing deep.

"I wish I'd thrown them away—better yet, not bought them at all. But Amie blew up at me."

"Can you blame her?"

August let out a long sigh. "I guess not. I don't think she'll ever trust me again. I don't know what to do."

Tripp leaned his elbows on outspread knees, hands clasped, staring at the ground. "Trust takes time. Even more if it has to be rebuilt. You got to give her time, August. And you have to keep your nose clean. To someone else, it might be just a couple scratch tickets, but to you . . ."

"I know, I know. It's a slippery slope." He licked his lips, stared at the parked cars along the downtown thoroughfare. "Grandpop forgave my debt yesterday. Not only that, but he paid off my school loans."

Tripp whistled long and slow.

"Right? I've never felt more undeserving. Never known true gratitude until that moment." He punched his thigh. "Everything was perfect."

"You can't change the past—you and I both know that. But you can spend the rest of your days living in the grace Grandpop gave you. The grace God gives you. And, maybe one day, the grace Amie will give you."

"How, though? How can I begin to make up for it all?"

Tripp leaned back on the bench. "August, you've already come so far. I know you, man, and I know you're not stupid enough to throw it all away over a couple of scratch tickets. But a weak moment's a weak moment, so you have to watch out for them. Give me a call the next time one hits. Promise?"

August swallowed, jaw tight. "Yes."

"As for Amie . . . she probably needs time. Show her you're getting your act together. Show her you don't plan on going anywhere."

"She's leaving for New York in September. Time is one thing I don't have."

"If you guys are meant to be, God will make a way, even if it's not in your timing."

August groaned. If Amie left for New York, she'd find a whole new world. Probably with a whole bunch of artsy-fartsy guys who understood what she meant when she said a painting was *ethereal* or *abstract*, or his personal favorite, *stimulating*. Ugh. Why'd she have to talk like art was some erotic pleasure?

Without warning, an idea came to him. He snapped his fingers. "That's it."

"What?" Tripp asked.

"I'll buy her some type of painting. There was one she fell in love with at the gallery down the street when we dated, but it was out of her price range."

Tripp's answer was slow. "That's a nice gesture, but do you

really think spending your first paycheck on a piece of art is going to convince Amie you've changed?"

"You have any better ideas?"

Tripp shrugged. "I guess not. But, August, don't go crazy. Despite how Amie might come off, I think deep down, she's a simple woman with a big heart who just wants to be loved. Wants to know she can trust you with her love."

August raised an eyebrow. Of course, Tripp would be an expert on Amie, wouldn't he? Amie had spent the entirety of her teenage years hung up on his older brother, after all.

August stood, brushed off his pants. "Thanks, big bro, but I think I can take it from here."

Tripp didn't really know Amie after all, just the infatuated Amie. She wasn't into simple. She needed big, extravagant, something ostentatious to show her he was serious about a future together.

"Wait, don't you want a ride back home?"

August shook his head. "I'm going to walk over to the Camden Falls Gallery and scope it out."

Tripp shook his head, but a small smile pulled at his lips. He hooked two thumbs in his pockets. "You know, there's other ways of gambling that doesn't involve scratch tickets and casinos."

August's feet itched to cross the green toward the waterfront, toward the gallery Amie had dragged him to when they dated. "It's not a gamble if it's a sure thing, big brother."

And he knew that, when it came to Amie Martin, art was a sure thing.

ᨀᨁᨀ

THE QUESTION WAS, *WHICH* ART WAS A SURE THING?

August crossed his arms and stepped back, looking at the paintings on the wall of the Camden Falls Gallery.

Truthfully, they more or less looked all the same to him.

Waves and boats and the Maine coast and a few nature pieces mixed with collage and three-dimensional items he didn't completely understand. Which painting had Amie gone googly-eyed for all those months ago?

If only he'd paid more attention.

"Is there anything I can help you find?" A woman in her forties with a flowing skirt and flowery scarf approached him.

"I'm just having a look, thanks." He didn't need anyone to pressure him into a sale. Surely, he'd know the right painting when he saw it.

A painting of the Curtis Island Lighthouse caught his eye. Simple enough. He supposed it was pleasant to look at. Perhaps it would remind Amie of their romantic evening the night before.

As long as it didn't remind her of the scratch tickets she'd found *after* their romantic evening.

He groaned. Another lighthouse picture caught his eye. Clean and crisp, it almost looked like a photograph. He leaned closer, noticing the slight, intricate brushstrokes. It was the Marshall Point Lighthouse, the one featured in Forrest Gump when he ran from one end of the country to the other.

Amie loved Forrest Gump. Cried her eyes out when Bubba died and when Forrest met his son for the first time, asking Jenny if he was smart.

His gaze roved over the painting until he almost felt like he was inside it. A sense of peace came over him. He could practically hear the lapping of the waves against the pilings, feel the warmth of the sun's rays on his skin.

Wait. He snapped his fingers. Amie was always asking him, "Doesn't this make you feel something?" when they visited art galleries. He'd never understood what kind of an answer she sought. Until now. Well, even if he couldn't find the actual painting she'd loved, this one had to be good if it finally made him "feel something," right?

August dropped his gaze to the price tag. He nearly fell over.

Sixteen hundred dollars? He scratched his forehead, cleared his throat.

"Excuse me, ma'am. By any chance are these prices negotiable?"

"Which painting are you interested in?" She walked around the counter.

August pointed to the canvas of Marshall Point Lighthouse.

"Ah." The woman placed her finger on her chin. "A fine oil painting. All of Mr. Bonita's work is quiet and reflective. It takes the viewer outside of time to the mystical, wouldn't you agree?"

August cleared his throat, noting how the woman hadn't yet answered his question. "Yes, I'd say so."

"I could give you ten percent off that piece."

Ten percent. One hundred sixty dollars, bringing the grand total to a number that was still quite high for his modest budget.

And yet, Grandpop had freed him from his debt. He could swing this. Think of it as an investment in his relationship with Amie, showing her how serious he was about starting over.

"I'll take it." He slid out his credit card as the woman flounced to the cash register to take his payment and then packaged up his purchase with foam board and bubble wrap, placing it sideways in a sturdy plastic bag.

August thanked her and held the painting as carefully as he might a newborn babe. He couldn't wait to see Amie's face when she saw his gift.

The bell above the door jingled and a young couple bustled through, the man opening the door for—

August stumbled, nearly dropping his painting.

Amie's sparkling eyes turned toward him, instantly dimming. He hated how his presence caused her light to grow faint. He glanced at the man, who looked to be in his early thirties. In khaki pants, a polo shirt, and messy gelled hair, he exuded a casual confidence in this place that August could only hope to possess.

He hated him instantly.

Amie'd been laughing with him, light and airy. But seeing August had zapped her joy, it seemed.

His chest deflated with sudden realization.

What good was his newly purchased investment in his relationship with Amie if she was already interested in someone else?

12

A
t the sight of August, all of the air drained out of my lungs and anger took its place. Had he followed me here, or somehow known I was coming? There was simply no other explanation for him being in an art gallery.

"August."

My gaze dropped to the package in his hands. No, he couldn't have known I was coming here with Luke. More likely, he was picking up a painting for his grandfather. Mr. Colton always had more taste than his youngest grandson, after all.

August nodded at me. A distant gesture that didn't hide his apparent hurt at seeing me with Luke. "Amie. Hi."

A moment of awkward silence passed between us. Luke came up beside me and held out his hand to August.

Luke was the picture of easygoing. There's a common mantra often used in meditation that encourages calm and flow, a state of ease. That's how I was fast becoming to think of Luke—flowing, calm. So very opposite of August and his unpredictable, volatile ways. "Hi. I'm Luke."

August hefted his package beneath one arm and held out a strong, tanned hand to Luke. "August *Colton*."

Did he think the Colton name meant anything to Luke, a virtual stranger in Camden?

"August's an old friend. Luke is a guest at the B&B. He's an artist."

August scratched his cheek. "Doesn't your mother have a policy about fraternizing with the guests?"

I raised an eyebrow. "Fraternizing? That's a big word for a surfer boy like you, isn't it?" As soon as the words left my mouth, my ears grew hot. What was I thinking being so ill-mannered, and in front of Luke, no less?

I opened my mouth to apologize, but August spoke first.

"I was just leaving." He glanced at Luke. "Nice meeting you." He walked out the door, his package tight beneath his arm.

Luke cleared his throat. "You still up for this?"

Wow, the guy was intuitive. I shook my head to be certain my hair covered my ears. Luke studied me with a warm smile. He must not think me rude as August just had. "Absolutely."

August had already ruined last night and a good chunk of my morning. I refused to allow him to ruin my time with Luke—a talented, mature, sophisticated, creative man.

Clearly, a better choice of a man to spend my time with. No matter how my heart lurched at the sight of August stomping away from the gallery.

I blinked, turning to Luke. "Where do you want to start?"

He gestured to the paintings closest to the door. "Here seems good to me." He walked over to a painting of a crowded boat dock at night. "What do you think?"

I bit my lip. What if he deemed me foolish and inexperienced? What if he laughed at my thoughts?

"Come on, now. There are no wrong answers in art."

I swallowed. "It's done well. Good contrast of light and dark. Great texture and color values. Very realistic."

"But . . ." he prompted.

"There's a feeling of chaos, like I can't breathe when I look at it. I suppose, overall, I'm not a fan."

He didn't say anything, and when I met his gaze, I caught him staring at me, lips slightly parted.

I shook my head. "I don't know what I'm talking about, right?"

He placed a hand on my arm. "No. No, that's not it at all. Your insight . . . it's quite good."

I blinked. "Really?"

"Absolutely. Interpreting and judging art is all about honesty. You have a perceptive clarity, Amie." He turned to another piece of birch trees and majestic mountains in the background. "What about this one?"

We went on that way for several more paintings, taking turns discussing each painting, inviting the woman who worked at the gallery to share her opinions as well. Eventually, Luke showed his paintings to the owner. By the time we left, she was begging for more of Luke's work.

I walked out of the gallery with a grin on my face, Luke by my side. "That is by far the most fun I've ever had at an art gallery."

He slung an arm casually over my shoulders. "Me too. You know, if I had you around, I'd bet I'd make even greater art."

My face heated. "I don't know about that."

He dropped his arm. "I'm serious, Amie. You get art. I'm glad we ran into one another today."

Heat coursed through me. Was this guy truly as pleased by me as he seemed? "Me too. Thank you, Luke."

"No. Thank *you*."

13

August was *not* a morning person.

So, when he set his alarm an hour early Monday morning in order to accomplish his surprise for Amie, he acknowledged that only Amie Martin could be reason enough to propel him out of his warm bed sixty whole minutes before he absolutely had to be at the office.

Then again, Amie Martin was the reason why he hadn't fallen asleep until three o'clock in the morning. She was the reason why getting out of his bed proved excruciating.

He staggered to the bathroom where he flipped on the bright overhead lights, splashed his face with water, and brushed his teeth. Coffee. He needed coffee.

He pulled on a pair of jeans and a button-down collared shirt and headed down the stairs.

Grandpop was usually up by now, brewing coffee and mulling over the newspaper, but this morning proved eerily quiet. August made himself a cup of coffee and poured it into his travel mug, adding cream and two sugars before grabbing a banana and heading to his truck.

As his brain came to life, so did the image of Amie smiling and laughing with *Luke* the day before. The *artist*.

Should he leave well enough alone? Accept that Amie would move on from him? Accept that someone like Luke—a sophisticated, put-together guy who liked the same things Amie did—was a better choice for her than someone like him—a recovering gambling addict who would choose to be on a surfboard any day of the week over staring at paintings on a wall?

August took a right turn and swiped a hand over his face.

No.

He refused to think this was the end of him and Amie, just when he came back home. Just when he finally gained his freedom from debt.

He wouldn't sit by twiddling his thumbs while Amie gallivanted around town with *Luke*. The other night he told her he'd move heaven and earth to prove himself. The painting he'd purchased yesterday, along with what he had planned that morning, would be a start.

🕉️

I TROTTED UP THE STAIRS OF COLTON CONTRACTORS, THEN juggled my lunch bag and pocketbook as I opened the door. Last night, as I planned my outfit—high-waist turquoise ankle pants, a cream tweed blazer paired with a black square neck tank and black pumps—I realized I actually looked forward to going to work.

The office work, though far from creative or stimulating, suited me. I was *good* at it. Good at talking to potential and existing customers. Good at organizing schedules and working on a list of tasks.

My only hesitation this morning was seeing August after the events of this past weekend. Memories of Saturday's picnic dinner followed by our argument diminished beside memories of Luke and I visiting half a dozen art galleries yesterday afternoon.

The man was brilliant. He'd shown me his other paintings, each more extraordinary than the last. Like a whole new world to explore and experience on canvas. The galleries we visited eagerly agreed to offer them on consignment. For a single afternoon, I breathed in the possibilities of a life of art. Luke actually made a living off his work.

And he hadn't gone to school.

He'd taken me out for a laidback dinner at *Fresh & Co.* In fact, everything about Luke seemed laidback. Almost as if he hadn't a care in the world. Or, as if the cares of the world didn't matter because he knew what he was about.

"Don't you ever worry what will happen if your art stops selling?"

Luke forked into his vegetarian meal of stuffed eggplant. "Worry only robs today of its light, Amie. My art has been selling for years. I'm not about to borrow trouble by expecting it to plummet. Expect good things. They'll happen."

Expect good things. Was it that simple? If I expected to save up enough money to live in New York City and attend Parsons, would it happen? If I expected to make a living with my art, would it happen?

Luke told me about his mother's death when he was only two years old. He'd been raised by his dad, who hadn't approved of him spending time at his art. His father wanted Luke to follow his footsteps in the corporate world, trading stocks.

"I couldn't do it, you know? All that noise. All that emphasis on money. All the pressure. In the end, I had to be true to myself."

I'd tapped my fingers on the wooden table beside my salad. "See? I so admire that. *That's* what I want. To be true to myself."

"What's stopping you?"

What was stopping me? I bit my lip, mulling over my life, my plans. "Expectations, I guess."

"Whose expectations?"

I shifted in my seat, unsure how much to share with this virtual stranger. Yet, what would it hurt? Luke was living my dream. He was smart, handsome, a paying customer at my family's business. Why shouldn't I trust him?

"My family's, I suppose."

He stayed silent, waiting for me to say more.

I licked my lips. "I'm the fifth Martin child. The youngest. The only one not to get a degree. No, that's not true. Josie dropped out of school but now she's some wildly successful author, so the degree is a moot point."

Luke leaned back, his dark gaze intent on me, deciphering my words. "So, you feel the only acceptable way to pursue your art is with a degree."

I shrugged. "I thought school might help me learn how to make money with it, at least."

"School takes thousands of dollars you could pour into inspiration or starting up your own art business."

"Clearly, you're not a fan of art school."

"I tried it. I guess it's good for some. Not for me. If you want to learn how to make money, get a business degree. If you want to learn how to make art, *make* art."

Make art. It sounded so simple. No doubt for Luke, it was.

"But what art?" A crazy question. He barely knew me, barely knew if I had what it took to make it as an artist.

"Only you can answer that. That's part of being true to yourself."

I pushed my salad aside, breathing in a deep breath and releasing it slowly. "The leaf lamps were the first creative thing I made that actually sold. That's why I've put so much effort into them."

"They're unique, they hold charm. I can see why they sell. Do you love making them?"

"I did the first few times. Discovering the process, the excitement in creating. Now, they all look the same to me. I'm burnt out with them."

"Then it's time to move on." Luke scraped the remains of his eggplant parmesan onto the side of his fork.

"But they're the only way I'm making money off my art."

"But they take hours of creative energy. You said you had a job as a secretary, didn't you?"

"A temporary one, yes."

"Put in your hours with your nine to five, save the rest to explore what's inside of you, to experiment with mediums you haven't tried before, or to invest in what you're passionate about."

I leaned back in my seat. "And not go to art school."

"No one can tell you what to do with your future. Only you have the answers to that."

Luke had opened a whole new world of possibilities to me in a single day. What would I do if I didn't feel the pressure to make money with my art? What would I explore? I thought of my jewelry making endeavors, my elaborate macrame hangings and hammock swings. I could sell any of those on my Etsy shop if I wanted. But is that what excited me?

I pressed my lips together before speaking. "I've always liked painting, but it's never been my strongest medium."

"You haven't given yourself over to it."

I squinted across the table at him. "No. No, I haven't."

"Painting—good painting—can't be planned like your leaf lamps. It has to flow from the soul."

My breaths grew heavy at his words. Intoxicating words. An intoxicating voice. A man who understood me and what I wanted. Could I have found my soulmate? His foot gently moved alongside mine beneath the table.

"I never thought of it like that." Our waitress cleared our

plates, and before the conversation diminished, I worked up the courage to ask the question I'd been longing to ask all day. Ever since I saw his painting, really. "Could I . . . could I watch you paint? Sometime?"

An easy grin spread across his face. I noticed one slightly crooked tooth, could almost glimpse the boy he'd been. Sequestering himself in his room to work on his art while his father planned a future on Wall Street for him. "I don't enjoy painting when I have an audience."

My chest deflated. "Of course. I'm sorry. I shouldn't have—"

"But I enjoy painting with other artists. Why don't you come to my room tomorrow after you're done with work? We'll paint together."

Blood rushed to my face. I was quite sure Mom wouldn't approve of me spending time in one of the guest's rooms, but we wouldn't be doing anything wrong. Making art. Together.

"Really?"

"Absolutely."

"I'm not very good."

He winked. "Maybe I could give you a few pointers. Or at least help you relax into yourself, find your creative spirit."

Was it just me, or was there more to the meaning of his words? A flirtatious quality, an insinuation?

I blinked, shoving the thought aside. Luke appeared genuine. What would it be like to be mentored by someone with his talent?

"Okay. I'd like that. Thank you."

We'd left the restaurant shortly after, and he hadn't given me more than a friendly wink when we arrived back at the bed and breakfast. The perfect gentleman. I could hardly wait to see him the next day.

But first, I'd have to get through the day with August. No biggie. I was the acting secretary of Colton Contractors. *Professional* could be my middle name.

I strode into the office, aware of the uncharacteristic quiet. Usually, I could hear Tripp and August talking about a project, or one of the guys on the crew in Tripp's office, discussing a punch list or a task for the work day. Mr. Colton's grunts and deep, booming voice had become background music in the office.

This Monday morning, however, proved eerily quiet. I placed my lunch in the refrigerator in the kitchen and walked to my desk. My computer already glowed with a screensaver that show-cased completed Colton Contractors projects, so someone must be here. Likely Tripp or Mr. Colton—both early risers.

I pulled out my chair and stopped short. A smattering of brightly-colored sticky notes adorned the sides of my computer screen. At the top, in a large rectangle, a fluorescent pink note read:

WHY WE SHOULD BE TOGETHER

August's handwriting. I blinked, slowly lowering myself to the padded office chair.

My eyes roamed the notes, skipping here and there to take in his words.

We make each other laugh.

Our favorite ice cream is mint chocolate chip.

I rolled my eyes. We'd probably need a little more than humor and a common ice cream flavor for the foundation of a rela-tionship.

We grew up together. I still have the ceramic teacup you made me even though I've never drank a cup of tea in my life.

I smiled. I'd almost forgotten about my pottery phase. Stacks of my old pottery had found its way into the basement of Orchard House—Mom too sentimental to toss the pathetic attempts.

Apparently, August had been sentimental about his teacup, too.

The thought of August keeping the little cup on his bureau or nightstand formed a lump in my throat as I continued to read.

You were born on a Monday, I was born on a Friday. You were born in the middle of the night, I was born in the middle of the day.

He seemed to be reaching with that one.

I'm a great kisser. Okay, you're pretty great at it, too.

Who was he kidding? I was an *amazing* kisser.

I sighed, remembering our first kiss. It had gone on forever, and I'd been enraptured by it. I hadn't wanted anything more, I simply wanted him to kiss me all night.

We both have amazing eyes. Can you imagine the gorgeous children we'd make together?

My face heated. August had never mentioned wanting children. Children meant long-term commitment. Marriage. Was he really thinking so seriously about me?

We know the deepest parts of one another—both the good and the bad. There's no one else I want by my side . . . forever.

I blinked away unshed tears.

Who was this man? Talking about children and forever and knowing the deepest parts of each other? I didn't want his words to seduce me. I wanted to forget about August Colton and the very real possibility of him breaking my heart. I wanted to pick him up and place him in a corner of my past I no longer had to deal with. I wanted to focus my attention on my art career. I wanted to devote my time to a man like Luke—a mature man who shared the same interests as me, who listened to me, who, I was quite certain, didn't have a gambling addiction.

My gaze fell to the bottom corner of the computer screen where a bold arrow pointed downward. I looked to see another post-it note with an arrow, followed by another, and another. Eventually, I came around to the other side of my desk.

I gasped. There, leaning on the back of my desk was a gorgeous oil painting of Marshall Point Lighthouse. A large mauve bow perched in the corner and a card with my name on it sat on the floor beside the painting.

Oh, August, what are you doing to me?

I knelt by the piece of art, studying the clean lines and fine brush strokes. Though nothing like Luke's impressionist paintings, I found myself drawn to the artist's use of color to create light at sunset. The stone pilings, the bridge to the lighthouse, even the tower of the light itself all reflected the striking glow.

In a rush of realization, I remembered August leaving Camden Falls Gallery with a painting similar in size the day before. Was this what he'd been doing? Not picking up a painting for his grandfather, but picking one . . . for me?

I blinked, tearing open the card. A relief painting of a boat in the ocean was featured on the front. A unique greeting card—one you couldn't pick up at a Hannaford's or Walmart.

Amie,
To say I'm sorry for what happened Saturday night isn't enough, but please know, from the bottom of my heart, I am sorry. You deserve nothing less than my complete honesty and integrity. I meant what I said—I love you, now and forever. Even if you never accept me, even if you hate me forever . . . Amie Martin, I will love you to my dying day.
I saw this painting and it made me feel something. A peace, a hope. That's never happened to me before, and it made me think of you.
Please, give me another chance. I only want to spend the rest of my days proving myself to you.
Yours Forever,
August

A tear slid down my cheek, and I tried to brush it away before Mr. Colton or Tripp walked into the office. I was on the clock, after all. This was entirely inappropriate.

And yet . . . his words. That *painting*. August may not have been speaking my love language when we dated, but he was most certainly speaking it now.

I startled at the sound of someone clearing his throat behind me.

"August."

He approached from the direction of his office, moving toward me with slow, cautious steps.

Still crouching on the carpet, I shook my head. "What are you thinking, August Colton? This is too much."

"Not for you. Nothing is too much for you. Please, Amie. Say you'll give us another chance. I'm crazy about you. Always have been, always will be."

I inhaled a quivering breath.

He continued. "I hate myself for hurting you. If I thought I could live without you . . . if I thought I could stand by while a guy like Luke sweeps you off your feet, I would. If I could fool myself into thinking it's what's best for you, I might be able to do it. And maybe I'm crazy or arrogant or full of myself, but I can't believe another guy's what's best for you, Amie. Because I'm what's best. I know it. To the core of my being, I know it. Because I'm the one who loves you."

He held his hand out to me, his skin tan and inviting and familiar, and I took it, allowing him to pull me to my feet.

"How in the world do you know what's best for me?" I whispered.

"This." He stared into my eyes, and there it was. The dizzying sensation, the consuming fire of passion that had always been ours.

He was right about one thing. Whether I wanted it or not, we were a part of one another. Our history alone had made it so.

I'd once read an article in a science magazine that said when two people who love each other touch, their heart rates and breathing rates align. I knew it was true, for it happened often between me and August. It happened now. Reason didn't stand a chance when our hearts were synchronized like this.

He breathed deep, spoke again. When he did, my brain scrambled, trying to believe the words I heard coming from his mouth.

"My love is like a red, red rose,
That's newly sprung in June.
My love is like the melody,
That's sweetly played in tune."

My face flamed. This couldn't be happening. Had he listened to an audio version of the poem? Because the sexy Scottish accent he pulled off was making my toes curl. "August, you don't have to . . ."

He pressed a finger to my lips.

"So fair art thou my lovely Amie,
So deep in love am I,
That I will love thee still, my dear,
Till all the seas gang dry."

He continued on and I tried not to melt beneath his words, his ocean gaze intent on me.

This was August, who struggled to remember two sentences for an eighth-grade science project we presented to the class. August, who hated poetry and reading, and even too much talk of romance.

And here he recited the entire Robert Burns poem, his words sucking the air from the room and making my legs like Jell-O.

When he finished, he didn't break my gaze. "I should have never gone back to school. I should have stayed until I made it up to you."

"Don't be ridiculous," I said, although I couldn't deny the power behind the thought.

"Give me another chance?"

I didn't answer right away, but when my gaze dropped to his mouth, he slowly lowered his lips to mine, as if testing to see if I might pull away.

I didn't.

Gently, he tasted my mouth. A kiss as soft as a feather, as rollicking as one of the thundering waves he loved to ride his surfboard. And then he pulled back, leaving me hungry for more.

"Is that a yes?" he asked.

I breathed around the passion tingling through my body. "We like the same ice cream? You think that's enough to build a relationship on?"

"Hey, I take my ice cream seriously."

A half-smile tilted my lips. "Do you really still have the teacup I made you?"

"It's a pen holder on my desk, but yes. Anything else you'd care to discuss? Maybe how gorgeous our future children would be?"

I tapped my chin and scrunched my face. "Except you walk around all day with your cell phone in your front pants pocket, likely killing the structure that would give us said future children."

He dug out his phone, threw it on my desk. "Never again. For the sake of our future children."

I rolled my eyes, but couldn't contain a giggle. I pushed away from him, biting my lip.

Giggling was not going to help anything. I needed to keep my head about me when it came to the younger Colton brother.

"August, I know your intentions are good, but what happens if we're running short on money? If we blow up at one another like we did when we broke up? We have little in common. What if we grow apart?"

He grabbed my hands with his own warm fingers. "I don't have all the answers, but I know I love you and I'm willing to work at this. I'm different, Amie. What we had—what we could have—is worth trying for. Please give us a chance."

His phone rang out, vibrating on my desk. A series of dings set off *my* phone, tucked away in my bag.

I jerked away from August. He scooped up his phone. "Tripp, everything okay?"

I read the group texts on my phone.

Josie: THIS BABY'S COMING! LIZZIE'S ALREADY
SETTLED WITH AMOS AND WE ARE ON OUR WAY TO
THE HOSPITAL!

Maggie: OH, YAY! PRAYING FOR YOU GUYS!

Mom: I'LL BE THERE AS SOON AS BREAKFAST IS
SERVED. CAN'T WAIT TO MEET MY NEXT
GRANDCHILD!

Lizzie: WOOHOO! (AMOS SAYS WOOHOO, TOO!)

I typed in my own excited words.

TRIPP BETTER GET YOU TO THAT HOSPITAL
PRONTO. IF THIS ONE'S ANYTHING LIKE ITS
BROTHER, YOU DON'T HAVE MUCH TIME!

I smiled, remembering how Josie's water had broken when
only Aunt Pris and I were home. Lucky for both of us, Esther had
remembered enough of her midwife days to help bring Amos into
the world.

I imagined meeting my new niece or nephew for the first
time, cuddling him or her in my arms as I'd done with Amos and
Maggie's daughter, Grace. While I'd never been one to get googly-
eyed over babies, my nieces and nephews were an entirely
different matter.

Oh. I was supposed to paint with Luke later in the day.
"Shoot." It would have to wait. I pulled up his number in my
messages and tapped out a quick apology along with a request
that we plan another time to paint together.

I slumped in my seat. I'd really been looking forward to

painting with Luke, but I looked forward to meeting my niece or nephew all the more.

When I finished, I looked up to find August staring at me. From the look on his face, he must have seen who I was texting. It irritated me when my face heated. I'd been doing nothing wrong.

With a ping of both regret and desire, I remembered the painting. The sticky notes. The card. That poem. I blinked, and slid my phone away. "I guess I should get to work so I have time to see my new niece or nephew later."

His jaw tightened, but to his credit, he didn't question why I texted Luke minutes after he'd confessed his undying love for me. "Me, too." A forced smile lifted his lips. "You think it's a boy or a girl?"

"Girl," I said. "Josie needs a daughter. What about you?"

"Boy. Amos needs a brother."

We shared an awkward laugh before he started down the hall, twisting at the last minute to point a finger at me. "Don't think our conversation's over, Martin. We have a major discussion in our future."

Did I want that discussion to occur? Yes, yes I did. But was it for the best? Wasn't someone like Luke—someone who understood me, who shared the same interests as me, the better choice? Luke had given me insight that made me rethink my entire life in just a few minutes. August had always given confusion, not clarity.

I couldn't reassure August. Not now. I wasn't there yet. Maybe I never would be.

And yet, there was no denying I wanted him. I studied his broad retreating back, longing for him to take me in his arms again, to kiss me with that same tender restraint.

I shook my head, forcing the longing away. From where he stood in the hallway, August's phone rang again. This time, he froze mid-step, rigid. His words echoed, rolling over the walls toward me.

"Grandpop? Grandpop, you okay?"

The tiny hairs on the back of my neck prickled, a thin sheen of sweat broke out on my skin.

August turned, starting back toward me, wide-eyed terror forming his face. "Amie, call 9-1-1 and send them to Pop's house!"

14

August's chest squeezed as he pressed his phone closer to his ear, as if that would transport him to his grandfather. By his side, to help.

"Grandpop, stay with me. I'm coming home now. Amie's calling the ambulance." He dove into his office to grab his keys off the desk.

His grandfather mumbled a gargling gibberish of words. Fear clamped down around August's throat. "Hold on. I'm coming," he croaked out. "I'm not going to hang up."

He passed Amie's desk, her eyes wide as she recited the Colton address to the dispatcher.

She scrambled out from behind her desk to open the door for him, placing a hand on his arm. He stopped, a millisecond in time that meant all the world to him.

"He's going to be okay," she whispered.

It was a silly thing to say. But nonsensical or not, it made him feel better. He bent to place a quick kiss on her temple before jogging down the stairs to his truck.

God, please.

He prayed silently between attempts at assuring words to his grandfather, now eerily silent. Once in his truck, he drove too fast. He couldn't lose Grandpop. He couldn't. Not now, not when he'd forgiven August his debts and they had the chance at a new beginning.

A new beginning that didn't include tumultuous teen years or the aftermath of a gambling addiction. They'd eaten dinner together last night for the first time since Tripp moved out. They'd *laughed*. August had teased his grandfather about popping the question to Aunt Pris. When Grandpop had returned the jest by mentioning Amie, August had confessed Amie's hesitation when it came to dating him.

He hadn't, however, confessed to the scratch tickets. He wasn't stupid, after all. He refused to disappoint his grandfather again, especially after he'd paid off all his debts.

Now, he wondered if he should have come clean. But no. How would that have helped anything?

It had been Grandpop's idea to recite poetry to Amie.

"Come on, Pops. Guys don't do that stuff anymore."

His grandfather had dipped his head and looked out of hooded eyes at August. "Maybe that's part of the problem with romance today. A little more poetry, a little less worrying about how you're going to skip ahead to the bedroom."

August cleared his throat. "I'm not—I mean, I'm not messing things up this time around. I realize what I had and I don't intend to lose her again."

"Then I suggest you memorize some poetry, young Colton."

August had shaken his head, a small smile pulling at his lips. "I'll think about it."

Now, August turned hard into the driveway and jumped out, running inside the house and leaving the door open for the paramedics. He called for his grandfather while hanging up his phone. Even if the older man couldn't answer, he wanted Grandpop to hear his voice.

To know he wasn't alone.

"Pops!" In the distance, sirens sounded closer. August scanned the kitchen and dining room. No sign of his grandfather. He tore up the stairs and rounded the corner, gripping tight to the solid wood banister.

When he reached the closed door of his grandfather's bedroom, he pushed it open.

His blood stilled in his veins.

Grandpop lay on the floor, clad in his two-piece striped pajamas. One leg splayed out at an awkward angle, the phone fallen from an outstretched hand.

August ran to him, kneeling beside his frail body. "Grandpop, I'm here. It's going to be okay."

But was it? His grandfather blinked, barely registering August's presence.

It hit him, then.

Grandpop had called *him*.

For some reason, that fact slammed him hard. He couldn't have known Tripp was busy having a baby, but he *had* known he hadn't felt well, or at least that something wasn't right.

And he'd called August for help.

August ran a hand over his grandfather's cool cheek, the notion that he'd failed the man who'd raised him fast taking root. "It's okay. They're almost here."

Sirens close, close, closer still. Voices outside the window.

"Up here!" August yelled, emotion thick in his throat. "Hurry, please." He dove toward the door to flag the paramedics.

Two uniformed men rushed into the room, one evaluating Grandpop, the other preparing a stretcher and asking August what happened.

"I was on the phone with him. He was slurring and mumbling."

"Okay. It sounds like you caught it quick. We're going to help."

August stepped back as they lifted Grandpop onto the gurney.

"You going to ride with us?"

"Yes." He didn't plan to let his grandfather out of his sight. Not now, maybe not ever.

He climbed into the ambulance, vacillating on whether or not to inform Tripp. Better not. Josie needed him, and they'd be at the hospital in no time. He refused to be selfish. Refused to call Tripp simply to hear his older brother's calm assurance.

He'd told Amie he'd grown up. Well, now was the time to prove it.

August closed his eyes as the ambulance tore onto the main road, sirens blaring.

God, I know I don't deserve for you to answer my prayers. But Grandpop does. Please, help him. He's old, but he's got so much more life in him still. I know it. Please, give me more time with him.

More time with Grandpop. Another chance with Amie.

Seemed he was asking for second chances all over the place.

The question was, would God grant them to a guy like him?

❧ 15 ❧

"Colton Contractors."

I pressed my ear to the phone. Without Mr. Colton or Tripp's direction, I floundered in the office. Yet, I refused to leave. Someone had to hold down the fort, and no matter how inadequate I might be, I was all Colton Contractors had at this moment.

"Miss Amie, it's Pedro. I can't get a hold of the Boss Man's cell. He in the office?"

Pedro was the foreman for Colton Contractors. I knew from last week that "Boss Man" was code for Tripp.

"I'm afraid not. He's busy having a baby at the moment. Anything I can help you with?"

"Oh, man. The baby decides to come today, huh?" He let out a long sigh. "Better let me speak to the Big Boss Man, then."

Big Boss Man. Code for Mr. Colton.

"Mr. Colton had an emergency, and August is with him. I'm sorry, Pedro. I don't think any of them are going to be available anytime soon."

Pedro released a mild curse, then apologized. "Sorry, Miss Amie. I have a situation, and I'm not sure what to do."

I blew a stray piece of hair out of my face. "Have you tried to call Josh?"

Maggie's husband was the other foreman at Colton Contractors.

"He's off today, chaperoning a field trip with the twins, I think he said."

"Looks like I'm your only option, Pedro." I tapped my long, polished nails on the desk, grimacing when I chipped the vegan, water-based nail color. "Sorry to disappoint. What happened?"

"I just got to the Trivino estate."

I racked my brain for the list of ongoing projects Colton Contractors had in the works. Trivino, Trivino, Trivino . . . ah, yes. The large in-law addition in Lincolnville. The family had taken a two-week trip to Florida. The plan was for the project to be completed by the time they returned home. As far as I knew, Pedro and his crew finished installing the kitchen last Friday.

"The counters are supposed to be installed today, aren't they?"

"I don't think that's going to happen, Boss Lady."

I raised my eyebrows. I was far from anyone's boss. "Why not?"

"We've got a water leak. A big one. Looks like the upstairs bathroom. Water's been soaking the new kitchen all weekend from the looks of it."

"Oh no," I groaned. "Oh no, oh no, oh no. How could this happen?"

"Hard to say. Not cold enough to freeze. It could have been when the plasterers hung sheetrock up there in the winter. Sometimes they can puncture a line."

I rubbed my forehead, pressing my eyes shut. "Listen, I'm going to the hospital later. I'll talk to Tripp then. Right now, I'll call the granite company and tell them to hold off."

"We're going to have to start from scratch."

I cringed thinking about the money that'd be lost on both

materials and time. "Don't touch anything yet. We might have to have pictures taken for the insurance company."

"Sure thing. Where do you want me and the crew to go for the rest of the day?"

Where did *I* want them to go?

I thumbed through the planner before me with a list of our ongoing jobs. A roof job scheduled for next week. But the shingles weren't being delivered until Thursday. We were still waiting for the permits for the Hill construction. Another crew worked in Rockport building a cabana. If I sent Pedro's crew over there, half the guys would be twiddling their thumbs.

My gaze landed on the last name on the list. Paulette Rivers. A widowed woman who wanted Colton Contractors to paint her kitchen and dining room. I'd finalized the paint colors with her on Friday.

"Can you pick up some paint if I give you the colors?"

Pedro groaned. "Ms. Rivers, right? We just painted her kitchen last year."

"She likes to keep things fresh. You could finish it today, right?"

"Sure thing, Boss Lady."

I threw back my shoulders. "I need to call her first, but I'll ring you back in a few minutes, okay?"

"Okay, Boss Lady. Good job today."

"Thanks, Pedro." I hung up the phone, my mind whirling with not only news of Josie's baby and Mr. Colton's emergency, but the major setback at the Trivino estate. Pedro's crew would be weeks behind.

I rang up Ms. Rivers, who assured me she had nothing on her calendar except for her prayer group later that night. Then, after I'd called Pedro back, I looked up the information for Colton's insurance company. This wouldn't be fun, but someone had to do it, and since I was the only one in the office, that someone was me.

WHY HAD HE BOTHERED TO COME TO THE HOSPITAL'S CHAPEL room?

But August knew why.

Because anything was better than sitting in that waiting room, waiting for someone to come out and tell him Grandpop was . . . was . . . He refused to let his mind go there.

The paramedic had said it looked like a stroke, but they couldn't be certain until they ran tests. A stroke. Would Grandpop lose his ability to walk, to write, to talk, to accomplish the simplest of tasks?

August had called the bed and breakfast and spoken to Mrs. Martin, who planned to drive Aunt Pris to the hospital as soon as she could get away from breakfast duties. He hadn't been able to hide the emotion in his voice when he spoke to Amie's mother, the closest thing he had on earth to a mother himself.

"I don't know if he's going to make it, Mrs. Martin."

"Oh, August. I'm so sorry." Mrs. Martin's voice cracked. "We're going to pray for him, that's for certain. We're going to put Ed in the Lord's hands and trust that He has a good plan for your grandfather. Whatever that is, honey. And when we get to the hospital, we're going to pray together."

He couldn't find the fortitude to disagree. He needed someone to tell him what to do. If Mrs. Martin said to pray, then he'd continue what he'd started the minute he realized Grandpop was in danger.

He'd prayed for hours in the waiting room, and when he couldn't take the cramped room any longer, he'd come to the chapel.

The room was small with five rows of wooden pews. Windows lined one wall, showcasing hospital gardens. An altar at the front stood naked without a cross or any other religious symbol. He supposed that made it more inclusive, which was fine enough.

Only right now, he longed for somewhere to put his focus. Anything, other than the vast abyss of nothing that the front altar seemed to offer.

He leaned forward to kneel, elbows propped on the pew back in front of him.

God, he started, but couldn't manage more words. Instead, he thought of Grandpop in the kitchen, pronouncing him free from debt. And when he insisted he didn't deserve it, what had his grandfather said?

That's grace, young man. It's what God's given me and it's what He offers you every day. It's what I'm giving you now.

"God, give Grandpop your grace," he whispered. "Give me your grace. Don't take him. I'd be lost. I need him more than you do, God."

A wetness spread down his cheeks, and he swiped it away. He was becoming a regular ninny lately—what was with him?

But if anyone deserved his tears, it was Grandpop.

He didn't know how long he knelt, begging for a miracle, but at some point, he grew numb to the physical and emotional pain. Silent. Still. Not exactly peace, but a quiet settled inside him.

Perceiving a movement beside him, he looked up to see Amie sitting a foot away.

He slid onto the bench. "What time is it?"

"Four-thirty."

He stood. "I've been away too long. I have to go check on Grandpop."

"They're moving him to a room."

August blinked. "He's—what did they say?"

"Aunt Pris told me. I thought you knew . . ."

He shook his head. "What did they decide it was?"

"He had a stroke. But they're hopeful his recovery will be good since he was able to get to the hospital so quick. They're giving him medicine and performed some sort of procedure that's supposed to break up the clot."

For the first time since that morning, August took a full, deep breath. "He—he's going to be all right?"

Amie gave him a small smile. "They seem to think so. Aunt Pris is insistent he will be absolutely fine."

August smirked. If anyone could will his grandfather better, it'd be Aunt Pris.

He slid to his knees again, hiding his face in his hands. *Thank you, God. I mean it. Thank you so much.*

The tears came again, this time born of relief. When they turned to quiet, shaking sobs, Amie knelt beside him and put an arm around his back.

"It's okay, August," she whispered. "He's going to be okay."

He nodded, lifted his head, and sniffed hard. "I've never heard better news." Not even when Grandpop had forgiven his debt. He hadn't realized how much his grandfather meant to him until he'd nearly lost him. How many other relationships in his life had he taken for granted? "I'm going to see him if I can."

"I'm going to stay here for a minute if that's okay."

"Of course. I'll catch up with you later. Did Josie have the baby yet?"

Amie broke into a grin. "A boy. Eight pounds, two ounces. No name yet."

His nephew. August's chest swelled. "Does Tripp know about Grandpop?"

She shook her head. "I don't think so. Josie only had the baby an hour ago."

"I'll catch up with him after I check on Grandpop."

Amie nodded and reached her hand out to him. He squeezed her fingers, soft and warm and comforting.

"Thank you, Ame. For everything."

"I'll always be here for you, August. Whatever happens."

He released her hand and turned to walk down the short aisle of the chapel. Her words left him with an empty feeling instead of one of promise. Had she meant she'd always support him, even if they weren't together?

He pushed open the chapel door, forcing such thoughts from his mind. Right now, he needed to focus on doing everything in his power to get Grandpop better.

The chapel door closed behind me and I soaked in the quiet, still thinking of August's quaking body beneath my arm, how he'd knelt as if in prayer, utterly boy-like and broken.

I blinked back my own tears just thinking about it. Thankfully, I'd been able to give him good news. I stared ahead at the empty altar.

God, are you there?

I wanted to thank the Creator of the universe for sparing August's grandfather, for giving me a new nephew, for allowing me breath and life and art and beauty and family. Why then, did I feel so distant from Him? So unsure of His existence?

Though I tried to shake the thoughts from my mind, this place inspired them. Quiet, peaceful, with spring flowers blooming right outside the glass wall of windows.

For someone who considered herself so in touch with nature and humanity and her own moral compass, shouldn't I also be in touch with the spiritual things in this world? Shouldn't I be certain of my faith, of what drove my very purpose? Instead, I'd always leaned on what felt right. Watching my family, I realized faith was sometimes *hard*. Did I really need more challenges in my life? Another reason to feel like a failure, unable to cling to an invisible God when the going got tough?

I thought of Luke saying I needed to be true to myself. Why, in this place where death and life coexisted so effortlessly, did that sound a bit hollow? I wanted to be more than true to myself, I wanted to be sure of my beliefs, to throw myself behind them with the passion they deserved.

God, show me who you are.

It was a simple prayer, but it was all I had.

I sat in silence, breathing deep, enjoying the quiet when I heard the chapel door open again. A heavyset woman with skin that matched the dark hair she wore in braids walked past me.

"Am I bothering you, honey?"

I shook my head and stood. "Actually, I was just leaving."

"Oh, please don't. Two or more are stronger in the Spirit."

I smiled, something about her warm brown gaze and friendly smile causing me to sit back down in the bench.

"Someone you love here?" She lowered herself to the end of a pew across from me, one row up.

"My sister just had a baby." I was about to tell her my boyfriend's grandfather had a stroke, but found myself caught on how to define August, so I clamped my mouth shut.

"Well, that is a happy state of affairs, now, isn't it?" Her brow drew downward. "Is the baby healthy?"

"Oh, yes."

"Good, child. Good. Nothing wrong with taking some time to thank the Lord for the blessings He brings us."

I swallowed. "My boss . . . he was kind of like a grandfather to me growing up, he's here too. He had a stroke." Why was I telling this lady these things? Did I need to give her a reason why I was in the chapel? It was a free country, after all. I could be here if I liked.

She tsked. "I'm sorry to hear that. Do they think he'll be okay?"

I nodded. "He seems to have a hopeful prognosis."

"Praise God for that." She was quiet for a moment.

"How about you?" I asked. "Is someone . . ."

"My husband. Started having seizures again. He's a diabetic. Thinks he can pop pills alongside his donuts and call it even. Stupid man." She sighed, shook her head. "But I love that stupid man. Love him more than life itself."

I bit my lip. Mom would offer to pray with this lady on the spot. But I was not Mom. "I hope he's okay."

"I hope so, too."

We were quiet again. "I should go, but I hate to leave you alone . . ."

"Oh, sugar, the Lord's my company. Besides, I have some sisters coming to offer me their encouragement. I'd be lost without my church family. You got a church family, darlin'?"

I cleared my throat. I went to church often because that's what the Martins did. Wake up on Sunday morning to head down the road to the historic white church on the green.

It wasn't that I didn't like it. The worship music was okay, but more often than not I tuned out the sermons. Any attachment I had to church was more over fond childhood memories with people I knew forever than anything to do with faith. But did I consider them my family?

The woman must have taken my hesitation as a *no*. "Church family's important. Real important." She dug in her bag and withdrew a card, reaching across the aisle to give it to me. "You come to my church. Be a part of our family."

I glanced at the card.

Abundant Life Church.
Where Faith and Life Meet.

Located in a town about twenty minutes south of Camden.

I smiled at her. "Thank you. I might just do that."

"You better, sweet girl. We all need a church family."

"I'll say a prayer for your husband."

"Thanks, sugar. His name is Joe. And my name's Kyra. And what's the name of your grandfather?"

I didn't correct her. "Ed."

"I'll be praying for Ed. And I look forward to seeing you Sunday."

I waved goodbye, unwilling to commit to such a venture quite yet.

Forty-five minutes later, I was gazing over the tiny, red features of my little nephew in my sister's arms. His nose regal, like his father's. "He's absolutely perfect."

Tripp grinned. "We're pretty attached."

"No name yet?"

He exchanged glances with Josie, whose hair lay pulled back and lumpy, likely from the toils of labor. I thought about August's comment regarding children, tried to picture myself in the throes of labor. Ick.

"What do you say? Will your mom throw a fit if we tell Amie before her?" Tripp asked.

Josie swatted a hand through the air. "Amie was the first person to meet Amos. It's only fitting she be the first one to hear our name for this little guy."

My heart swelled. Josie and I had as much in common as the day does with the night. We got on one another's nerves. Yet, beneath it all—sometimes, *really* deep beneath it all—we held a special bond. Our hardships and arguments had made our peaceful moments all the more precious.

"We're naming him Edward, after my grandfather," Tripp said.

"But we're going to call him Eddie."

"Oh, I love it! Little Eddie." I allowed the name to roll off my tongue, savoring it as much as I savored the sight of my new nephew, all swaddled up to his mother, a tuft of dark hair poking out from his blankets. "I won't tell anyone, I promise. Wait until his big brother meets him. Did Lizzie bring Amos over yet?"

Josie stifled a yawn. "They're on their way. Actually, I better feed this little guy before they get here."

I gave an awkward hug to my sister, scared to hurt her with my embrace. She offered me a brilliant smile. "I'm glad you saw him first, Ame."

I blinked back tears. "I love you, sis."

"Love you, too."

"I think I'll go dig up something to eat." Tripp kissed Josie on the top of the head, then did the same with little Eddie. I bid goodbye one more time and then walked out of the room with Tripp, closing the door softly behind us.

We started down the hall. "Seriously, Tripp, I didn't want to say anything in front of Josie because I know how touchy she can be, but he looks just like you."

He grinned. "I know."

I laughed.

"How'd things go at the office today?"

My thoughts stalled. "Um . . . we had a lot going on." News about the Trivino project could wait, but Tripp should know about his grandfather now that little Eddie had safely arrived, shouldn't he? August wanted to handle it all on his own, but it wasn't right. He needed his brother.

I cleared my throat. "Your grandfather actually had an incident today, Tripp. He's here in the hospital."

Tripp stopped walking, his eyes growing wide. "What? What happened? Is he okay?"

"He had a stroke. They think he'll have a good recovery. That's all I know. I'm sorry."

He strode fast down the hallway, jabbing the elevator button with his thumb. "Where is he? Why didn't anyone tell me?"

I scurried to his side. "You were having a baby. Josie needed you—all of you. There's nothing you could have done. August has been doing nothing but waiting for hours."

"What floor?"

"I—I don't know."

The elevator door slid open and we stepped inside the empty space. Tripp pushed a button for the first floor.

"I'm so sorry, Tripp."

He leaned one hand against the wall, jaw tight, eyes closed.

I reached out a hand to his muscled arm. "He's going to be okay."

He placed his hand on the back of mine and nodded. "Thanks."

How many times had Tripp comforted me after Dad died? We both knew firsthand that things didn't always end okay. Weird to be on the giving end of comfort, but also . . . right.

He straightened, releasing my hand as the doors opened. I watched him stride down the hall, and as I followed, I realized that whatever romantic feelings I'd held for Tripp in the past had finally and truly slid into their rightful place as sisterly affection.

I released a long breath, an insatiable need to find August and make sure he was doing okay surging within me. I'd given comfort to Tripp, and now, more than anything, I wanted to make sure I could give the same to his younger brother.

❧ 17 ❧

August stared at the grandfather clock as it chimed eleven times in the empty house. He didn't move, simply gazed out into the dim room, inhaling the scent of his grandfather still clinging to the stuffed armchair August sat in—leather and books and Old Spice. Across the room stood a bookcase with all Grandpop's favorites—The Lord of the Rings trilogy, The Odyssey, Jurassic Park, and a smattering of other books by Ray Bradbury, Charles Dickens and George Orwell. He even had some Calvin and Hobbes thrown in there.

August's gaze fell to the end table where Grandpop's well-worn Bible lay. He closed his eyes, picturing his grandfather in this very chair, feet propped up, Bible in hand. It seemed Grandpop spent as much time in this chair reading the Holy Book as he had simply closing his eyes with it on his lap. August suspected he fell asleep often like that, but he also knew his grandfather prayed in that position as well.

August raked a hand through his hair. He'd gone to visit his grandfather earlier in the day. Four days in the hospital had brought little improvement. Though Grandpop could speak, it was through slurred words. August had fed him dinner that evening and the process had been humbling, for both of them. Mashed potatoes falling out of his mouth, and chicken pureed so his grandfather could get it down.

Grandpop had shaken his head in frustration, refusing to eat, which in turn produced frustration in August. "Come on, Pops. You have to eat to get your strength back."

His grandfather had waved a hand through the air. "Leave," he'd said without the full "l" sound at the beginning.

And August had.

Was this his grandfather's life now? He'd been so strong, so quick-witted. Would he be reduced to being pushed around in a wheelchair, struggling to feed himself or accomplish any of life's everyday tasks? And what about the business? How would they survive without his dynamic personality running the show?

Still, the doctors said it would simply take time. He thought of Amie, the extra hours she'd put in at the office, how she'd even brought over a lasagna her mother had made. They'd sat on Grandpop's back porch and eaten it together, sitting beside each other until the stars came out.

He swallowed, the memory of her nearness both comforting and disconcerting. He'd loved Amie before Grandpop's stroke, but this past week had glued her into his heart. What would he have done without her?

Sighing, he picked up Grandpop's Bible, flipping through the pages. Though the last time he'd read scripture on his own was in elementary school, the worn pages called to him now.

God, help me.

He'd never prayed more in his life than he had this last week. And although Grandpop was still ill, a strange knowing that God was with them filled his spirit, starting the moment he'd been in the hospital chapel and Amie had told him his grandfather would recover.

He continued flipping through the pages, stopping at a place in the middle where Grandpop had underlined a few verses.

Show me your ways, Lord.
Teach me your paths.

August allowed his head to fall against the back of the chair. Strange, but this was becoming the desire of his own heart. Why, when he'd grown up in the church, when he'd always been familiar with the teachings of God, did he not care until now, when so much seemed to be up in the air?

He continued reading, his thoughts stalling as he read the next couple of lines.

Do not remember the sins of my youth
And my rebellious ways;

He closed his eyes. It was almost as if this psalm were written with him in mind. He glanced at the heading. A psalm of David. Right. The rock-slinging shepherd boy who'd stolen someone else's wife and had her husband killed.

David might be able to give August a run for his money in the sin department. And yet, David ran after God, and God saw his heart, didn't he?

According to your love remember me,
For you, Lord, are good.

August slid to his knees, turning to face the chair and lean into it, burying his face in the pillow.

I'm sorry, God. I treated my grandfather like dirt when all he did was love me. And I've done the same to you, too, haven't I? Forgive me. If it's possible, don't remember my sins, either. Give me a new life. Help me live for you. Show me your ways.

When he lifted his head sometime later, he breathed deep. A knowing that something had changed deep inside of him left a light feeling in his chest. Akin to how he'd felt when Grandpop released him from his debts, but this time, the feeling burrowed far into his soul.

August stood, pacing the living room, alive with excitement, already seeking to prove himself to God so He didn't regret forgiving him.

August would start by being more patient with his grandfather. By continuing to visit him every day, to take care of him however he could. Maybe he'd bring him his Bible and read it to him, pray with him. He'd read Jesus's words. How many times had he ignored them during sermons? Now, he could hardly wait to dive into the words. Pops would like that, wouldn't he?

August scooped up the Bible, eager to experience more. This book held wisdom. How had he not seen its power before?

Show me your ways, Lord, he whispered, closing his eyes and flipping forward, putting his finger on a random page. For a brief moment, the act felt a bit like gambling. To throwing a pair of dice and anticipating the result.

But this wasn't the same at all. Didn't the pastor at church even say that every bit of God's Word was useful? August wasn't gambling, he was trusting.

He opened his eyes and read. He was in the book of Proverbs. He followed his finger, which had landed squarely over verse twenty-two.

He who finds a wife finds what is good
And receives favor from the Lord.

He let out a short exhalation of breath. Was this what he thought it was? Was God telling him to find a wife? He leaned back, thinking of Amie, how he already had been on the road to pursuing her.

Did he need to quit dilly-dallying and lay it all out there? To prove beyond a doubt that he was serious about her being the only one for him by proposing?

He shook his head. But surely, she'd turn him down flat. What then?

And yet God had just used words from this book to draw August so he could make his peace with Him. Was it so preposterous to think He might use more words to propel August toward another path for his life?

August had wanted a way to prove himself to God. And he

planned to continue doing all he could for Grandpop. But what if the Lord was asking him to do even more?

Amie had walked alongside him this week like they were the best of friends. She'd taken care of him, she'd *cared*. And while they hadn't shared so much as a kiss, his love for her had grown.

He stood, decided. He jogged up the stairs to his bedroom where he dug in the back of his top dresser drawer. Finally, he pulled out a ring box and opened it. Inside, lay a single diamond— his mother's. Tripp had received their father's watch, August had received their mother's wedding ring.

He placed it on his nightstand, falling to his knees once again at his bedside.

I'll do it, God. I'll trust you to show me the way.

18

"August, I'm leaving!" I called down the hall of Colton Contractors.

It wasn't terribly professional. But this working girl was bone tired from her second week of work, not to mention all the running around I'd done, trying to fill the shoes of both Mr. Colton and Tripp. Enough phone calls to make my head hurt. An employee on Josh's crew who hadn't turned in his hours last week yet magically expected an overtime paycheck this week. The insurance mess at the Trivino place. And then there were the permits we hadn't yet obtained for the Hills.

Turns out pulling teeth was easier than pulling permits with the building department. While the process wasn't hard, no one at the department seemed to be in a rush to give me said permits. My next move would be to head down to the building department with coffee and donuts and a pretty smile. I wasn't above groveling.

And then there were the subcontractors. Sure, I could get them on the schedule. But whether or not they actually showed up seemed to be anyone's guess. After ignoring my phone calls for three days straight and not showing up for a job, I was about ready to fire the electrician Colton used.

Man, I could use a foot massage. Maybe a bath with Epsom salts. Oh yes, that sounded heavenly.

"August!"

He emerged from his office. "Sorry, I didn't hear you. Heading home?"

"Yes. I still haven't heard from Circuit Craig. I'd fire the guy if I were you."

"Circuit Craig, huh?"

"There are a lot of subs. I have to remember them somehow."

His mouth inched up in a smile. "What's your nickname for Tim?"

The plumber. "Toilet Tim. Sheetrock Stu. I couldn't think of a painting name for Larry, though. Roller Larry, maybe? Anyway, I'm tired. You heading to see your grandfather tonight?"

"For a little while. I was actually wondering if I could take you out to dinner? A way to thank you for all you've done this week."

"August, I don't need you to thank me. I need you to get a hold of Circuit Craig."

"I don't mean just for the business, Amie. I mean for me. I . . . I'm not sure I could have gotten through these last few days without you."

My face warmed. While I'd never been the emotionally supportive type, something fierce had welled up within me after I'd seen August break down in the chapel on Monday. An urge to step in and comfort, to care for this man I'd grown up with, this man I'd loved at one time. Maybe still did.

It was a complicated love for sure. More romantic than friendly, more passionate than brotherly. And yet, I also knew I couldn't be swept up in it, especially not when he was vulnerable.

With our history, with how close our families were—things were bound to be complicated. Sometimes, especially on a day like today, I longed to escape. To fly free to New York. To be selfish, not worry about anyone but myself or care about disappointing August by not reciprocating his feelings.

And then there was Luke. After I cancelled our plans Monday night, he'd asked every day to reschedule. I'd put him off to spend time with August.

"I don't know, August. I'm pretty tired. I kind of feel like staying in."

"I'll get takeout, then. Maybe we could eat at the bookshop."

I gathered a breath. "Sure. Yeah, that sounds good." Better than I wanted to admit.

I liked August's company. If only that didn't have the potential to become a problem.

And yet, August had certainly proven himself this last week, hadn't he? Visiting his grandfather, taking care of him, arranging for rehab, handling things at Colton Contractors.

"Great." He grinned, and it was the first full smile I'd seen from him all week. That smile . . . "Seven-thirty okay?"

"As long as I can wear sweatpants."

"You got it."

"And no make-up."

"You're beautiful without it."

"And I want a foot massage."

He winked. "Now *that* can definitely be arranged."

I couldn't help the giggle that escaped. I wasn't supposed to be flirting, but after a week of so much heaviness, a little laughter and light conversation felt good.

"See you then."

I drove home, smiling at August's comment about me being beautiful without makeup. When I pulled into the driveway, my phone dinged, signaling a text.

Luke.

You free tonight for some painting?

I groaned. I wanted to paint with Luke. I *really* wanted to paint with Luke. But I'd already given August my word.

To spend time with him, tucked away in the bookshop by the cozy fireplace, snuggled up in my sweatpants, wasn't the worst evening I could imagine. Comfortable, familiar. Not exactly safe, but . . . August.

I'm so sorry, I can't. Tomorrow?
After breakfast?
Sounds great.

Luke had been at Orchard House for over a week. Either he was having some wild inspiration here in Camden or his art was selling like crazy.

I walked into the Victorian and slipped off my shoes. The sound of female voices came from the sitting room. Probably Aunt Pris's quilting circle. I better steer clear.

I headed for the fridge and opened the door. Ew. Only sparkling waters in plastic bottles. I tried to keep the glass bottles stocked myself. BPA chemicals and all of that. Josie hadn't believed me when I told her that plastics imitate the effects of estrogen in the body, effectively disrupting well-balanced hormones. After googling it, she'd given me an apology.

Yet, apparently, we were still bringing these endocrine disruptors into the house.

I growled, chastising myself. I was a working woman. I could go out and get glass bottles of sparkling water anytime I wanted.

Stop being critical, Amie. Stop being critical.

"That you, Ame?" Mom called from the sitting room. I bit back a groan and shuffled into the next room to see five elderly women and Mom bent over pieces of fabric and needles.

"Hey. You guys look busy." I sat in a chair beside Miss Esther, Aunt Pris's oldest friend.

"We're making a quilt for Ed." Aunt Pris didn't look up from her work where she appliquéd what looked like an apple onto a block of fabric.

"That's so nice. I'm sure he'll appreciate it."

I studied my aunt. She'd aged this past week, additional lines on her face, her mouth thinner than before. My heart went out to her. It stunk that she'd only just been reunited with the love of her life and now he was in the hospital in such serious condition.

"He won't appreciate it," Aunt Pris said. "He'll say we made too much fuss."

"That old coot. He can stand to learn a little humble gratitude, if you ask me," Esther piped up.

Aunt Pris lifted her head, her eyes snapping. "Ed Colton is the most humble man I know, and don't you forget it."

Nina Tinkham, my old elementary school art teacher, lifted her silver head. "She didn't mean anything by it, Pris."

"Yes, I did. I meant what I said. He's an old coot." Esther nodded her head as if to cement her words. I glanced at mom. Esther's dementia came and went, sometimes erupting in cantankerous bursts. "That man is so full of himself, he thinks the world revolves—"

Mom stood. "Esther, would you help me in the kitchen for a moment, please?"

"What? Now? But I was just—"

"Only for a moment. I'm making your stuffed cabbage this weekend and I think I copied the recipe wrong."

Esther pushed off her chair to stand. "No one makes it like I do, you know."

Mom guided Esther from the room.

"Someone needs to learn some humility, but I'm not sure it's Ed." Cora Sinclair, wife of the president of the bank down the street, raised her eyebrows and the group tittered.

All except for Aunt Pris. She lay aside her quilting block and stood. "If you'll excuse me for a minute, ladies."

She shuffled out of the room, back straight. A moment later, I glimpsed her sneak out of the back door. I excused myself.

I found my great aunt sitting in one of the chairs outside the bookshop. Mom had set up a small table with two chairs outside the door, and it had a homey effect. Though the bookshop was closed now, I knew Lizzie had come in earlier in place of Josie.

"You okay, Aunt Pris?" I lowered myself to the seat alongside hers, inhaling the scent of lilacs.

"I don't need coddling, child."

"I'm not coddling, I'm questioning. There's a difference."

I detected the slightest twitch at the corner of her mouth. Aunt Pris and I had a special relationship . . . an understanding I'm not sure she had with any of my other siblings. Though she'd never admit it, she appreciated my quirks. My spunk. I wondered if I reminded her of herself in her younger years.

She sighed, long and deep. "Don't get old, child. It's not fun."

"I'm sorry," I whispered.

"You have nothing to be sorry about. Age is a fact of life, I guess. It's difficult seeing the physical bodies of those I love deteriorate. First Esther's mind, now my Ed . . . always so headstrong. It's breaking him to not be able to do the things he loves."

"August said the doctors expect him to recover." I ended the sentence on a high note, as if to instill hope into my words.

"I hope so." She stared off into the orchards, as if seeing another time, another place.

"Can I ask you a question, Aunt Pris?"

The merry chirping of birds filled the silence between us before she spoke. "I don't think my saying no is going to stop you."

I laughed. She was right on that count. "Why haven't you and Mr. Colton gotten married? I mean, you've been dating for more than a year, you love each other . . . don't you want to be by his side when he comes home?"

She swallowed, and I noted the wrinkles at her neck, the skin loose and fragile. "I'd feel foolish getting married at our age. Whoever heard of such a thing?"

"Since when did you start caring about what people think?"

She smiled. "Good point."

"Is it because you don't want to leave Orchard House?"

"Are you trying to kick me out, young lady?"

I shook my head. "Orchard House will always be yours, Aunt Pris. You know that. But . . . I don't know, don't you feel a part of your heart belongs with Mr. Colton?"

"You always were quite the romantic, weren't you?"

I shrugged. "Always cheering everyone else on, anyway."

She eyed me. "How is young Colton?"

"Oh, you know, Colton men." I rolled my eyes.

"If August is as stubborn as his grandfather, I *do* know."

August was stubborn all right. Stubborn on not taking no for an answer. But did I even want him to?

"August and I are . . . complicated."

"Believe it or not, I understand, young lady."

It struck me then that although my aunt was in her eighties, we likely shared similar heart struggles.

"He threw me out of his hospital room today." Aunt Pris whispered, her vulnerable words saturating the springtime air between us.

"Oh, Aunt Pris . . ."

She sniffed. "I know he didn't mean it. Esther's right. He is an old coot. It's hard for him to let me see him so helpless. I've always been headstrong, always known what I was about. But that man wrecks me. I love him so much it hurts."

I reached out a hand and placed it on her own cool one, the blue-green veins of her hand like rivers marking her skin.

"I want him to get better, of course I do. But even if he didn't get better, there's nowhere else I'd rather be than by his side. Helping him."

"Maybe it's time for you to give him a taste of his own medicine."

She cocked her head in my direction.

"Being stubborn, I mean. Don't take no for an answer."

She stared straight ahead, into the large back window of

Orchard House where the breakfast nook sat, the kitchen beyond. "You know, you just might be right, young lady."

I nodded. "It's about time someone around here started realizing that."

"You wouldn't have time to drive your old aunt to the hospital, would you?"

I glanced at my phone. August wouldn't be here for a few more hours. I supposed my sweatpants could wait. For the sake of love. For the sake of Aunt Pris.

"You bet."

❦ 19 ❦

August walked into his grandfather's hospital room holding his breath. Grandpop lay sleeping, mouth hung open, the left side of his face droopy.

August lowered himself to the now familiar chair by the bed. His grandfather opened his eyes and blinked.

"Hey, Pops. How's it going?"

The older man grunted, eyeing him.

"Just came from the office. We got ahead on a few jobs this week." He didn't mention that one of the jobs was painting Paulette Rivers' kitchen—not exactly a job that raked in the dough, but a job nonetheless. Also no need to mention the Trivino job or the fact that the Hill permits were taking incredibly long. Or Circuit Craig. No need to mention Circuit.

Dr. Mansfield entered the room. Funny how his balding head, dark-framed spectacles, and white coat had become comfortingly familiar in this place. "August. Perfect timing. I was just about to outline your grandfather's rehabilitation plan."

A flash of annoyance passed over August. This information was important. Shouldn't they have ensured either he or Tripp were present?

"We'll be discharging you tomorrow, Mr. Colton, and moving you to our inpatient rehabilitation unit. We estimate your stay there to be two to three weeks. The staff will work with you to improve your mobility as well as help you restore some of your verbal and communication skills before you go home."

August worked his tongue around in his mouth. He should ask questions. If Tripp were here—why *wasn't* Tripp here?—he would have all the right questions.

Instead, Dr. Mansfield continued. "As we talked about before, there are three factors which will determine the extent of your recovery. First, is the extent of the damage to your brain. Your stroke, while understandably alarming, was not as severe as it could have been. We were able to break up the clot early and I'm optimistic regarding your recovery. The second factor, of course, is your age, but you were in good health prior to the stroke. The third—and the factor that will play most importantly into your long-term recovery—is your determination and will to recover."

August grinned. "If Grandpop has one thing, it's determination—isn't that right, Pops?"

His grandfather grunted, noncommittal in tone.

"Do either of you have any questions?"

Pops stayed silent.

August searched his brain. "Not right now, Doctor, but if my brother has any questions, can he give you a call?"

"Absolutely. I'm here for the rest of the day and I'll be in tomorrow morning."

He thanked the doctor and after the man left, August turned to his grandfather. "One step closer to home."

Home. They'd have to hire a private nurse, wouldn't they? Grandpop couldn't be in the house alone, at least not right away. He made a mental note to talk to Tripp about plans for Grandpop's homecoming.

August held up his grandfather's Bible. "I brought this for you. Been reading it a little bit myself, actually."

He couldn't be sure, but he thought Grandpop raised his eyebrows. It wasn't that he couldn't talk—he seemed embarrassed to. His words sounded like a mouthful of marbles, and although August could make them out most of the time, the older man chose to abstain from speaking more often than not.

August continued. "I read Psalm 25, actually."

Still nothing from Pops. August swallowed. Well, if his grandfather wouldn't speak, he'd fill the space with words.

"It was weird, you know? Like for the first time ever, I think . . . well, I think God was speaking to me."

Nothing.

August flipped open the Bible. "Some of it was underlined, so I'm thinking the words might have meant something to you, too." He glanced at his grandfather, who stared straight ahead, blinking. "I could read it to you since you're not one for talking these days. If you want."

No objection.

August cleared his throat and began. "In you, Lord my God, I put my trust. I trust in you; do not let me be put to shame, nor let my enemies triumph over me."

Sudden emotion clamped down on August's throat. What was with him lately? But something about reading the holy words to Grandpop in his helpless state filled August with immense comfort. They'd never shared a bond of faith—that had been for Tripp and Grandpop, not for August. But here, now, despite Grandpop's inability to speak well, the words seemed to wind around them and unite them.

He finished out the psalm, the last of the lines clinging to his spirit.

My hope, Lord, is in you.

He swallowed, leaving the Bible open on his lap. "Pops, when you forgave my debt, you told me you were giving me what God has already given me. But I didn't completely understand, not until last night. I didn't understand how . . . " *How he loved me even though I didn't deserve it*, was what he wanted to say.

Slowly, Grandpop reached out his right hand—the one which still had adequate function—to August. August lifted his head, grasping the older man's cold, wrinkled hand. He squeezed. When his grandfather squeezed back, holding August's gaze for the first time since his stroke, he saw in those warm gray eyes, felt in the slight pressure of the fingers around his, all the words Pops wanted to speak but couldn't.

And it was more than enough.

❧

"YOUNG LADY, I AM QUITE CAPABLE OF SEEING MYSELF TO A hospital room." Aunt Pris stepped out of the elevator and shuffled along at a rather clipped pace down the halls of the hospital.

"Just doing my civic duty." I grinned at my aunt. "Man, you sure can walk when you want to. Maybe you ought to take Lizzie up on one of her hikes."

"I do not need an audience while I humiliate myself in front of that stubborn man. Do you understand me, Amie Martin?"

I nodded. "Can't I say hello to Mr. Colton?"

Aunt Pris slowed. "Of course. He'd love to see you."

When they approached his room, Aunt Pris knocked on the partially open door before entering. I followed, my heart tripping over itself at the sight of August hunched over, clasping his grandfather's hand. When he caught sight of us, he straightened.

Mr. Colton pulled his hand away from his grandson at the sight of Aunt Pris.

"Hey, Mr. Colton." I walked over to give him a gentle hug. "How are you feeling?"

He shrugged one shoulder. I tried not to stare at the limp left side of his face.

"We just got word they're breaking him out of here tomorrow." August placed a Bible on the tray beside his grandfather. "He'll be in the inpatient rehab for a couple of weeks before he gets to go home."

Aunt Pris nodded. "Good. That's exactly what I came to talk to him about."

August glanced at me. "Okay . . ."

I cleared my throat. "Perhaps we can give them a minute, August?"

"You bet." He stood, placed a hand on his grandfather's shoulder. "I'll be by a little later, okay Pops?"

Another grunt before we exited the room, closing the door lightly behind us.

"Walk me to my truck?" August asked as soon as we were in the hall.

I gripped his arm, shaking my head and putting my fingers to my lips as I craned my head toward the door of Mr. Colton's room.

August's eyes widened in an *Are you serious?* look but he didn't drag me away.

I took one step closer to the door. Aunt Pris's voice carried easily into the hall. The woman had never been softspoken, and for that I was grateful.

"You're a stubborn man, Ed Colton. But I can't pretend I haven't been the same. You asked me to marry you last year and I said no, not because I didn't want to, but because I thought it was foolish at our age."

I shared a surprised look with August. Mr. Colton had proposed to Aunt Pris? She could have told me that during our patio conversation.

My great-aunt continued. "I see now that I was wrong. You clearly think you can get rid of me easily when we hit our first bump in the road, but you can't. I'm here to stay, Ed, for as long as the good Lord gives us. Maybe there's only one way for you to believe me on that. So, I'm accepting your proposal. I'm sorry it took so long."

Mumbling words from Mr. Colton.

"What's he saying?" August whispered, drawing closer to me. The scent of his familiar woodsy cologne overpowered that of the hospital smells of latex and disinfectants, and I inhaled him deeply.

"Shhh, I don't know," I whispered back, leaning closer to the door.

Aunt Pris spoke again. "If you think I'm going to let you return to your house without me, you have another think coming, Ed Colton. We're getting married, and that's final. I'm moving into your house while you're in rehab and we'll have Pastor Mark marry us as soon as you're home. It'll all be good and proper."

More words I couldn't make out from Mr. Colton. Then, quieter words from Aunt Pris. "I want this, Ed. More than anything. We belong together. I'm sorry I didn't accept your proposal last year—I was scared. Scared to leave my home, those kids, all I've ever known. But you, Ed . . . you are my family. And where you are is home. No matter how long your road to recovery, there's nothing more I want than to be by your side."

Something that sounded like angry words came from Mr. Colton, and then Aunt Pris was crying. I clenched my fists, wanting to barge in and defend her. Here she was, pouring out her vulnerable heart to Mr. Colton—something I had urged her to do—and he dared make her cry? I put my hand against the door but August's fingers gripped my arm with a gentleness that belied their strength.

"I know, Ed. I know. And I'm sorry we may not get that. But it seems our relationship is destined to be one of second chances. And second chances can be beautiful, too. Don't deny us that now. Please. I love you."

And then there was quiet. I peered around the door to see Aunt Pris laying her head on Mr. Colton's frail chest. Tears pricked my eyes, but I wiped them away.

Slowly, I backed away from the door, dragging August with me. Once we were out of earshot, he spoke. "Was that what I think it was?"

"She proposed." I couldn't keep the smugness from my tone.

"But it sounds like he proposed first. Last year, even."

"Does it matter? They're getting married now." I pushed the button to the elevator.

"Did you hear him say yes?"

"They were all cuddled up together. He said yes. Either that, or she didn't give him a choice in the matter."

"Anyone ever tell you you're too nosy for your own good?"

I flipped my hair over my shoulder. "I'm curious. There's a difference. Besides, I didn't see you backing away."

The tips of his ears grew pink.

"And why wouldn't he say yes?" I mused.

"Because he'll think your aunt is just pitying him."

I bit my lip as we stepped into the empty elevator. "She loves him. She wants to be by his side."

"It would have been nice if she made up her mind before now," August grumbled.

"She's been on her own her entire life, and the one time she did get married it was because her parents wanted her to, and it turned out to be a disaster. Independence . . . it can be hard to give up, you know?"

August studied me. The elevator dropped, causing my stomach to jolt. At least, I told myself it was the elevator.

"It was good of you to bring your aunt here when I know how much you were looking forward to those sweatpants."

I tilted my head back and groaned. "Oh, I was!"

He laughed. "Is it okay if I still come over?"

"Only if you bring gluten-free pizza."

He wrinkled his nose. "They make that?"

The elevator doors opened and I stepped out. "With goat cheese and mushrooms and bacon."

"One sec. I better write this down." He dug his phone out of his front pocket, but didn't miss me eyeing him. "Come on, Ame, give a guy a break. You want me to start carrying around a fanny pack to put my phone in? And they don't fit right in a man's back pocket, so what's a guy to do?"

I shrugged. "But you promised . . . they make man bags."

"Man *purses*, you mean."

I couldn't help the smile pulling at my lips. His tongue poked into the side of his cheek as it often did when he concentrated.

Good grief, I wanted him to kiss me. Right now, in the hospital corridor. I wanted his hands on me, his mouth against mine. He could push me up against the wall for all I cared. I shivered, the thought creating waves of want pulsing through me. Was it fatigue or was it seeing Aunt Pris and Mr. Colton cuddled up on that hospital bed, both wrinkly and old but clinging to love as if that was all that mattered in the world?

When August lifted his head from tapping out my order on his phone, he did a double take when he saw my gaze upon him. "I am not getting a man bag."

I giggled at how he'd misread my stare. Better off, probably. "A briefcase then."

He shook his head. "I'll see you in a little?"

I nodded. "Although who knows how long the love birds will be. I'll text you." Impulsively, I leaned over and gave him a peck on the cheek.

When I pulled away, he wore a goofy grin. "I'll never wash this cheek again."

I rolled my eyes. "Goodbye, August."

I watched him exit the hospital, already wishing I were back in his presence. I thought of Aunt Pris's words to Mr. Colton.

Where you are is home.

How was it possible I was coming to feel the same way about August? Was it simply all the time we'd spent together this week or, was it as I suspected, more? And if it was more, how would I know when trusting August Colton with my heart was actually the wise thing to do?

❧ 20 ❧

"**A**mie!"

I whirled at the sound of the masculine voice, my hand on the back door of Orchard House as I held it open for Aunt Pris.

Luke jogged toward us in khaki shorts and a polo, a joyful expression on his tanned face. He carried a backpack portfolio case. He looked great. All earthy and artsy and carefree.

I turned to Aunt Pris. "I'll catch up with you later?"

She eyed me for a moment before stepping into the house. "Thanks for the ride, dear."

Once she was inside, I closed the door and flashed Luke my brightest smile. "Hey."

"Hey, yourself. I've missed seeing you around here. Busy woman, huh?"

"It's been quite a week. I looked for you a few times but didn't see you around."

"I've been exploring. This place is gorgeous. Inspiration everywhere I look—I can't get enough."

I scrunched up my nose. "Inspiration in Camden? Really? I wish *I* could find it." I shrugged. "It's one of the reasons I'm looking forward to art school. A new place to be, new experiences, new vision."

"Nah, art school keeps you too busy to be inspired."

"But at least I'd be doing *art*." Not filing insurance claims and sorting through subcontractors and hounding after the building department. Though I appreciated my job at Colton, knowing it was temporary got me through each day.

One side of Luke's mouth lifted beneath day-old stubble that made him all the more ruggedly appealing. "You're making art too hard." He took my hand, pulled it gently. "Come with me. All you have to do is trust inspiration is yours for the taking. I'll show you."

I bit my bottom lip. I wanted to go with Luke, but August was coming. With gluten-free pizza. I remembered our time on the elevator, and a rush of anticipation swept through me.

"Amie, trust me. Don't think so much. Art is all about feeling," Luke said.

He was so persistent. And he *wanted* to teach me about art.

"I—I only have an hour. Let me go change into some jeans?"

He grinned. "I'll be waiting."

Two minutes later, Luke was grabbing my hand again, pulling me toward the orchards. Up the hill we climbed, and though I'd never been much of a nature girl, I didn't mind the journey this time. Whenever I slowed, he slid his hand up to my elbow or pressed against my back, guiding me forward. "I found this amazing spot today."

He led me to the brink of the orchard where a forest of pines began. The edge of Camden Hills State Park. We climbed over an old stone wall and up a small hill. Luke's hand often brushed against my arm or my back as we worked our way over the hilly terrain together. Whenever he assisted me over uneven ground, I kept wishing he'd just keep hold of my hand. A flutter worked its way up my stomach until heat broke out over my entire body. *Desire*, much like what I'd felt for August in the corridors of the hospital, was calling to me with his every unexpected touch. What if *Luke* decided to push me up against a tree and kiss me deeply? A surge of want coursed through me at the thought.

If both August and Luke could stir such breathtaking longing within me, perhaps there wasn't just one perfect man for me.

"You know, I've been thinking about you all week." Luke clasped my hand and pulled me up a small, steep slope.

I swallowed, holding his hand tightly, willing him to not let go again. "You have?"

He stopped, faced me. The towering trees threw shadows across his face. "Yeah, ever since we hung out Sunday. Whenever I've been painting, I've wondered what you'd think about what I'm doing. What you would say to make it better. I'm having a hard time with the thought of never seeing you again." He took both my hands, ran his thumbs ever so lightly across my knuckles. Drew closer.

My chest grew tight in an entirely pleasant way. I pulled breaths through my lips with effort. Wow. *Wow.* It seemed Luke didn't know how to speak one unflattering word. How in the world could I respond to such a statement? I hadn't been that insightful . . . had I?

I licked my lips before speaking. "I . . . I wonder if all this talking isn't hindering us from finding the inspiration we're looking for?"

For a split second, his eyes glazed over and I worried I offended him. But then it was gone, in its place an easy smile. "Of course. You're right. Let's go find our inspiration."

He continued pulling me deeper into the forest, his hand warm in mine.

Trying hard not to breathe heavily so Luke wouldn't realize how unused to hiking I was, I looked at the greens and browns of it all, not seeing anything particularly rousing. If I'd been alone, I'd have given up by now. It was probably time to go back anyway.

If August arrived at the bed and breakfast early, I didn't want him to see me with Luke.

"I don't know, maybe I was wrong. I don't think I could find anything out here pretty enough to paint, and we should probably head ba—" My sneaker hit an exposed tree root and I stumbled hard, releasing his hand to break my fall. A jolt of pain scraped against my knee and wet earth soaked through my jeans.

Luke crouched beside me. "Are you okay?"

I pushed myself up, brushed the dirt off my hands. I breathed deep.

And then I saw it out of the corner of my eye, just past Luke. Huddled beneath a massive tree. A cluster of purple.

Luke brushed what I assumed to be dirt off my cheek and whispered, "See? I knew I was right. You can definitely find beauty out here if you keep your eyes open."

I drank in the vivid color. "I do see it." I crawled forward to find a beautiful cluster of picture-perfect mushrooms. So many shades of purple on a single plant, the sun shining on the tree in the background. Beautiful.

Luke crouched beside me and let out an amused chuff. "While those are certainly beautiful, I hadn't meant the mushrooms."

I met his piercing, dark gaze. Warmth stealing over me so fast it made my head spin. Was I imagining the way he was looking at me?

"You, Amie, are far more captivating. The way the wind is tangling up in your hair, even the dirt on your cheek—" He held up a finger. "Stay right there. I want to sketch you." He dropped his backpack on the ground and drew out a sketchpad and charcoal pencil. With practiced movements, he began.

I held my breath, feeling both silly and exhilarated by the attention. Less than ten minutes later, he ripped off the paper and handed it to me.

I clutched it, trying to believe my eyes. Is this how Luke saw me? The simple lines formed me—yes, but this me was like none

I'd ever seen. Strong, confident, beautiful, and yet the dirt smudge on my cheek, the wind moving through my hair, some deep part of my eyes, gave me a wisdom and splendor beyond my years.

"It's amazing."

His gaze landed heavy on me. "Patience is the key to finding what you're looking for. Art and life—they're not made for rushing."

I smiled. "And I was about to give up. But then, I never would have seen these mushrooms. You never would have sketched . . . this." Maybe Luke was right. Maybe there was inspiration in Camden . . . or anywhere. Maybe hikes weren't as bad as I told Lizzie every time she tried to drag me out here.

"Let's not go back. Let's stay out here together and watch the stars come out, see what other inspiration we can find."

"I—I have plans. I'm so sorry." And I was. Stargazing with Luke sounded amazing. But I was hungry and August would soon be at Orchard House. Mushrooms sketching would have to wait.

His Adam's apple bobbed hard with a swallow, his face pinching a bit. "Maybe we can paint together tomorrow morning after breakfast then?"

How could I disappoint him? "I'd love that."

He stood and helped me up. "Let me walk you back to the house."

We hiked in silence back toward the orchards. Had I bruised his ego? But no, he was simply drinking everything in, patiently awaiting his next burst of inspiration.

With our fingers entwined, I tried to pull my attention off the softness of his hands to the beauty that I would surely find if I kept my eyes open, as he said. Unfortunately, keeping my feet under me so I'd not embarrass myself again kept me from noticing much but the grasses we trampled between us.

When we reached the patio, Luke lifted my hand to his lips, those penetrating eyes boring deep into my soul. "Until tomorrow, dear Amie."

The sound of a truck pulling into a parking spot tore my attention from Luke.

August.

He stared at me, and then Luke, who walked back toward the orchards with long, confident strides. My stomach churned, and this time it wasn't from hunger. I waved to August, who climbed out of his truck.

"I'm just going to get my sweatpants on," I called, hoping to avert a scene.

He nodded, mouth tight.

Unable to help myself, I chanced one last look at Luke, small in the distance. What in the world was I getting myself into?

21

He was lovesick. Or maybe a pushover. Why else was he still planning to do what he came to do after seeing Amie all friendly with Luke a moment earlier? And the way that guy looked at him as he passed—as if he won a contest, as if he were better than August.

But no. He needed to get a hold of himself. Showing Amie his jealous streak was not the way to win her over. Besides, Luke was a guest at the bed and breakfast. Amie interacted with guests all the time. She had a right to talk to the guests. Surely, he read more into Luke and Amie's exchange than warranted.

He drew in a few deep breaths, grateful Amie was inside so he could gather himself, focus. He grabbed a bag from the passenger seat, biting down a curse as he strapped the newly-purchased fanny pack to his waist and dropped his cell phone inside.

This was bound to please her. Sure, he felt like he'd jumped straight out of an eighty's aerobics special, but his creative attempt was certain to bring a smile to her lips—and make her forget about whatever Luke had just said to her.

He grabbed up the pizzas from the passenger's seat and prayed no one would spot him as he crossed the driveway toward

148

the bookshop. Thankfully, the sun had nearly dipped below the horizon.

He opened the door of the bookshop, the bell above jingling merrily. Dim accent lights highlighted the bookcases. Two lamps at the far sitting area near the fireplace created an intimate setting. He set the pizzas on the large coffee table.

A moment later, the bell jingled again and Amie breezed in, plopping herself in a large armchair, sweatpants on. "Those smell heavenly. I am starving."

So, they weren't going to talk about Luke. Great. There was probably nothing to talk about, anyway.

She stretched and uncurled her legs, then stopped, a sharp burst of laughter erupting from those perfect lips. "What . . . what are you wearing?"

"Oh, I think you know."

She hid her mouth behind her hand, and he barely made out her words through the giggles. "They probably make camo ones or something a bit more . . . manly."

"Are you saying I can't pull off hot pink?"

Now, she was doubled over laughing. "Take it off, August. It's too much. Take it off!"

"No can do. It's for the sake of our future children."

She shook her head. "I cannot take you seriously with that thing on."

He opened the box of gluten-free pizza and slid two slices onto a paper plate. "It just so happens you're going to have to get used to it. When our children are born with ten fingers and ten toes, you'll thank me."

She leaned into the arm of the couch, a fresh burst of laughter erupting from inside her. The sound—the best he'd probably ever heard—caused him to finally break, his own gusty laughs barreling up his chest.

"You win!" she called out. "I can't. There's no way I can eat with you wearing that thing. I'll be choking on my food all night. Take it off, August."

He raised his eyebrows and took a step toward her. "Amie Martin, are you telling me to take off my clothes?"

She tossed a throw pillow at him. "No! I'm telling you to take off that oh-so-attractive accessory."

"But then wherever will I put my cell phone?"

"On the table. Back pocket when necessary. We'll have to compromise. That thing goes against every fashion bone in my body."

She giggled again, and he grinned, his fingers hovering at the straps on the fanny pack. "First, you need to say it one more time."

"What? August, I'm not telling you to take your clothes off no matter how much you beg."

"As much as I loved hearing that, I'm talking about the part where you tell me I win."

She flopped back on the chair. "Must you be such a child about it? I'm hungry and—"

He raised an eyebrow. "Amie . . ."

She huffed, her lips twitching. "Fine. You win. You happy now? I'm starving."

He unclasped the fanny pack and threw it aside. "Too bad. It was starting to grow on me."

She giggled, taking the plate he offered her. The scent of cheese and sauce and bacon wafted through the air. Moaning, she took a bite, chewing carefully. "The world was just made right with this slice of pizza."

He opened the other box of pizza—meatball and bacon and all the gluten he could imagine—and slid a slice onto his plate. He sat on the couch beside the chair she occupied. "How was Aunt Pris when you drove her back home? She say anything?"

Amie nodded through a mouthful. "They're engaged all right. But she doesn't want to make a big deal out of it. Normally, I'd be against such nonsense—a wedding is a big deal no matter what age you are—but I think she wants to be sensitive to Mr. Colton's rehab. They're going to be married quietly. Maybe once fall comes, if your grandfather's up to it, we can throw them a small party."

August lowered his plate. "I can't believe it. Pops is getting married again after all these years."

"They love one another. It's the right thing for them."

August blew out a long breath. "He has a long road ahead of him."

"Aunt Pris is good for it. She's not one to back down or run away when the going gets tough. I just hope you can handle her for a roommate."

August's mouth fell open.

Amie poured herself a glass of water from the pitcher she'd brought over. "Don't worry, once Cragen warms up to you, he'll stop licking your ankles."

He groaned. "Oh man. The *dog*." The dog *and* Aunt Pris. August had never lived beneath the same roof as a woman. Or a dog either, for that matter. But Grandpop's house was plenty big enough for all of them, wasn't it?

Then again, maybe if his plan fell into place, he wouldn't have to worry about being a third wheel in his own home. Maybe he could begin building a new life soon with the woman he loved by his side.

They finished off their pizza, talked about little Eddie, the cutest kid August had ever seen. He asked what art Amie was working on, but she'd grown quiet, saying she'd been too busy to be creative.

When they were done, August cleared the plates and sat back on the couch. "How about that foot massage?" He held out his hand and she allowed him to lead her to sit beside him on the couch. She lay down, propping her head on the sofa arm and resting her feet on his lap.

He gently took her slippers off, staring at her small, tanned feet, her toenails polished a deep red. He rubbed his hands together before placing them on her soft skin, the gesture ten times more intimate than it had been when they'd been dating. Softly, he began stroking the arch of her foot.

She moaned, and he nearly forgot himself, a longing to take her onto his lap and kiss the living daylights out of her overwhelming him. But that wouldn't do. Especially not tonight. Especially with the conversation he intended to have.

"I really do miss your foot massages, August." She spoke in a sleepy tone. Man, what he wouldn't give to wake up beside this woman every day, to hear that sultry voice before he went to bed, the first moment upon rising.

His hand slid up to her shin. He squeezed. "I hope that's not all you miss about me."

She smiled, though her eyes stay closed. Yeah, she definitely missed more than his foot massages.

They stayed quiet several more minutes as he rubbed her feet. Her body grew heavy, relaxed, at his side. A clock on the other end of the store ticked quietly, counting the seconds.

He swallowed, moved his tongue around his mouth. "Something happened to me last night."

She opened one eye.

"I had an . . . experience, I guess. There's no other word for it."

She shifted slightly, sitting up straighter. "Everything okay?"

"Oh yeah, not a bad experience. Like a moment of clarity—about God, life, everything."

"Wow. Sounds deep."

He breathed around the notch in his chest. "It was. Amie, I've screwed up a lot in life, but I've never known what I wanted more than now. I see my future. And I can't imagine it without you."

She pulled her legs back, curling them under herself. "August . . ."

He shook his head. "Just let me finish. Please." He turned to her. "I love you, Amie Martin. There is never going to be another woman for me. I promise to live all of my dying days trying to make you happy." He shifted, pulling the ring box from his pocket.

"August . . ." Her voice wavered.

"If you want to go to school in New York, take me with you. If you want to pursue your art here in Camden, I'm on board. If you want to be a secretary forever, I don't care. I don't care what you do Amie, as long as I can be a part of it." He opened the box, exposing his mother's diamond solitaire. "Marry me, Amie. I'll love you forever."

22

I stared down at the simple but beautiful ring August held out to me. It sparkled beneath the dim lights of the bookshop, demanding I accept this unexpected turn of events.

Was August for real? I grappled for words—a rare occurrence for me—and opened and closed my mouth. Shook my head. "Are you serious?" I scrunched myself farther on the other side of the couch, as if pushing myself away from the ring—away from August—would make it all disappear.

I wasn't even sure I wanted to *be* with August. An hour ago, I'd been romping around the woods with Luke, helping him make art. Wishing he'd push me up against a tree . . .

August lowered the box, and I could have kicked myself for the way his entire face fell. "Not exactly the response I was hoping for."

Wait. He was serious. *How* was he serious?

I closed my eyes, shaking my head back and forth. "I don't understand. We're not even really dating."

"I just—I felt sure this is what I was supposed to do."

"But *why*?" I winced at the hard edge to my words. Josie had once accused me of being callous with other people. Though I hated August for putting me in this situation, I didn't want to hurt him further.

His ocean-blue gaze met mine. "Last night, I felt God was telling me to ask you to marry me."

I raised my eyebrows, shot to my feet. "Let me get this straight. We're not even dating, I told you I wasn't sure we should date, and you thought the next logical step was to propose to me in the same place your brother proposed to my sister over pizza boxes because God told you to?"

He raised his hands, palms up. "This week made me realize how fleeting everything can be, how I don't want to waste time. I don't want to be in a hospital bed when I'm eighty-five, finally having the love of my life agree to marry me."

"Well, August, that's a lousy excuse to propose." And yet, as the words left my mouth, I couldn't quite let go of the ones August had just spoken.

The love of my life.

There was no doubt in my mind August actually viewed me as this. And while I couldn't deny the hope that had sprouted in my chest over the past week that a relationship for us was possible, I also couldn't deny that this was the last question I ever expected. I struggled to trust August, so he asked me to marry him? And what about my confusing feelings for Luke?

I lowered myself back to the couch. We'd been having a lovely time. Why'd he have to go and ruin it?

He pressed his lips together and closed the ring box with care. For the first time, I wondered about the ring. The box looked a bit worn at the edges, as if it held history. Oh. *Oh.* Was this his mother's ring?

"I guess I made a mistake," August whispered, standing. "I better go."

A sudden burst of intense affection erupted in my chest. I held my hand out, brushed his arm. "August, don't leave now. Not like this."

"What else is there for us to say, Amie?"

I hated this. Hated how my denying August's proposal meant the death of whatever we'd been building this past week. Why did it have to be that way?

"We were just starting to get close again. I don't understand how you thought this was anywhere near the right thing to do."

"I thought . . . I love you. We've known each other forever. What more do we need?"

"Trust," I whispered. "Time. Your grandfather is going through a tough time right now. Aunt Pris is moving in with you. With everything happening, we need to take things slow."

Luke was right, August was wrong. Patience was always the better way.

He laughed, but it lacked humor. "Spontaneous Amie Martin finally wants to be reasonable."

I swallowed. "I'm sorry, August. I don't want to hurt you. Can we take things slow? Please."

"What about Luke?"

Burning fury whirled like a twister inside me, beginning in my stomach, traveling to my chest, erupting in my throat, and bursting out on my tongue. "You can't be serious. You're jealous of Luke? You don't want me to be with him so your answer is—is—?"

"That's not what I—"

I stood again. This was all a mistake, wasn't it? Us hanging out again? Hadn't I vowed to only be friends? "Maybe you should leave."

His jaw firmed, his eyes sparked. Even so, with quiet acceptance, he stood, pocketing the ring box. "I don't know why my heart insists on loving you, Amie Martin. But thanks, you sure are trying your best to cure me of it."

My heart pinched as he turned and walked out the door, the merry bells of the bookshop jingling, oblivious to our argument. I flopped back on the couch, the headlights of August's truck shining out of the corner of my eye as he backed out of his parking spot and drove down the drive.

My gaze landed on the hot pink fanny pack, August's phone probably still inside, and my bottom lip trembled. He'd spoken of our future children when he'd given me the painting, and I hadn't discouraged him. Maybe it was my fault he'd proposed. I slumped back on the chair. I pictured August holding that small ring out, hope in his eyes, and a warm tear slid down my cheek. Was I a horrible person?

Then again, maybe this was all simply dreadful timing. It wasn't my fault Luke had come into my life. Should I ignore the possibilities his arrival created? The possibility of filling my days with someone who loved art as much as I did? We could be free, seeking out our next subject, romping about cities and country-sides, staying in hotels and inns around the world.

I didn't want to hurt August. But that's what we seemed best at doing—hurting each other. Perhaps, that was enough of a reason to admit that August and I were simply not meant to be.

23

"**Y**ou did what?"

August clenched his eyes shut and rubbed his forehead. "You heard me."

When August opened his eyes, he saw Tripp leaning over splayed legs, staring at him intently. The massive fireplace beside him rose two stories until it met up with the cathedral ceiling of Tripp and Josie's home.

"Oh, man. This was your answer to keeping Amie in Camden, I take it?"

"What was the answer to keeping Amie in Camden?" Josie stepped into the room and sat beside Tripp, leaning back and closing her eyes. "They are both asleep. Finally."

Tripp squeezed Josie's knee. "You should head on upstairs and get some sleep. I'll take first shift."

Though Josie looked ready to fall asleep on the spot, she shook her head, opened one eye. "First, I want to know what's the answer to keeping Amie in Camden?"

August stuck his tongue inside his cheek. He'd already humiliated himself. What did it matter if he told Amie's sister? She'd find out sooner or later.

"That wasn't why I did it. I thought . . . I thought it was the right thing. I proposed to Amie tonight."

Josie shot up, fully awake. "What? I didn't know you two were even back together. That girl . . . I know I've been busy lately, but I'd appreciate it if someone in this family would keep me in the loop." She shot a glare at Tripp.

"We're not back together." August raked a hand through his hair.

Josie cocked her head. "You're not back together, but you . . . asked her to marry you?"

He blew out a long breath. The more it sank in, the more he realized how ridiculous it all was. "I had a pretty crazy experience last night. I felt like God was speaking to me. Forgiving me. Asking me to start new."

Tripp blinked. "Are you saying what I think you're saying?"

August shrugged. "Yeah, I guess I am. I gave my life to God."

Tripp stood. Slapped him on the back and enveloped him in a bear hug. "August, that's great. I couldn't imagine better news."

Josie hugged him next, but once she pulled back, she shook her head. "But what does this have to do with asking Amie to marry you?"

In as few words as possible, he outlined his encounter in Grandpop's chair the night before, as well as the random events that had prompted him to ask Amie to be his wife.

Tripp and Josie listened carefully. When August finished, Tripp's mouth tightened. "I'm sorry, August. I can understand why you might have been thinking God wanted that for you, but who's to say He meant for you to ask Amie the next day?"

"I know, I know. I jumped the gun. Obviously."

"Did you pray about it?" Josie asked.

August shook his head. "I thought it was clear, you know?"

Tripp sighed. "I suppose it's not outside God's power for Him to speak to you that way, but you know . . . the Bible isn't a magic roulette wheel. It's meant to be read in context, prayed over, studied."

"Now you tell me."

Tripp chuckled. "Either way, I think it's safe to say Amie knows how serious you are about her now."

"I'd say so."

They talked a bit more, including coming up with a plan for when Grandpop returned home. Before August left, Tripp and Josie prayed for him.

"Thanks, guys." He stood. "I'm sorry I missed the little men. Maybe I could stop by tomorrow?"

Josie smiled. "Anytime. You're always welcome, August."

He swallowed, a surge of gratitude and longing rushing through him at the sight of his big brother standing with his wife in the gorgeous new home he'd built with his own hands, his two sons sleeping upstairs. Would such a thing ever be for August? More importantly, if he ever obtained it, would it be Amie by his side?

❦

THE NEXT MORNING, I TRUDGED DOWN THE STAIRS, THE SCENTS of bacon and waffles and the happy clamor of my family greeting me as I hit the last step. I blinked at the number of bodies spread in the kitchen and sitting room. With me and Bronson the only two Martin siblings still at home, I'd grown used to quiet mornings. Aunt Pris mulling over a crossword with her tea, Mom bustling around the kitchen serving breakfast.

But this morning was a happy mess of kids and babies and siblings. Lizzie came into the kitchen through the butler's pantry, a stack of empty plates in hand. "I think that's it, Mom. All the guests are fed."

I had something to do after breakfast, didn't I? I scrunched my eyes, still felt I was in a hazy dream after August's proposal last night. I hadn't slept well—a rare occurrence for me.

"Oh good, Sleeping Beauty's finally up." Bronson poked his girlfriend Morgan in the side and gestured toward me.

I waved a greeting and stumbled my way around Asher's wheelchair to the coffee maker. "Ha. Ha. It's only nine-thirty. I had a rough night."

Maggie's son, Isaac, sidled up to me, showing me a Lego truck he'd built. I crouched down, examining it. "That's impressive, kiddo. I like the colors you picked."

Maggie placed her hand on Isaac's shoulder. "Why a rough night, Ame?"

I shook my head. "I don't want to talk about it."

Bronson elbowed Maggie. "As long as the ozone's depleting and people are feeding their kids foods with dyes in them, there's a reason for Amie Martin not to sleep well—isn't that right, little sister?"

I gave him the dirtiest pre-coffee look I could muster. "What's the occasion, anyway? Why's everyone here?"

Josh elbowed Bronson. "Bronson asked us to come over for breakfast."

Mom spun around the kitchen, grabbing flour, sugar, and eggs to make more waffle batter. "Next time, Bronson needs to give the cook a head's up."

"Sorry, Mom. I'll take care of clean-up today. Josie coming?"

"She said she could get away for about an hour before Eddie'd need to eat again. She should be—"

"Sorry I'm late!" Josie sang as she burst into the back door, a travel mug of coffee in hand, a dripping wet raincoat slung over her head. "Driving away from that baby is nearly the hardest thing I ever had to do. This better be important, Bronson."

"Omelet or waffle, honey?"

"Waffle. Thanks, Mom." Josie turned to Bronson. "Spill it. It better be good, too, like you finally popped the question or something."

I hopped up to one of the chairs at the island, rolling my eyes. "Bronson and Morgan haven't even been dating a year, Josie. Give them a break."

But Bronson's goofy smile and Morgan's shining green eyes as she looked up at my brother belied my words. My jaw dropped. "You've got to be kidding me."

Mom blinked, the batter poised over the waffle iron dripping and steaming. "Bronson?"

Bronson clasped Morgan's hand. "We're engaged. I asked her last night."

The room erupted. Mom left her spot in the kitchen to envelop Bronson and Morgan in a hug. Maggie and Josie did the same. Asher shook Bronson's hand, Lizzie jumped up and down, even Aunt Pris sat beaming from her corner.

I urged my legs to work, to lower my body off the chair. It wasn't that I wasn't happy for my brother. I loved Bronson. And Morgan was the best thing that ever happened to him. But what with Aunt Pris and Mr. Colton's abrupt engagement, August popping the question to me, and now my brother announcing his plans to marry, I couldn't help wondering what force had taken over our family.

I studied Bronson and Morgan, staring at each other like two lovesick teenagers, and something lurched in my stomach. Why had I been so blatantly rude to August last night? He'd bared his heart to me, confessed his undying love. I'd been relaxed, enjoying his company, the way he rubbed my feet with so much care and attentiveness, how he made me laugh with that ridiculous fanny pack. The proposal seemed to come out of nowhere.

While I didn't doubt August loved me, accepting his proposal didn't make sense, not with my uncertainty. Bad enough I couldn't fully trust him not to gamble, now I felt he'd gambled with my heart. And to use God as a scapegoat. What was he thinking?

Bronson draped an arm around me when I finally made my way over to him and Morgan for a congratulatory hug. "I'm so happy for you guys." And I was. I refused to let August ruin this moment for me. Bronson and Morgan deserved every bit of happiness a lifetime with one another would produce.

"Thanks, Amie." Morgan grinned, and I couldn't help but notice how she'd changed over the past year. When she'd first arrived at Orchard House last spring, she'd been quiet and reserved, haunted by the events surrounding her from one horribly irresponsible decision in high school. Now, she glowed. No doubt because of my brother, but also because she seemed to finally put her past behind her.

I sidled my way over to Aunt Pris. "Don't you think now might be a good time to share your big news?" I whispered.

Aunt Pris's mouth tightened as she gave me a dry look. "I don't want to steal your brother's thunder."

I giggled. "Are you kidding? They'll be so happy for you."

"Happy about what?" Josie shoveled in a bite of waffle drenched in syrup.

"Now you've done it." Aunt Pris glared at me, but her eyes twinkled, belying the fact that she did very much want to share her news.

"Okay, spill it, Aunt Pris. Once this waffle's done, I'm going home to my baby."

Lizzie sat in the chair on Aunt Pris's other side, orange juice in hand. "What's Aunt Pris spilling?"

The room quieted, all eyes on Aunt Pris. The older lady cleared her throat, tapped her fingers on the side of her plate—an uncharacteristic nervous gesture I'd never seen from her.

"Though the circumstances aren't ideal, and though I wish Ed could be here when I tell you this, we've decided to get married."

"Aunt Pris, that's wonderful," Mom said.

"It's about time," Josie said.

"That dog." Bronson grinned at our aunt.

Though the celebration was more subdued, considering Mr. Colton's circumstances, it was no less heartfelt.

"It's more practical than sentimental. I plan to move in as soon as Ed's out of rehab. He never would have allowed me to live with him otherwise."

Josie cut her waffle with the side of her fork. "Oh, Aunt Pris, you're not fooling anyone. You are head-over-heels in love with that man. Don't try telling us otherwise."

Aunt Pris blushed, and in it I glimpsed the pretty young woman who had first fallen in love with Ed Colton. How many regrets did she hold?

A flash of August holding out that ring box to me the night before appeared in my mind's eye. How he'd said he didn't want to wait until he was old to marry the love of his life. I tried to picture myself an old lady like Aunt Pris. Would the day ever come when I regretted my response to the question August asked the night before?

A knock on the pantry door. Luke stuck his head around the corner. "I'm sorry, but is there any way I could have some more coffee?"

Mom's hands fluttered to her throat. "Oh, my goodness, I'm so sorry. I'll be right out."

Luke's gaze caught mine, a question in his eyes. Right. Our painting session. I nodded and he smiled warmly before disappearing.

No. I had not made a mistake last night. If the day ever came when I would accept August's proposal, I would make certain he was the *only* guy for me. I deserved that much, and so did August.

24

After my sisters had left the house and Bronson stood at the sink dutifully doing dishes, I sneaked into the guests' living quarters through the butler's pantry. To my disappointment, Luke was nowhere in sight.

I glanced up the stairs, hesitating at climbing them with the intent to knock upon the door of a guest—strictly against Orchard House rules. Yet, Luke had invited me to his room to paint. I was an adult with an appointment to keep. There was nothing wrong with seeking Luke out.

I climbed the stairs swiftly, praying Mom wouldn't slip through the connecting door that led to our upstairs living quarters to start cleaning the guest rooms. Probably not. It was still early. She usually kept an eye on the cars, knowing what guests owned which cars so she could ensure they were gone for the day before she made quick work of cleaning the rooms.

At the top of the red carpeted stairs, I veered left and knocked lightly on the door of the Thoreau Room.

"Coming!" Luke's deep but gentle baritone came from the other side of the door, and without warning, my heart sped up. When he opened the door, my breath caught. His dark hair fell in front of one eye and his short-sleeve button-down shirt was open partway at the collar. In loose-fitting jeans and a paintbrush in hand, he gestured me inside. "Amie, hope I wasn't too forward knocking on the door this morning. I couldn't wait another minute to see you."

I couldn't hold his gaze. "Really?"

"Really."

"How long will you stay?" I whispered.

"I'm not sure. I booked ten days, but I wouldn't mind staying longer. Right now, this place is working with my muse. Although I think Maggie said there's another reservation next weekend. I'll play it by ear."

I sighed. What would it be like to travel the country—the world, even—to seek out inspiration for my art as I pleased?

He cocked his head. "What?"

I couldn't meet his gaze. "I was just thinking how amazing it must be to come and go as you please, to wake up and have nothing to do but make art."

"Hey, now. I have to sell the art, too. That's work. But yeah, it is pretty amazing. Lonely, sometimes, but I guess that's the price I pay for being a traveling creative."

Lonely. Huh. I'd never thought of that.

I gestured to the corner where plentiful windows had created the ideal place for Luke to set up his easel, paints, and a drop cloth. Two easels, actually. My breaths came fast at the thought of creating alongside a master artist like Luke.

"Are you starting a new project?"

He nodded. "We both are."

I grinned. "I hope you're not disappointed."

"Impossible. Art is art. Trust what I've told you already. You have a good eye, now it's time to show me what you can do."

"I hope you're right."

"Don't overthink. Great art comes from being."

Being. I could *do* that. Just be. Kind of like meditating or deep breathing. I didn't need to do anything but be present. Alive.

A flash of memory came to me. The hospital chapel, the woman named Kyra. Why would I think of her now?

I cleared my throat. "Too bad it's raining out. I'd love to find those mushrooms again."

"Outdoor inspiration is good, but we have the inspiration of our minds. Close your eyes. Picture what you want to draw. Focus on the light and where it's coming from, the colors, rich or muted, the shading, the focal point. But start with the light. Always start with the light."

I closed my eyes. What did I want to draw? Something that elicited peace. Home. Or maybe a faraway place that spoke of adventure. I pictured the orchards with their blooming white buds, rich in the sunlight. Camden Harbor, the streets of France. Then I thought of that hospital chapel with its large windows displaying beautiful gardens. Good grief. What was with me and that chapel?

I thought of Kyra's invitation to her church. Would I go? Should I go?

I shook my head and opened my eyes to see Luke studying me. "I don't know. It's hard to feel inspired with you staring at me like that."

"You can't fault me for getting my own inspiration, now, can you?"

I looked away, my face heating. "Maybe this was a bad idea. After seeing your work, I don't know how I thought I'd be able to—"

"Relax, Amie. The art will come." He stepped closer, the attraction between us palpable.

How could I paint like this, with him so near I could smell his aftershave?

"What if I help you?"

I bit my lip and nodded, holding my breath.

He placed a brush in my hand and came behind me, grasping my fingers with his own warm ones. Though his body didn't touch mine, I felt the heat of it close to me, the slight brush of his shirt against my back when he leaned forward to dip my brush in a yellow ochre and dab it in the middle of the canvas. He added some white, blending it together in expert, free strokes by guiding the movement of my own fingers. Some lemon yellow and more white, then a blending of paints on our palette to create a peach hue.

After a few minutes, I relaxed into him, enjoying the fluid movements, sinking into their effortlessness, pretending they were my own. Red and blue and blending and mixing until a gorgeous sunset sky formed above a calm waterfront. Fifteen minutes into our painting, Luke's chest pressed against my back and I didn't resist. What we created—what he created—was the most gorgeous painting I'd ever done.

Once the canvas had filled, he squeezed my hand, the warmth of his words brushing against my neck. "You finish it."

This time, I didn't hesitate. Luke had taught me something in these last fifteen minutes. Not only technique, but a rhythm to his style of painting. It suited me, and I fell into it. But I didn't trust it wouldn't leave me, so I grasped it, sank into it, forced myself into the canvas while consciously blocking out my surroundings.

Using a darker color, I defined the water and the rocks at the bottom of the page with slight shadows. I blended the entire landscape, lightening up the water where the sun shone, defined the clouds with the same white. I stood back and eyed the work, darkening the line of the horizon. When I finally placed my brush in a cup of water, a soft smile rounded my lips.

"You're a natural."

I blinked, having nearly forgotten that I wasn't alone. I looked at the beauty we'd created on the canvas, felt certain I could repli-cate it on my own, felt hungry to do so, even. Gratitude bubbled up within me and I flung my arms around Luke's neck. "Thank you."

When I moved to part from him, though, his arms held me. I froze, my hands still around his neck as I tried to decide if this was what I wanted. Luke smelled of acrylic and canvas, of eucalyptus and mint.

"Amie," he whispered against my hair. His mouth drew toward mine and I sank into it. His kiss was like diving into a hot tub. All warm and shocking and hungry.

I pulled back. "Didn't you say everything in life was better when it wasn't rushed?"

He dropped his head before giving me a charming smile. "I did. Of course, you're right. But you can't blame a man for being enraptured when a woman like you throws her arms around him, can you?"

I laughed softly. "You're forgiven."

A pinch of guilt scratched my conscience. Here I was, all too ready to forgive Luke for getting carried away when I'd flung some really hurtful words at August last night for jumping the gun.

Ever so slowly, Luke's hands loosened. "Maybe it's okay to get carried away sometimes. Maybe great art can be made that way, too."

My brow furrowed. Was I imagining things, or was he speaking about more than just paint and canvas? "I should go. I promised Mom I'd help her clean rooms today."

"Don't go. Please. Here, clean slate." He carefully moved the piece I'd just finished off to the side and placed a fresh canvas on my easel. "Now that you've warmed up, let's see what you can do on your own."

I bit my lip. The mood had shifted. I wondered if I might have lost whatever I'd gained when I'd finished Luke's painting.

"Amie, the last thing I want is for you to feel uncomfortable. Believe me. I like teaching art, especially to someone with your potential. Am I attracted to you? You better believe it, but the last thing I want to do is get in the way of you and your art. I want to help you thrive."

I swallowed. He was attracted to me. He wanted to help me. "I—I would like that."

He brushed a strand of hair from my face. "Come on, let's paint." He turned to his own palette and canvas, began deft strokes as he blended colors with effortless simplicity. Watching him, I wondered again how easy it might be to fully give myself over to someone like Luke. Ambitious, talented, carefree. To spend our lives encouraging one another in art, traveling the world, working alongside one another just like this.

But when I imagined leaving Camden, to my surprise an ache started in my breastbone. An ache of homesickness. I probed it, searched out its source. But it wasn't homesickness for Orchard House, or even Mom and my siblings.

The person that caused the ache was the same one who drove me crazy. The same one who had held that small, humble ring out to me the night before.

I needed to release August Colton once and for all. Here, with Luke, rested beautiful possibilities. And I'd ruin it all if I kept myself stuck on August. Worse, I'd lead him on more than I already had. If I loved August and I respected myself, I needed to free him. Now, once and for all.

❧ 25 ❧

August leaned back in his office chair on Monday
morning and lightly kicked the side of his desk, staring
at the plans on his computer screen until the lines
blurred.

He needed to use the bathroom. Morning coffee was funny
like that. But a trip to the bathroom required leaving his office,
walking by Amie at her desk. He'd glimpsed her this morning in a
skirt and white, lacy blouse. If she didn't look so good all the time,
maybe this would be easier. Maybe he could walk by her without a
second thought about Friday night.

Who was he kidding? Amie Martin could be having her worst
hair day, have no makeup on, and be covered in sewage, and he'd
still think she was beautiful. He'd still love her.

None of that made seeing her any easier, though. Bad enough
she'd dropped off the fanny pack with his phone in it at the house
on Saturday afternoon, leaving it at the doorstep without so much
as a hello.

Lucky for him, Tripp was back in the office, taking care of the
many logistics Grandpop wouldn't be able to get to in the near
future, if ever. August was once again relegated to backseat

brother. And that was perfectly fine by him. It was where he felt most comfortable, after all.

When he thought his bladder might burst, he finally left the office, praying Amie was on the phone. She wasn't. He walked by her without saying a word and on his way back, he pretended to look at something on his phone.

"So, you're just going to ignore me?"

Why did he insist on loving this woman? What about her sassy attitude and snippy comments attracted him? Did he *enjoy* rejection? Did he enjoy a relationship that was so much work?

"I'm not ignoring you," he ground out.

"Wait."

He turned, hating how a part of him lifted with hope at the one word. Maybe he needed to spend more time surfing. Or take up a new hobby. He'd been entirely too invested in Amie since he'd returned to Camden. He didn't even have a life. Work, tending to Grandpop, and Amie. How pathetic. He vowed to seek out some waves that very night. Maybe take up fly fishing. Wait— why did that pop in his head? He didn't even know the difference between fly fishing and regular fishing.

"I'm sorry," she said.

He leaned closer. "What's that? I couldn't hear you. I *thought* I just heard Amie Martin apologizing, and that can't be right."

She scowled at him, looked as if she wanted to hurl the desktop monitor in his direction. "Don't make this harder than it has to be, August." Her eyes were slits, her voice like the sharp point of a dagger.

His body grew soft. "You're right. I don't want things to be awkward between us."

She scribbled something on what looked like a deposit slip, then picked it up and tapped it lightly against the top of her desk. "Me neither." She shuffled papers and checks around on the desk, apparently flustered. "I like hanging out with you, but you caught me completely off guard and—"

"Amie, I know. It was a mistake. I'm sorry."

And yet, if she'd said yes to his proposal, no doubt he'd view it as the best decision he'd ever made. But she hadn't. And really, could he blame her? He'd thought God had been speaking to him. How had he screwed up so badly?

Their gazes met, but she broke the connection first. "I'm sorry too."

"So, where does this leave us?" It took every last ounce of his pride to push the words out of his mouth. But he had to know. Would Amie break things off for them for good? And yet, technically they hadn't even been dating, so did that relegate him back to the friend zone?

She pressed those moist, pink lips together, and his heart physically hurt, for he knew what she would say before she said it. Because whether she liked it or not, he knew *her*. Better than he knew almost anyone else on the planet, aside from Tripp, maybe.

"I think we should take some time away from one another. Figure things out. Cool off, you know?"

No. He didn't know. She was leaving in six weeks. She'd hang out with Luke, they'd talk about art and museums and probably paint together and bond over color and light and texture and shading. Luke would kiss that perfect mouth, he'd take her in his arms and she'd melt into him. He'd—

August clamped his eyes closed, trying to block out the unpleasant visions. He couldn't hyperfocus on "winning" Amie. He refused to obsess over Luke. Besides, he'd be gone any day now.

"Whatever you want." It took everything within him to push the words out. Yet playing the jealous want-to-be-lover didn't appeal to him. Neither would it win Amie's heart.

"Please don't be mad at me, August," she whispered. "I couldn't stand it. Especially with everything going on with Mr. Colton. Please know I'm still here for you."

"I'm not mad at you." He could never stay mad at her—not for long, anyway. "I think I'm more mad at myself." He forced one side of his mouth into a small smile and turned back toward his office, the truth of his words hitting him hard.

He pictured Amie in the bookshop, doubled over in laughter over his fanny pack. What he wouldn't give to go back to that minute, to keep that blasted ring in his pocket.

He ducked into his office and closed the door. He slid into his desk chair and rubbed his temples.

God, I know talking to you is new for me, but I need help. Big time. Tell me what to do. Really, this time.

A picture of Grandpop's Bible came to mind, and he blinked. Not sure he'd try that tactic again, what with all the trouble it got him.

The Bible isn't a magic roulette wheel . . .

Maybe he'd read scripture differently next time, start with the Jesus stories and read entire chapters at a time. Not that Jesus would give him a magic answer about Amie. But it seemed Amie had made up her mind. And if he knew one thing about the youngest Martin, it was that pushing her wouldn't help.

Maybe, in order to show her he really loved her, he needed to do the hardest thing in the world.

Let her go.

※

I HADN'T INTENDED TO GO TO THE BANK TO DEPOSIT THE SMALL batch of checks for Colton Contractors until the end of the day, but after my encounter with August, I needed escape. I'd make my deposit at the bank and then stop at *Bowa* and order myself a Thai Curry Bowl for lunch. Maybe I'd treat myself by adding some tofu. Yes, an emotional crisis like this called for tofu. Or maybe simply some potato chips.

My stomach growled. Yes, potato chips were in order. I'd stop by *French and Brawn* to grab a bag to eat with my Thai bowl.

Maybe I'd find a spot in the park, stare out at the harbor, and grumble into my bag of potato chips.

I ground my teeth together and tapped my fingers on the steering wheel of my jeep. I passed a Golden Retriever and its owner. The dog had just finished doing its business—on the sidewalk, no less—and the young man was now walking away.

Without picking up his dog's waste.

I growled and put my blinker on, rolling down my window and pulling over to the left side of the road. A minor traffic violation, but one I would willingly make to set Dog-Doo Man straight.

"Hello! Excuse me!"

The man looked startled. To be fair, he looked to be the sort that startled easily. Thick glasses behind wide eyes with a mop of curls. Shoulders that hunched into themselves. Probably a few years older than me. Definitely old enough to know how to pick up his dog's poop.

"Don't you think you should pick that up?"

The man blinked, his mouth working. A strong gust of wind blew through my car, and hid the man's face behind his dark curls.

"I just think it's extremely inconsiderate to leave that, don't you?" I tried to temper my voice so as not to be rude. I simply wanted the man to see the error of his ways—I didn't want to be nasty. "You see, once I was walking down this very sidewalk with a pile of books in my hands. My sister loves books."

This guy could be the bookish type. Perhaps I could ease into the conversation with a mention of my older sister. "Maybe you know her. Josie Colton? No, sorry, she uses her maiden name as her pen name. Josie Martin?"

The man blinked at me and his dog whined, seeming to want to jump up into my Jeep, which would never do. I'd be vacuuming up dog fur forever.

I cleared my throat. "Anyway, I was walking on this very sidewalk with a stack of books. I couldn't see where I was going to save my life, much less my Christian Louboutin boots. I stepped *right* in a pile of dog-doo. I mean, Christian Louboutin boots—isn't that an absolute *travesty*? Do you know how expensive those are? Not that I bought them full price—I'd never pay that much money, not with children starving in this world, but they were ruined. Ruined! And all because of someone's inconsideration."

"I—I ran out of doggy bags. I was going to go back to my house and get some, come back and clean it up."

Bet your backside you weren't, buster.

I reached over to my console where I kept an empty plastic bag from Hannaford for car trash. "Here, take this. I'm happy to donate."

The man reached for it. "Th—thank you."

I gave him a bright smile. "My pleasure."

We stared at one another for a minute until he bent down and picked up the waste. I waved before putting my directional on and continuing on my way. "Have a good day!"

I sighed deep as I watched the man hold the bag out at arm's length and look around. This guy would never forget his doggy bags again, no doubt.

I pulled into the bank, feeling slightly better that I had made boring Camden a marginally more pleasant place to live.

I grabbed my purse on the seat next to me and headed into the bank, slipping my hand inside my bag as I stood before the long teller's desk. My fingers hit my wallet and my cell phone. I opened my purse wider, expecting to see the deposit slip and checks from the clients that had come in over the weekend.

Nothing.

"Can I help you?" A woman behind the teller counter with hair the color of strawberries smiled at me. Her name was Eden. I'd struck up a conversation with her about hair stylists in the Camden area the last time I'd made a deposit for Colton.

I blinked, shook my head. "I'm sorry, I must have left my deposit in the car. I'll be right back."

I whirled around and pushed open the heavy door. Once in

the parking lot, I opened the passenger door of my jeep. There. The deposit slip had fallen onto the passenger side floor. I must have put the deposit on the seat instead of tucking it into my purse as I normally did. I'd been in too much of a hurry to get as far away as I could from August.

I pushed the seat back, searching beneath it for the two checks I was to deposit. One, a smaller check of a few hundred dollars from Paulette Rivers and another larger one—a hundred-thousand-dollar deposit for the Hill project.

My skin grew warm as I leaned my head down to peer beneath the seat. My heart lifted at the sight of a slim paper. I pulled it out. Ms. Rivers' check. Great, but not the one I would have preferred to find.

I placed one knee on the passenger's seat and peered between the seats and the console. Nothing but a few potato chip crumbs. I folded the seat and peered in the back, lifting floormats and placing my cheek against the floor to examine in between and under the seats.

My breaths came fast as panic bloomed in my chest. No. This couldn't be happening. I had not lost a hundred-thousand-dollar check.

I leaned against the partially-opened door of the jeep and sucked deep breaths in, forcing them out long and slow to calm myself. After my fourth breath, I gathered my harried thoughts.

Think logically, Amie.

The check hadn't up and disappeared. It had to be somewhere.

I closed my passenger door and walked around the jeep, sliding into the driver's seat. I started the engine and headed back toward the office.

I must have left the check on my desk. I'd filled out the deposit slip there. When I picked up the small pile, I must have left the larger check behind without realizing it.

I drove back to the office, pulling haphazardly into a parking spot and trotting up the stairs, barreling through the door, and dropping my purse on the floor as I scanned my desk.

No check. I lifted the desktop calendar, searched the floor. Nothing. I opened the top drawer of my desk in case it had fallen inside, emptied the rubbish bin beneath my desk. My pulse hammered against my temples, throbbing within my body. A thin sheen of sweat broke out along my upper lip.

This couldn't be happening. This couldn't be happening! Where had it gone?

I sat on the floor alongside the upended trash, forcing in deep breaths through my nose.

Okay. I needed to run a play-by-play. Hadn't that always worked when I'd lost things before? The time I'd borrowed Josie's pens to sketch our dog Scrabbles, I'd retraced my steps and found them at the bottom of the stairs. The time I'd misplaced my keys after a yoga class. The time I'd lost my favorite earrings.

I squeezed my eyes shut, concentrating. I'd made out the deposit slip and carried it and the checks to my jeep. I was certain I had. I remembered searching the top drawer of my desk for a paper clip but realized I'd run out on Friday and hadn't replaced them. In order to retrieve a new box, I'd have to walk by August's office to the supply closet, and that was the last thing I'd wanted to do.

Had I slipped the deposit into my purse? No, I hadn't wanted to crinkle the checks. I'd placed them on the passenger's seat. They couldn't have leapt out my window. The only time I even had my window open was . . .

My thoughts stalled as I remembered the gust of wind that had swept into my car as I spoke to Dog-Doo Man. That must have been why the deposit slip wasn't on my seat and Ms. Rivers's check was underneath it. But then why would the Hill check not be in the car as well? It couldn't have swept out my window without me noticing.

My blood froze. Unless the Hill check had flown off the seat into the open Hannaford bag I kept for trash. Unless I'd handed a hundred-thousand-dollar check to the stranger to clean up his dog poop with.

I groaned as my blood continued to flow again, my heart pumping so wildly I grew lightheaded. Leaving the trash, I grabbed my purse, stumbling down the stairs and to my car. I had not done this. I had not! That check was not only a lot of money, it was needed to start digging the Hill foundation, to put in the concrete forms and order framing material for the house. If I lost it, Tripp would be furious. How could I ever face him or August again after I'd been so careless?

I pulled out of Colton Contractors a bit too fast, retracing the route back to the bank, all the while searching for the stranger with the Golden Retriever. He couldn't have gotten far, could he?

I traveled a mile past the spot where I'd seen him, stopping to ask several passersby if they'd seen a man with dark hair walking a golden dog. No one had.

I drove up Bay Street and its side streets on the chance the man had walked up one of them. But the only person I spotted walking a dog was a short woman with a Yorkshire terrier. A half-hour later, I pulled back into the parking lot of Colton Contractors, utterly defeated.

Even if I did find the man and his dog, what would I say? Can I please have the poop bag back so I can retrieve my hundred-thousand dollars? The check was certainly ruined. The bit of dog-doo I'd seen on the sidewalk hadn't been exactly well-formed.

Unless the man saw it in the bag before he retrieved his dog waste. Could he have taken it out just to spite me, the lady who refused to mind her own business and look the other way at the social disgrace of allowing his dog to make a mess on Camden's sidewalk?

Oh, why couldn't I keep my nose where it belonged? Why did I feel the need to add my two-cents in whenever I perceived a wrong? And really, why hadn't the man been a responsible human being and simply cleaned up his dog-doo?

One more time, I dragged myself into Colton Contractors. I picked up the trash I'd left on the floor and made my way to Tripp's office, knocking lightly on the partially-opened door.

"Come in," he said, without looking up.

"Hey, Tripp." I spoke in a soft whisper, shame clinging to the edge of my voice.

He looked up. Good grief, he looked tired. Dark circles had taken up residence beneath his eyes and for the first time I noticed a faint gray splattering of hair at his temples. Little Eddie must be giving him and Josie a run for their money. Not to mention the stress of taking care of Mr. Colton and running the business. Finn was coming to town soon, too. While Tripp tended to get along with Amos's father, sometimes he got worked up about impending visits.

The last thing he needed was my bad news. Tripp had trusted me. I was supposed to be a help, an asset to the business. Instead, I'd proven Bronson right—I was flighty after all. Too caught up in my own problems, in my own love life, to perform a simple task like making a deposit at the bank.

"What's up, Amie?"

I hadn't seen him yet this morning. Usually, he'd ask me how my New York plans were, how my weekend had been. Some sort of small talk. But he appeared distracted now, his pen poised over his paper like a bookmark, holding his line of thought.

If my confession could wait, I would have put it off. But there was a hundred-thousand dollars on the line. And while I had a good hunch it lay at the bottom of the doggy bag, I couldn't be certain.

I stepped forward. "Tripp, I need to tell you something, and you're probably going to be mad."

Not the most professional statement of my life. But I wasn't sure professional would get me anywhere. Playing the Josie's-little-sister card might.

But Tripp leaned back and groaned, giving up on whatever thought his pen held by tossing it alongside the stack of papers on his desk. "I'm not sure I can handle much today, Amie. But I guess I'm the boss now. What is it?"

I winced at his already-frustrated tone, and dragged in a deep breath. "First, I want to tell you how much it means that you've taken a chance on me in this position. I don't take that lightly and—"

"Amie, out with it."

My jaw dropped at his abrupt tone.

He closed his eyes. "Sorry. Go ahead."

"I lost the Hill check, Tripp. I'm so sorry."

He stared at me a moment, not seeming to comprehend my words. Slowly, his brow furrowed. "What?"

"Well, I think I know where it is. But I don't know where it is. And even if I could find it, I don't think it would be . . . depositable," I finished on a weak note.

Tripp shook his head. "What do you mean, you *think* you know where it is?"

Though each word was like pulling teeth, I summed up the events of the morning the best I could, ending on the realization that the Hill check was in the bottom of the dog waste bag which was in some stranger's trash who lived within a four, maybe five-mile vicinity—how far did one walk a dog?—of downtown Camden.

Tripp's jaw grew rigid. Without a word, he stood, walked into the foyer, and began searching my desk. Then the trash, just as I'd done.

"I already looked—"

"I'm looking again," he growled.

"Tripp, I'm so sorry. I know you trusted me and I know I let you down. Maybe I should go to the bank, ask them to put a stop payment on the check?"

"I don't know if you can do that on a cashier's check. Regardless, the Hills would have to request that at their bank since it was their check."

"Oh."

"We needed that money, Amie. It's going to be a process to have a check reissued, and it's not a great first impression of our company to the Hills."

"I know, Tripp. I'm so sorry."

"What's wrong?" August emerged from the hall, staring at the upended trash.

I opened my mouth to speak, figured it would be better to hear my failures coming from my lips rather than Tripp's. "I lost the Hill check."

August went around to the other side of the desk. "Are you sure? Checks don't just walk away. It has to be here somewhere."

Tripp straightened. "Oh, it's somewhere. Amie here was saving the streets of downtown Camden with it, offering it to poor unsuspecting dog owners as a way of cleaning up their pet's mess."

My eyes stung. "I'm so, so sorry. I can call the Hills, do some research as to the best way to go about fixing this."

Tripp shook his head. "You've done enough. I'll take care of it. I can handle everything." He stomped back to his office, shutting the door a bit too hard behind him.

Through wet eyes, I glanced at August. A horrible part of me wanted to blame him for making me so distracted this morning, but I knew deep down, it wasn't his fault. I wasn't cut out for this job. Something I should have realized from the very beginning.

August stepped forward. "Don't mind Big Brother Bear this morning. He got a total of forty minutes sleep last night. Amos was throwing up and the little guy wouldn't settle. He's under a lot of pressure, he's worried about Grandpop, Finn is driving in tomorrow . . ."

I shook my head. "You don't have to make excuses, August. I messed up. I never should have taken this job, especially not with . . ."

With you here.

It had not been a good idea for August and I to work under the same roof for more than one reason. Good grief, it probably wasn't a good idea for us to be under the same roof at all, considering our history.

"It was a mistake, Amie. It's not unfixable. It happens."

I dragged in a wobbly breath, taking slight comfort in the fact that my tears hadn't yet spilled over. "I think it's best I step away."

August nodded. "Sure. Go take your lunch. When you come back—"

I shook my head. "I mean, I think it's best I resign from Colton Contractors."

"Are you kidding? No way. You've done a great job. The business needs you. Tripp needs you. *I* need you."

We stared at one another. Why did things have to be so complicated between us? Why did I have to find those scratch tickets in his glove box on that most glorious date? Why had he asked me to marry him when we hadn't even been dating? I didn't even know if I was the marrying type! Did he not know me at all? I wasn't like my sisters—responsible, grown-up Maggie, or Josie who always knew exactly what she wanted, or even like sweet Lizzie. I was me. Just Amie. I had strong opinions and stronger beliefs.

And, in the end, all the opinions and beliefs in the world couldn't hide the fact of what I was—a total screw-up.

26

August watched Amie walk out of Colton Contractors, her bag hanging at her elbow, her hair uncharacteristically tussled.

It took a lot to defeat Amie Martin, but it seemed this afternoon had done it. He might have acknowledged he needed to let her go, romantically, but he'd been comforted by the fact that he'd still see her every day, still hear her voice down the hall from his office, still walk past her desk to see her biting her bottom lip in concentration. He couldn't deny the irrational hope that he'd wear her down eventually. He and Amie were meant to be together. Period.

August gritted his teeth and opened Tripp's office door without knocking. His brother looked up, raising an eyebrow.

"Can I help you?"

"You shouldn't have been so hard on her."

Tripp sighed and leaned back in his chair, clicking the top of his pen. "So, you think every time an employee loses a hundred thousand dollars, I should bat my eyes and look the other way? Maybe offer them a raise?"

"That's not what I mean and you know it."

184

"August, I can't treat Amie special just because she's Amie. If Eileen had—"

"You can't compare Eileen to Amie."

"Why not? Because in twenty years, Eileen has never—not once—lost a single check on her way to the bank. They were hired for the same job, August. You simply can't see straight when it comes to that girl."

August clenched his fists. "I am seeing straight. I see that you just bullied your only secretary into quitting her job."

A flash of something passed Tripp's face—regret, maybe? "She quit?"

"Yes."

"What did she say?"

"That she thought it was best for Colton Contractors if she resigned."

Tripp raked his hand through his hair. "I'll talk to her."

August breathed around the knot in his chest. "Thank you."

"But August." Tripp looked out his office window to where a maple tree shaded lush green grass. "She might be right."

"She was doing a great job, Tripp. It was one mistake."

"A big mistake. A mistake that will affect our company."

Our company. August couldn't deny how those two words called to him, made him feel at home, as if he belonged.

"I know it's not the best impression on the Hills, but—"

"The money," Tripp said. "I'm waiting on the insurance money for the Trivino debacle. I had to go ahead and order new materials without being reimbursed. Not to mention, the Peterson project. They still haven't given us the final payment."

"What? Why not?"

Tripp rubbed his neck, wincing at the pressure. "There's a massive hole in the wall we need to fix. My guess is one of the kids found Mr. Peterson's hammer, but they're claiming it was our guys."

"So, let's get in there and fix it."

"Josh is there today, but things will still be tight until we get that check and the Hill one sorted out."

August scuffed the bottom of his shoe on the wood floor of Tripp's office. "Colton must have savings. Why are we so dependent on a couple of checks?"

The corners of Tripp's mouth turned downward. "Grandpop keeps the savings in CDs. They matured last week. He has a grace period of ten days, but I didn't plan on bothering him with it all."

"You're not on the accounts?"

Tripp shook his head. "Just as a beneficiary. Besides, this shouldn't even be a conversation we're having. Colton is not in a dangerous place—we just got caught with some bad timing."

"Amie didn't deserve how you treated her. You said she didn't deserve special treatment, and you're right. But if Eileen lost a check, you would have handled it a little more graciously."

Tripp rubbed his hands over his face. "I need more sleep." He exhaled long and slow. "I'll talk to Amie. I can't pretend I'm happy with her carelessness, but you're right, I could have handled it better."

"Thank you."

Tripp picked up his pen, tapping it on the edge of his desk. "Anything else?"

"We need to talk about the wedding, but maybe we should save that for outside of office hours."

Tripp blinked. "What wedding?"

"Grandpop and Aunt Pris's."

"Excuse me?"

August snapped his fingers. "No way—Josie didn't tell you?"

"She's been a little busy . . ."

"I can't believe I forgot to mention it to you the other night." Considering he'd been trying to mend his own broken heart, he supposed it wasn't that unbelievable.

"You're pulling my leg."

"I'm not. Aunt Pris proposed to Pops on Friday. He said yes."

"And I'm only just hearing about this now?"

"You've been up to your eyeballs in dirty diapers and toddler vomit. I guess we'll excuse you."

"So, you're telling me on top of running a business and figuring out how to father a newborn, I have to plan a wedding?"

"They don't want anything fancy, considering Grandpop's rehabilitation. But I thought we should at least cater a lunch at the house in order to show them our support."

Tripp massaged his temples. "Yeah. Of course. But I can't think of that now. Actually, I bet it's the sort of thing Amie'd be great at organizing. After I straighten things out with her tonight, I'll mention it." He returned to the papers in front of him. "Now, if you'll excuse me, I had a boatload of work to get done *before* I had to track down a hundred-thousand-dollar check."

"Sure thing." August left his brother's office. He reached for his phone to text Amie, his thumb hovering over the cell phone keypad in their running text thread. Text or call? Text or call?

He cleared his throat, moved his thumb to the "message" button.

Tripp's going to call you tonight. He realizes he was a total goon.

His finger hovered over the send button before Amie's words from earlier came to him.

I think we should take some time away from one another.

Would he have texted Eileen if Tripp had gone off on her?

No. He would have kept it professional, let his brother handle it. If he wanted to show Amie he respected her, maybe it needed to start here, with not sending this text.

He deleted what he'd written and placed his phone on his desk.

He'd stayed away from Amie for an entire year after they'd broken up. It was possible.

Why then, did this time around feel one hundred times more difficult?

27

I was going to be okay. If I could just do some deep-breathing exercises to activate my vagus nerve, I would get a handle on this situation and not plummet down the dark hole of despair and depression.

I lay on my bed, blocking my right nostril while breathing in and out through my left nostril, then blocking my left and performing the same exercise with my right.

I'd taken part in a webinar last month that outlined the importance of the vagus nerve—the main nerve of our parasympathetic nervous system. Sometimes, stress and poor eating and living habits could damage it, but there were ways to activate it, to increase immunity and the relaxation response, the opposite of the stress response. Like the alternate-nostril breathing.

Although no matter how hard I attempted to concentrate on the breathing, all I could think about was that hefty check under a pile of dog waste, the look of pure disappointment Tripp had given me when I'd confessed what I'd done.

I lowered my hand, breathing regularly. Still, my heart sped up and tears pricked my eyelids. My vagus nerve was definitely not activated. I could take a cold shower. That might work. Singing was another option, but even if I was musically talented, I didn't feel like belting out a tune just now.

No. What I felt like doing was burrowing under my covers and never coming out until it was time for me to leave for New York in the fall.

The thought of New York caused the tears to spill over. I swiped at my nose with the sleeve of my blouse. Unless I could find a decent paying job, and fast, I wouldn't be going to New York. Perhaps I'd never escape Camden.

Oh God, tell me what to do.

My breaths came faster, panicked. What was wrong with me that I couldn't perform a simple task like making a deposit? Why did I have to be so flighty, so aimless at life, so very un-Martinish?

I sniffed, tried to sit up to get a better handle on my rapid breathing. But it was no use. It continued, and I allowed my body to get carried up in it. Forget my stupid vagus nerve. Who cared, anyway? None of my other siblings cared about their vagus nerves and every last one of them had figured out life. They had a strong faith, a strong relationship with their special person, and each one of them was on the road to success in their particular careers. Maggie, being a kick-butt mom and running the business side of the B&B, Josie with her hundreds of thousands of book sales, Lizzie with her record deal, and even Bronson, changing the lives of each kid who stepped into his classroom and running a camp for kids who might not otherwise get a chance at such an opportunity.

And how was I doing?

I didn't want a nine-to-five job—if today didn't prove I wasn't cut out for such a life, I didn't know what did. I wanted adventure. I wanted to be done with Camden. Maybe renovate an old camper and drive across the country, painting landscapes of America. I wanted to live simply, to connect to nature. I wanted to be more like Luke, not having one iota of a clue what town I would make my home in on any particular night. I wanted a life that was anywhere but here.

When the thought of traveling with August popped into my mind, I pushed him out.

Enough of August. August wanted marriage and the family business and Camden. August was familiar and safe. August was family.

And family . . . family would just roll their eyes at what I wanted. I thought of Bronson, ridiculing the spiritual group I'd tried to start, of Josie complaining how sensitive I was, and even Mom, who wore such a patient, saintly smile when I spoke of things that were important to me—art school and faith groups and yoga and the environment and organic foods and the overuse of antibiotics by well-meaning doctors.

I could not bear to tell them what I'd done with that check. The worst part was, they wouldn't be surprised. Bronson and Josie had probably placed bets on how long I'd last at Colton, anyhow.

I was done with this life. I needed more. I needed to find a place to fit in, a place to belong.

And it sure as anything wasn't Camden, Maine.

"Everyone thinks Amie Martin's impulsive," I mumbled to myself two minutes later as I strode out of my bedroom down the hall. "I'll show them impulsive."

I'd come up with the thought two minutes earlier, and I didn't allow myself to entertain the pros and cons of it. Instead, I allowed the possibility to settle deep within my mind, where miraculously, it slowed my breathing. I grew calm, relaxed. If my instincts were urging me toward this idea, then it must be right. Right?

Though no one had been downstairs when I came home an hour ago, I chose to avoid my family altogether now. I unlocked the second-floor door that connected our upstairs living quarters to the bed and breakfast guestrooms. I closed it behind me and walked quietly across the red carpet until I reached the Thoreau room.

I knocked lightly on Luke's door. He probably wasn't there. It was a gorgeous day—no doubt he was out painting some beautiful piece to sell in one of the shops downtown. He'd told me paintings specific to the location often sold better than those set in a foreign locale.

I startled when he opened the door. His shirt was buttoned only partway, revealing a muscled tanned chest. His hair stood on ends, but it earned him a boyish, appealing look.

"Amie." A slow grin spread over his face and it churned warm in my belly. Had it only been two days ago we'd painted together in his room?

"Hey, Luke. You busy?"

He opened the door wider, revealing a suitcase on the vintage luggage stand in the middle of his room. He gave me a sheepish smile. "Just packing up."

My jaw trembled. "You're—you're leaving?"

"I think it might be time to move on. I'm starting to get a little antsy and I'm ready for a new adventure." He reached out a hand and I felt the pulse in his wrist throbbing.

For a moment, my heart seemed to do that thing it had only ever done with August. Synchronize. Keep in step. This man understood me. I was antsy. I was *so* ready for a new adventure.

"How do you know when it's time for a new adventure?" I whispered.

His grin retreated; his gaze probed deeper. He seemed to know what I was asking, without me even saying it.

"I search out beauty and I find it in every corner and crack of every place I visit." His chocolate gaze melted into me. "Sometimes, it's too hard to find beauty. When you realize it can't last forever, you move on before it can break you."

My skin heated. I remembered him admitting he was

attracted to me. He thought me beautiful, worthy of admiration. He thought I had potential. That I could create art if I wanted to.

"Let me go with you." My next words were scarce a breath of air. They whooshed out between us. I didn't know what I was asking. I had little money, little to contribute. But it didn't have to be forever. I wasn't running away exactly. I was taking life by the horns and seeing what it offered. I wasn't settling for Camden, or even four years of school that couldn't offer me a guarantee of making it in the art world. I was stepping out and helping myself to the future I wanted.

I licked my lips. "I could work odd jobs wherever we go in order to contribute. I could sell your art for you—I'm a great saleswoman. You could teach me what you know."

A smoky desire simmered in his eyes. He reached out and pushed a lock of hair behind my ear. "I'd like that. And I hope, in time, we could be more than partners in art."

I bit my lip. "I think I'd like that. I just—I don't want to jump the—"

He shook his head, pressed a finger to my lips. "We can take things slow. It's never good to rush anything you're passionate about, right? Best to let it build and percolate in art, as well as in love."

Yes. We would be a great team, exploring a burgeoning relationship alongside making and selling art. What could be better?

He pulled me gently into his room and closed the door, taking the sides of my arms in his hands. "Amie, this is what I'd hoped for. I admit, I wasn't prepared for the amount of talent I saw in your painting the other day. Believe me when I tell you, you do not need art school."

He *had* seemed taken aback by my painting of the mushroom. Maybe he didn't know what to expect. Even I had surprised myself at how easily it had come. Almost as if the mushroom was simply hidden on the canvas, and it was my job to uncover it with simple brushstrokes. It *was* my best painting yet.

"You showed me what I want, Luke."

He squeezed my hands. "Let's do this, together."

I nodded, certainty surging within me. "I feel like if I don't get away, I'll shrivel up and die."

Even as I said the words, I pictured August holding out his mother's ring to me. I blinked back the slight prickles behind my eyelids.

"I was going to leave today, but Maggie said the room's free for another night. We could leave tomorrow, give you time to say goodbye."

I shook my head. If I didn't leave now, I'd lose the courage. "I can be ready in half-an-hour."

"Okay," he said slowly. "You're sure?"

I pressed my lips together, nodded. "Are you sure you don't mind me coming along?"

His handsome face spread into a genuine smile, his dimples lighting up the room. "Amie My Waitress, there's nothing that would make me happier."

❦ 2 8 ❧

I scribbled a note for Mom and left it on my bed before throwing toiletries and as many clothes as I could fit into the smallest suitcase I owned. Luke would have his van packed full of art supplies and canvases—I didn't want to take up any more room than necessary.

Though a part of me didn't feel right about leaving without saying goodbye, I quieted that part by telling myself this was only temporary—an art camp of sorts. Not every aspiring artist had the chance to travel the country learning from someone with as much talent as Luke. I wasn't betraying my family. I was being brave, courageous. I was testing the waters of life, stepping out of my comfort zone in order to find my true purpose, my true calling. Who could fault me for that?

Still, guilt wormed through me as I lugged my suitcase through the private door of the second-floor, checking to make sure Mom's car was still gone. Maggie was at the twins' field day. Luke had already checked out and simply needed to leave the key on the dresser of the Thoreau room. No one would see my departure.

As Luke helped me bring my suitcase down the stairs, I

thought about my car, alone in the driveway. When he opened the back doors of his work van, I bit my lip. "Should I bring my car, maybe?"

"It's up to you. But you might be blowing through a lot of gas money. I have to admit, I was looking forward to having your company on the ride."

Right. What was the point of an adventure in separate cars? And who knew how far Luke would travel. I hadn't asked, hadn't even really cared. But with my limited savings, I couldn't afford to squander gas money. I'd need to pay for food—and what about lodging? I couldn't gallivant around with Luke at all the fancy inns and bed and breakfasts around the country and not pitch in.

We hefted my suitcase in the back of his van lined with paint supplies, canvases, easels, palettes, tables, display panels, drop cloths, and tents.

"There's an art festival in Bar Harbor this weekend. That'll be our first stop. You want to bring some of your lamps? I have room, and I bet you'd get some buyers."

I pressed my lips together. I didn't have any lamps except for those on consignment downtown and in the Orchard House bookshop. For a brief moment, I thought about ducking back into the Victorian and searching Maggie's desk for the bookshop key, but the thought of Mom pulling in while I did all that was more than I could bear.

I shook my head. "Can we just go?"

Luke, hands still on the back door of the van, stared at me. "You sure you want to do this?"

I nodded, forcefully. "I admit, my mom won't be happy, but I'm a grown woman. I can make my own decisions." I was tired of not being taken seriously, of not fitting in. Here, with Luke and the chaos of all his beautiful art supplies, his free-spirited, wandering lifestyle, perhaps I could find myself.

But he didn't stop staring at me with those deep eyes. "I agree.

You are a grown woman, capable of making your own decisions. So why are you afraid to face your mom, then?"

Heat rushed up my neck and into my face, but instead of embarrassment, obstinance rose in my belly. "Are you going to let me come or not?"

He gave me an easy smile, shook his head. "Of course."

I gave another hard nod as he shut the back doors of the van. I climbed into the automobile. It reminded me of the van Josh drove for Colton Contractors, although instead of the scents of sawdust and machine oil, it smelled of acrylic and canvas. I reached for my seatbelt and clicked it into place.

Luke put the van in reverse. "Ready?"

"Absolutely." We drove down the driveway, the tables and art supplies rattling in the back. I glanced at the orchards, now a brilliant shade of green, and then at the front veranda of Orchard House. Without provocation, I remembered the many family gatherings and picnics, the first time Mom and Aunt Pris had announced they'd be joining together in the Orchard House Bed and Breakfast venture.

It had been hard to leave the home I'd grown up in. I'd been the only Martin sibling to drag her feet about the move. But in the end, it hadn't mattered. It was the right decision for our family. I only wish someone understood how difficult it had been to leave all the memories that included dad behind in our former house.

I blinked the thought aside as Luke turned the van north and away from Orchard House. Mom would be upset, and Lizzie might be heartbroken, but Josie would probably get a haughty I-told-you-so attitude and Bronson would roll his eyes, as if this were just another one of my ploys to gain attention. Maggie might understand, if she could get past her hurt.

I pressed my lips together. I'd text Maggie and Mom soon. I didn't want them to worry. This wasn't about our relationships; this was about me doing what I thought best for me.

The thought gave me pause, for no doubt if spoken aloud in front of my siblings, someone—probably Bronson—would accuse me of being selfish. Whatever. There was nothing shameful about chasing the wind.

And right now, the wind was leading me far away from Camden, Maine, sweeping me away to bigger and better things.

🕊 29 🕊

August had never known a man more stubborn than his grandfather. If this stroke couldn't jolt the mule-headedness out of him, he didn't know what could.

In rehab, the order of the day seemed to be two steps forward, one step back. And after the day he'd had at the office with Amie breaking up with him for good, then quitting—not to mention a stressed older brother trying to take on the world—a stubborn octogenarian man was more than August could take.

"Don't be upset, Pops. That was good. You're making progress here, don't you think?"

Grandpop glared at him.

"You want me to quit talking to you like you're a toddler, is that right?" August asked.

Grandpop nodded, crossed one arm over his chest and shot daggers at the fork he'd just hurled across the room. It lay against the opposite wall, bits of white rice and chicken gravy on its tines. August had cut up the chicken that was Grandpop's dinner, leaving small pieces alongside the rice and mixed vegetables. But the older man had refused to eat.

"Then maybe you should stop acting like a toddler." Once

August realized the words had left his mouth, he wished to snatch them back. But it was too late. And maybe Pops needed to hear the truth—the hard truth.

He lowered himself to the chair beside his grandfather's bed. Pops simply continued to stare at the fork. "Listen, Grandpop, I'm sorry you're going through this. And I know it's not fun to feel like you're learning all the basics over again. I hate it, and I hate that you have to do it, and I know you don't want to eat or talk in front of anyone because it's embarrassing."

His grandfather still didn't move, but August could tell he was listening.

That would have to do.

He remembered his grandfather reaching out to him in the hospital on Friday after he'd shared how David's psalm spoke to his heart.

"Pops, what matters the most—what makes you, you—is still inside you, still intact. You've got to let go of your pride. It's only hindering you."

An unintelligible noise came from the older man before he started muttering, "If you . . . think me . . . be-being laid up is going to m-make me listen to wisdom from a twenty-three-year-old boy, you . . . have another think . . . coming."

The words were barely intelligible, and yet they were music to August's ears. He leaned closer. "Sorry, Pops. I'm not sure I could hear that. Come again?"

"I s-said, I'm not listening to a young whippersnapper l-like you!" This time, the words were a bit clearer, definitely more forceful. Grandpop sat back, motionless at the strength of his own words.

August grinned. "I heard you that time, loud and clear."

"I—I s-spoke." Amazement tinged the older man's voice. "It almost s-sounds like me."

August leaned over splayed knees. "You can do this, Pops. I know you can."

His grandfather blinked, and August cleared his throat. "Grandpop, you've never given up on me. Never. Even when I was mad with addiction and stole thousands of dollars from you, you stuck by me, got me the help I needed. You didn't make things easy for me, but I appreciate that now."

Grandpop swallowed, the motion seeming to take much effort. This would be a long road. But it wasn't an impossible road. Especially if August had anything to say about it.

"Pops, it's my turn to stick by you, now. I know you have Aunt Pris, and that's great, but I want you to know I'm not going anywhere. Me, Tripp, the Martins, we're with you through thick and thin. We're going to get you through this. And we're going to be praying like crazy along the way."

His grandfather's bottom lip trembled and he shook his head back and forth.

"We're in it for the long haul whether you like it or not," August continued. "You've poured your life into others—especially me and Tripp. Maybe it's time to humble yourself and let us pour into you."

A shiny tear slid down the older man's cheek, finding a path through the deep crevices and folds of his skin. He swiped at it with his good arm. "Hard . . . for a s-stubborn old c-coot like me."

August smiled. "But not impossible, right? In fact, I seem to remember you telling me that with God, all things are possible."

One side of Grandpop's mouth lifted. "D-didn't think you were listening."

"I was," he whispered. Their gazes caught and they shared a smile. August straightened. "Did Aunt Pris visit today?"

He nodded.

"Then you know she has a moving van arranged for next Saturday, right? That woman plans to have the house in tip-top order and handicap accessible by the time you come home."

Grandpop huffed. "How's the b-business?"

August searched for a way off the topic of Colton Contractors.

"Hanging steady." Not a complete lie. "Tripp told me to say hi. He doesn't think he'll make it over tonight."

Tripp would be at the office late. Amos still didn't feel well, and Tripp didn't want to bring any viruses into the rehab facility. August hoped his brother had called Amie by now to straighten things out. He hoped he'd walk into Colton tomorrow to see her sitting at the desk in the business foyer, her posture straight, her brow slightly furrowed as she perused the emails through the thin haze of her oil diffuser.

Man, would he never get over her? Would he ever be able to release the idea of them being together? He didn't think so.

"B-better off. He has a new b-baby. N-no sense wasting t-time on an old fart like m-me."

"Pops, you're the best fart around."

That earned him a smile.

"How about I get you another fork and we try eating again?"

The older man narrowed his eyes at August and August held his hands up in defense.

"Sorry, sorry. Honestly, not trying to talk down to you. I'll go get you a fork so you can scarf down this meal like a manly man, okay?"

Grandpop growled. "M-more like it."

August laughed as he picked up the fork on the floor and walked out of his grandfather's room. His phone vibrated and he dug it out of his back pocket.

Mrs. Martin.

Huh, that was odd. Unless she wanted to talk about the dinner he and Tripp planned for Aunt Pris and Grandpop? Maybe Tripp mentioned it to her.

"Hi, Mrs. Martin."

"Hey, August. I hate to interrupt your evening, but I'm wondering if Amie is with you? She was supposed to go over the bookshop inventory with me and Josie, but that was an hour ago. She's not answering her phone. I'm starting to get worried."

Something unpleasant settled in his chest. "I'm sorry, I haven't seen her since early this afternoon."

"Oh. Well, that's okay. I just thought you might have a better clue than I do."

"Can you track her?"

Mrs. Martin laughed softly. "You know, Amie. Loves her privacy. She never did approve my request to track her."

"Sounds about right." He swallowed the lump in his throat. "Tripp was supposed to talk to her. She was . . . upset when she left work. How about I give him a call and ring you right back?"

"I'd appreciate that."

"No problem."

"Thanks, August."

As soon as he hung up with Mrs. Martin, he fetched Grandpop a new fork and called Tripp.

"What's up?" his brother answered.

"You ever talk to Amie?"

Tripp sighed. "Still buried beneath a mess of contracts, project bids, and I just got off the phone with the Hills. They're none too happy. I wouldn't be surprised if they pull out altogether."

August groaned. His first official plans for Colton and he wouldn't be able to even see them to fruition. "That rots, man. I'm sorry."

"I'll call Amie before my head hits the pillow tonight, I promise."

"Okay, let me know if you talk to her. Mrs. Martin can't seem to get a hold of her."

Silence on the other end of the phone.

"I'm sure she just got lost in some art gallery, probably has her phone turned off." August spoke the words to reassure himself as much as to reassure his brother.

"Yeah. Okay. I'll call her soon. Let me know if you need anything."

"Thanks, bro."

August strode back into his grandfather's room and presented him with the fork. "Pops, as much as I know you want an audience while you finish your dinner, I have to split."

"Everything . . . okay?"

"Just the youngest Martin driving me crazy again."

Grandpop grunted.

"Right?" August answered, trying to make light of Amie's disappearance. "Those Martin women will be the death of us yet. Especially now that we'll both be living with one."

His grandfather's eyes sparkled for the first time since he arrived at the hospital. It lessened the slight ache in August's chest.

"Maybe next time I come, I'll sneak you a steak." He winked, gave the older man a firm squeeze on his good shoulder, then exited the building and started for his truck.

Where could Amie be? And why did he think it his place to worry about her?

Because you love her, that's why.

Because his heart didn't like to listen to his brain. And because if Amie's mom was worried, then perhaps it was his place to worry, too.

30

Two hours after leaving Orchard House, Luke pulled the rickety van into a rundown motel. Seaside Motel and Cottages, the bright blue sign read.

I shifted in my seat, my backside sore from the drive and my head aching from the constant rattle of the art supplies in the back. I'd ignored the calls and texts coming in from Mom, deciding I'd message her once we were settled. I must have tensed during the drive, for as I climbed out of the van, my back protested, stiffening. I needed a yoga session.

We walked toward a bright pink sign that announced *Office*. I craned my neck past the main building to see a slew of small blue cottages. It wasn't horrible, really. It just wasn't exactly what I'd pictured. Certainly not as elegant as the Orchard House.

I tried to brush off the ungrateful thoughts. I'd assumed Luke stayed at high quality inns because he stayed at our bed and breakfast for so long, but maybe I shouldn't have presumed that much.

At the front desk, Luke spoke to the older man, reporting his name and handing over his credit card. When I reached for my wallet to give him some cash from the stash I'd withdrawn from the bank on our way out of Camden, he gestured for me to put it away.

"You can get it next time, after you've sold some of your art."

I gave him a closed-lipped smile at his show of confidence.

The older man behind the desk possessed dark eyes beneath bushy brows that seemed to stare hard at me, as if trying to figure me and Luke out. I looked young for my age, and I hoped he didn't think I was a minor, hoped he wouldn't call the police. "Number six," he said, handing Luke a set of keys.

We drove down the parking lot a bit, finding number six at the far end of the main building. Luke jiggled the key in the door and opened it. The faint scent of cigarette smoke and Lysol hit me and I coughed into my sleeve.

Luke placed his suitcase on the floor. "Home sweet home for the next week or so."

My gaze swept over the tiny room. A single queen-sized bed perched in the middle with barely enough room on either side to walk around. I cleared my throat. "Is there a pullout somewhere?"

Luke chuckled. "I don't think so. A queen's plenty big enough for two, though. Unless you want to take the floor?"

I crossed my arms over my chest and rubbed my arms. "N-no, that's okay."

He turned toward me and placed his hands on either side of my arms as he'd done in the Thoreau room earlier that day. He kneaded my skin, and I tried to relax into his touch. "You can trust me, Amie. It's going to be okay." He pulled me toward him, planted a chaste kiss on my forehead, then turned to his suitcase. "I can't always afford to stay in places as nice as your family's. In fact, I sold a painting to a Camden client and they gave me a gift certificate to the Orchard House. I guess they'd bought it for their son, who couldn't get away. I was grateful, no doubt. Gave me a reason to paint Camden, but more often than not, it's places like this where I make my home. I've been known to sleep in my van a time or two, as well."

I choked. "Your—your van?"

"Yeah. It's all part of the adventure, you know? The experience of a wandering artist. I thought about writing a blog once but could never get up the energy to start it. Maybe that could be a project we work on together."

The way Luke spoke, I was being given an amazing opportunity. Maybe life wouldn't be . . . comfortable, but I was living it. I was experiencing it, striving toward my dreams.

Luke's phone rang and he pulled it from his front pocket. Hmm, I'd have to tell him the dangers of cell phone radiation on the prostate when we got a bit more comfortable with one another.

His brow furrowed. "Oh, hey, Hannah."

My blood froze. Mom.

I backed away from Luke, as if my mom could sense me with him, and then I hated myself for acting like such a child. Hadn't I been telling myself all along that I didn't need Mom's permission to do as I pleased?

I planted my feet on the carpet of the motel room as Luke continued talking.

"Sorry I didn't get to say goodbye. I left the key in the room. I hope you received it?"

A moment of silence. "Yes, yes she's with me. Would you like to talk to her?"

He held his phone out to me, and I considered shaking my head violently, forcing him to lie for me. But that was not acting like an adult. If I truly felt I had nothing to be ashamed of, why hide from my mom?

I reached for the phone, warm from Luke's hand, and raised it to my ear. "Hey, Mom."

"Amie." Mom spoke my name in a single exhalation of relief. "I've been out of my mind with worry."

"Sorry . . . I left a note . . ." I tried to instill a breezy quality into my tone, as if all of this was no big deal. But even I could tell how miserably I was failing.

"Oh. I didn't see anything. I mean, I don't ask a lot of you. I know you're an adult, but I do ask for consideration." She was rambling, something she only did when she worried. "Josie and I were waiting an hour for you to show up for the shop inventory."

I winced. I'd totally forgotten about our plans. "Mom, I'm so sorry. I completely forgot."

I heard dishes clinking and pictured her at the kitchen sink, filling the dishwasher after dinner. "So, you plan to be home late tonight then, I take it?"

I swallowed. I should have put the note on the kitchen counter instead of on my bed, but if I were honest with myself, I'd wanted to give Luke and I some time before our plans were discovered. Now though, I couldn't skulk away with a simple note. "I won't be home tonight, Mom."

The tinkling of the dishes stopped. "Okay . . . is there a time you *will* be home?"

"No," I whispered. "I'm going to hang out with Luke for a bit. We're attending an art festival in Bar Harbor. He's going to teach me what he knows about painting and selling art."

Silence. I could practically feel Mom grasping for words.

"Amie, you barely know him."

"I'm not a little girl, anymore. I can take care of myself." Even as the words came out, I realized how they sounded like the words of an adolescent instead of a twenty-three-year-old woman. But Mom was *treating* me like an adolescent instead of a twenty-three-year-old woman.

"What about your job? Colton Contractors is depending on you."

"No, they're not. Tripp made it perfectly clear today that he can handle everything without me." He and August would run the business without me better than with me. At least they wouldn't offer huge checks to strangers to clean up their dog waste.

"Where is this coming from, Amie? What about saving up for New York, planning for—"

"Luke doesn't think I need art school."

"And what is it Luke thinks you need?" An angry edge sharpened Mom's words.

"Experience, Mom. Life. Studying art."

Mom released a long sigh. "You're going to do what you want no matter what. I just wish you had thought this through more."

"This is right for me," I whispered. "I'm sorry it was so sudden, though. I'm sorry I didn't get to say goodbye."

"You don't have your car . . ." For the first time since Luke handed me the phone, my mom's voice broke. "What if you need something? What if you want to come home?"

My heart softened. "It's not the eighteenth century, Mom. I can call an Uber."

Another long sigh. "Please call me if you need anything at all. Anything, okay? I'm here for you. I'll come get you anytime, day or night, no questions. I love you."

I sniffed. "I love you too, Mom. Tell everyone I'm sorry I didn't get to say goodbye."

"I will. Bye, honey."

I hung up, suddenly cognizant of Luke staring at me. I handed him his phone.

"Everything okay?"

"Uh-huh," I murmured, turning to my suitcase as he disappeared inside the bathroom. If this were to be my new home, I better start getting used to the stained wallpaper, the carpet where I imagined a thousand different microscopic fleas and dust mites lived . . . the shower. Ew, the shower. I hadn't brought my flip-flops to protect my beautiful feet from toe fungus.

I looked around the living space, which included the bed, a small sitting area, a kitchenette, and a bathroom, and it struck me.

I was living with a man. A man I didn't know from Adam. A

man who was not my boyfriend, not my husband. For a split-second, I doubted my decision to drive away with Luke, but then I remembered the conversation I had with my mom. It would be absolutely humiliating to come running home before I'd been away for one night. I didn't like to be wrong, ever, but I really didn't want to be wrong about this.

It was an adventure, that's all. A grab-life-by-the-horns adventure. Starting now.

Luke walked out of the bathroom. "Toilet's clogged. I'm going to track down a plunger. In the meantime, I wouldn't go in there if I were you."

He gave me a charming grin and I raised my eyes, trying to pull off an amused expression when I was anything but tickled.

A grand adventure, indeed.

31

August stared at Mrs. Martin from where he stood in the small foyer of the living quarters of the bed and breakfast. He attempted to breathe around his tight sternum, but fought to suck in a breath. He turned away from Amie's mother, stared out the window to the darkening sky.

"She—she left? Like, for good?"

Amie's mother lowered herself to a chair at the breakfast nook. "She's always been unpredictable, but I never would have expected something like this."

"With Luke. She ran away with Luke." He made himself say the words, each one clawing into the tattered pieces of his heart. Amie *really* hadn't wanted him. She'd run as fast as her pretty little feet could carry her away from his mother's diamond ring. She'd run away from her family, from everything she'd ever known. Away from him. Toward *Luke*.

He released a frustrated growl, slapped a hand against his thigh. "I—I just didn't know they were serious." And how could he? He and Amie had been practically dating the last few weeks. Even if they hadn't been official, he deserved more than hearing this news secondhand, and from Mrs. Martin, no less.

"I don't think they are." Mrs. Martin rolled the edges of the cloth placemat on the table. "She said he's going to teach her art."

He paced into the kitchen, and then back. "I bet that's not all he wants to teach her," he growled.

"August."

He hung his head. "Sorry. It's just—how can she do this? Up and leave everybody who loves her?"

Amie's mother bit her lip. "Believe me, I know how frustrated you are. When I spoke to her on the phone tonight, I wanted to give her a good tongue lashing. But the reality is she's a grown woman. She's trying to find herself. She's hurting, although I don't know why. Any harsh words would only push her farther away."

He exhaled, long and slow, trying to cast out the pain of the news. "She had a bad day at the office. She quit. But I didn't expect anything this drastic." Again, he paced into the kitchen, in front of the double ovens, and back toward the breakfast nook. "Should I go after her? What if she's not safe with this guy? What if—"

"Running after her would only show we don't respect her. She needs to figure this out herself. If she doesn't do it now, it might be in New York. I think it's time for me to step out of the way." Mrs. Martin placed a gentle hand on his arm, and he sank onto the chair beside her. He knew what she was on the verge of saying —that he needed to step out of the way, too.

"I just love her so much, Mrs. Martin. Why does it have to be so hard?"

She swallowed, and he noticed the faint strands of gray at her temples. "I've always thought you and Amie would find your way to one another. And perhaps you still will. But for now, I think the best thing we can both do to show Amie our love is also the hardest thing."

"What's that?"

"Letting go."

He gritted his teeth. Hadn't he had that same thought earlier at the office? But that was when Amie was still in the same town, a phone call away. Now, he doubted she'd even answer his call.

"It doesn't mean we don't care, August. And we can place her in the arms of Someone who cares as much, if not more, than we do."

He nodded and grasped her hand when she offered it. They bowed their heads as Mrs. Martin prayed for Amie's safety and protection, that she would find whatever the Lord would have her discover, and above all, that she would know His love.

When she finished, August echoed an "Amen," and squeezed her hand.

"Thanks for always being there for me," he said, surprised by the emotion clamping on his throat. "You're the closest thing I've ever had to—to a mother, and I want you to know I appreciate you always being there for me. Never giving up on me."

"Oh, honey." She wrapped him in a hug and he sank into her warm embrace. "We all need a bit of grace, and if Amie ever decides to come home, that's what she'll need too."

❧ 32 ❧

The first seventy-two hours, I was able to fool myself into thinking everything was going swimmingly. Sure, the bathroom was disgusting, and sure, I wished I had brought my own sheets from home for the bed, but there was an upside. Spending countless hours at one of the biggest art festivals in New England was inspiring, breathtaking, and downright awesome.

I'd helped Luke set up his tent and display his paintings. I'd spoken to potential customers about his work, and when I'd sold a rather pricey painting on our first day, he'd given me the most dashing grin. I felt like we were a team, that this could work forever and ever.

Sure, most of the time, the paintings didn't sell. We had to talk to about three hundred customers for every one sale, but I *was* a good saleswoman. During the lunch hour, Luke encouraged me to walk around and talk to the other vendors and artists, to gain "inspiration."

And I did.

Luke wasn't the only one traveling the world to sell his art. A woman from Ukraine sold beautiful jewelry. She sent most of the money back home to help care for an ailing brother. One man made art out of newspaper, another sold lotion derived from bee pollen.

Everywhere I looked, creativity thrived, and I felt certain Luke was right—experience was the best teacher. I couldn't wait to make my own art, to display it in the tent alongside Luke's.

When I might do that, however, remained a mystery. We dragged ourselves out of bed before sunrise in order to bring the paintings to the festival tent and set everything up in an aesthetically pleasing manner. Vendors wouldn't pack up their supplies until dusk, and sometimes, if the crowd was especially thick—we'd stay until well past nightfall.

We ate greasy food and my stomach ached often, probably from too many unfamiliar preservatives. I cringed when I crawled into bed, praying the staff did indeed wash the sheets with hot water, laundry detergent, and—even though I was generally against it—bleach. I spent way too much money at a local craft store on paint supplies I couldn't afford. The numbers on my bank account app decreased significantly.

Luke stayed well to his side the first night we slept in the same bed. I have to admit, it *felt* intimate. Though we didn't touch, the simple act of sharing a bed with a man hit me in a way I hadn't expected. I chastised myself that first night, and flipped on my left side, facing away from Luke. I'd *actually* slept with August. There was nothing disgraceful about sharing a bed with Luke in this manner. Unless one of us wanted to sleep in the bathtub, we hadn't any other options. Luke was helping me—paying for these accommodations, however lacking—paying for my food, exposing me to all this great art and talent.

The second night, we went out to eat with a couple who sold unique glass art. Though I usually avoided alcohol, I indulged in a beer along with Luke. It was the first time I'd seen him drink, and he became even more charming, more funny, more passionate about creating art. And not just his art. He was excited about my paintings, bragged about my leaf lamps, and told our companions I was the next Claude Monet.

It was an exaggeration—I knew it, and so did he. But one thing was clear—Luke believed in me.

He'd forgotten his wallet at home that night, and I picked up the bill for all four of us, thinking it was the least I could do for all he'd done for me. And when we climbed into bed that night and he pulled me toward him, I allowed it. We fell asleep that way —nothing more than me cradled in his arms. I couldn't deny it felt good to be held, good to be wanted, needed even. We were a team.

The following night, after a heated makeout session, I'd grown suddenly and violently ill. Likely the greasy, nonorganic food. I'd made it to the toilet just in time, and had immediately felt better, although weak.

I'd faced the wall when I climbed back into bed, intense homesickness overtaking me alongside Luke's soft snores. When I woke up in the middle of the night, Luke stroked my shoulder. I blinked my eyes open, my heart racing. The lights from the motel sign splashed blue onto the wall.

"Amie, are you okay?"

"I—I think so."

"You were crying."

I swiped at my eyes. My hand came away wet.

"I—I don't know why."

"Do you miss home?" he asked.

Did I miss home? It had been three days. Was this just a passing homesick phase, or would I chicken out after only a few days of living my new adventure?

I didn't answer, just shrugged, and I wasn't certain if he saw the gesture by the light of the motel sign. He continued stroking my arm, and I must have leaned into it a little because it *was* comforting, and I did miss home, and I did feel alone, even with him, even knowing I could go back to Orchard House whenever I wanted.

His hand made a wider sweep, inching toward my shoulder blade and, after a few moments, down to the curve of my waist. I lay there, almost frozen.

I liked Luke. In many ways, we seemed perfect for one another. I knew he was attracted to me, and although he didn't stir to life my nerve endings in the same way August had, the draw between us wasn't purely one-sided, either.

He inched closer, his body heat warm and not unpleasant. It would be so easy to turn toward him, allow myself to sink into that solid body. But I'd gone this route before, and though there was nobody else I would have rather lost my virginity to than August, I told myself a long time ago that just because I slept with one guy did not give me free license to give my body away to anyone on a whim.

Luke said we'd take things slow. In my mind, that meant months. But maybe his definition of slow was different.

I shimmied just a centimeter away from him, and he retracted his hand. I waited for his now-familiar snores before I was finally able to relax enough to fall asleep.

The next day, Luke left his wallet in the motel room again, and even though I offered to go back and get it for him, he insisted it'd be easier if I paid for our meals and he reimburse me later.

As I handed over my debit card to a lady in a food truck selling Greek Gyros, a slow dread crawled over me as I looked at my bank app. How had it drained so quickly? If I spent this much in three days, what would this mean for the rest of the summer? I wasn't making money with my art—I hadn't time to make art. Neither was Luke paying me for my help at his booth. No, that wasn't true. He'd paid for the motel outright. But how was this going to last? And what did I assume? That Luke was simply rolling in the dough from his art that he could afford to completely support me, a near stranger?

As I chipped in the last of my cash for dinner, also covering the tip, I faced the very real fact that this—whatever *this* was— was not going to work.

Luke drank more than usual that night and as I crawled into bed and he stumbled, I fought discouragement. Yet again, I had failed at one of my endeavors. Selling my leaf lamps as a way to earn a living? Fail. Starting a spiritual group to dig into the possibility of real faith? Fail. Scoring my first real job by working at Colton Contractors? Fail. Saving up enough money to live in New York come fall? Epic fail.

And now, stepping out into an adventure that I thought had the potential to change my life. Such an undeniable failure, and after only a few days.

"Luke," I murmured as we lay in the near dark.

He turned toward me, wrapping a heavy arm around my waist. "Hmm?"

He was barely coherent. Better to talk to him tomorrow in the light of day.

He pulled me closer, nuzzled his face in my neck and started kissing the tender skin below my ear. "You smell so good."

I closed my eyes, sinking into the cocoon of being desired. Luke was far from perfect, but he didn't expect me to be anyone else. And though I was coming to realize his flaws, I also knew he believed in me—believed I *could* do this art thing.

His lips trailed to my collarbone and then back up until they met my mouth. He smelled of beer and fried onions, but I tried to block it out. Tried to live in this moment and not worry about the cares of tomorrow. Did I really have to slink back home and admit I'd failed, again? Yes, I missed my family. My heart ached at the thought of little Eddie not even knowing who I was. I missed Mom and Maggie and dear Lizzie, even Bronson, who'd texted me several times the last few days. None of his words were condemning, only caring. Josie, too, tried calling several times and texted me a dozen, saying if I ever wanted to talk, she was always a phone call away.

My eyes smarted. My family did love me. They may not understand me, but there was no denying they loved me.

August was the only one who hadn't reached out.

The thought stung as I imagined his anger and hurt at finding out I'd skipped town. With Luke. I'd scoffed at August's jealousy of the wandering artist, but now I was in his bed, allowing him to pull me close and kiss me. Maybe August had seen this coming all along. Or maybe I'd simply played out what was expected of me.

Pushing August to the farthest corner of my mind, I turned into Luke's kiss, meeting his hot passion with my own. My response made him all the more eager, and he deepened the kiss, probing my mouth with his tongue, running his hands up my waist and searching beneath my shirt. Groping.

But it all felt so very wrong. In one decided burst, I pulled away from him. "I'm sorry, Luke. I shouldn't have—I mean, we shouldn't."

With strong arms, he dragged me toward him. "Amie, don't tease me like this. Why shouldn't we be together? Lovemaking is one of the most beautiful forms of art."

His words disgusted me. How many other women had he "created" this type of art with? We weren't in love. I'd thought—what had I thought? That Luke was my knight in shining armor. My savior. Someone to whisk me away to a magical land of freedom and art. But this—beer-soaked, prickly-whiskers, drunk Luke—was not what I imagined. Neither were my drained bank accounts, this disgusting motel room. How had I been so stupid?

I pushed out of his arms and for a moment, he fought me, raking my body against his. Fear clamped around my throat. If I screamed, would anyone come to help me? And did I deserve to be helped? I'd gotten into Luke's bed of my own volition. What did I expect to happen?

"I don't want this, Luke," I said with a firmness that belied my trembling insides. "I'm leaving."

"What?"

"I'm going home."

"Now?"

"Yes." I couldn't stand to be in this place another moment. Yes, it would be humiliating dragging myself back to Camden, but I deserved the humiliation. At least I would be home.

I pulled on the jeans I'd worn that day over my pajama shorts and flipped on the light, hurrying around the room to grab my phone, toiletries, clothes.

Luke sat up in bed. He swayed. "Don't leave, Amie. Come back to bed. I'll be a good boy." He giggled at this last remark and my stomach churned.

"I'm sorry, Luke."

His gaze turned hard. "Fine, then. I don't need you. I was fine before you came along." Each word he spoke was a struggle as he sought the right one.

I moved faster as he inched toward the edge of the bed, grabbing for my hand. I snatched it away, picking up the bag of my new art supplies.

He sneered. "Don't bother with those."

I froze. Part of me knew I should turn and march out the door, not give him another moment of my time, but apparently, I sought out torture. I waited.

His face contorted into an evil grin—like the Grinch in the original Christmas movie, all self-absorbed and heartless. Who was this man?

And still, I stayed, waiting for what I already knew would come.

"You don't have talent. Not enough to make it out here in the real world, anyway."

My bottom lip trembled. "You're drunk. You don't mean that."

I dragged my suitcase toward the door, the bag of art supplies clutched in my other hand.

"You're just a child, playing in finger paints, convinced you're creating a masterpiece. You'll never get anywhere. I'm doing you a favor telling you now."

I gritted my teeth, considered hurling my art supplies at him.

The worst part was, I knew he was right. How could I have any talent when I didn't stick with any one form of art long enough to commit myself? My art wasn't any different than my spiritual group, than my job at Colton, than my relationship with August. The truth was, I didn't have enough depth to see any of it through.

I opened the door without a goodbye or a backwards glance and dragged my suitcase through it.

The summer night held a chill, but finding my sweatshirt would involve unzipping my suitcase in the middle of the motel parking lot. Instead, I continued walking as far as I could from room number six, and then onto the sidewalk of the dark street. Once I felt certain Luke wasn't going to come after me, I dug out my phone and searched for an Uber but blanched at the price it would cost to take one all the way back home. It was more than I had in my bank accounts combined, more than I had in cash.

If only I hadn't been such a stickler about staying credit card free. Once again, I thought I'd known what was best—never going into debt so that I never had to climb out of debt. But a credit card sure could have come in handy now.

A sob worked up my throat and my hands shook as I scrolled through my recent texts. I hovered over Mom's name, pressed the small arrow beside it that gave me an option to call or facetime.

But like me, Mom didn't sleep with her phone. I'd have to call the bed and breakfast line, risk disturbing guests at this late hour. Besides, Mom's alarm would go off in a few hours—she'd never make it back in time to serve the morning meal.

I exited out of Mom's information. Maybe Maggie? But that

would involve dragging her away from a husband and three children to drive in the middle of the night to come get me. Lizzie would be here in a heartbeat, but I also knew the drive would frighten her—she wasn't a fan of driving unfamiliar roads in the dark. She'd probably wake Asher and they'd both come to get me. I groaned. Hard enough to face my humiliation with one person, never mind two people who shared their disapproval over me. I considered Lacy, but my friend had to teach classes in the morning. As a respectable business, she couldn't cancel on her customers.

I blinked back more tears and sat on top of my suitcase. The wind rustled the trees behind me and I shivered, darkness shadowing my spirit. I breathed in a long breath, then scrolled to the person I'd wanted to call from the moment I walked out of that motel room door.

33

A s a rule, August didn't believe in sulking. It accomplished nothing and it made for disagreeable people. So, when he found out Amie had run away with Luke—he couldn't think the man's name without a burning arrow of rage piercing his heart—he forced himself to keep moving. To throw himself into the business, willingly taking on the secretarial tasks in addition to his architectural ones. He collaborated with Aunt Pris on the details of her move, he built a ramp for the house with nothing but a YouTube video and a single call to his brother. He visited Grandpop. He did not think of Amie.

Okay, that was a lie. He thought of her all the time. Wondered what she was doing, if she thought of him, if she missed home.

Nights, however, were a different torment altogether.

August threw the covers aside and lay his bare feet on top of them, the cool air rushing over his heated skin. Another dream about Amie. This time, she was crying, calling out for him.

A bunch of malarkey, obviously. Something his own conscience conjured up to satisfy his ego. He groaned and slid to his knees at the rectangle area rug beside his bed. "God, take care of her. Show her your love. Bring her home."

This had become a habit for the last several nights when he couldn't sleep. Though there was nothing he wanted more than to call Amie, or even text her, Mrs. Martin had been right. He needed to let her go. As much as it killed him to do so, what other options did he have? Amie had made it clear she didn't want him. He had to respect that.

By the time he climbed back into bed and was finally about to doze off, his phone rang. He fumbled for it, swiping right without fully trusting his eyes at the name that lit his screen.

"Hello?"

"August?" Her voice was tiny, scared. He sat up in his bed, instantly on high alert. He swore to high heaven that if Luke had hurt her, he'd kill him with his bare hands.

With much effort, he tamped down his emotions. He was still learning a lot about following Jesus, but he knew one thing—killing was definitely frowned upon. "Amie? Are you okay? Where are you?"

She sniffed. "I'm okay. I'm sorry to call so late."

"You can call me whenever. Whenever, you hear me? I will always be here for you."

A sound like a soft sob came and went. He held his breath. For a moment, she didn't speak.

"I'm leaving now. Where are you? I'll be there as fast as I can."

She told him, and he was out of the house in three minutes, his heart simultaneously soaring and frightened at this turn of events. He tried not to think of the many circumstances that could have led Amie to call him in the middle of the night.

God had answered his prayer. Amie was coming home. He could only hope she wasn't broken beyond repair.

⚜

BY THE TIME AUGUST PULLED UP TO THE BENCH I'D SAT ON FOR the last two hours in downtown Bar Harbor, faint rays of light cast themselves over the eastern sky. Self-consciously, I brushed my hair with my fingers, remembering the day I'd seen him in his truck in the Hannaford parking lot. Remembering how I'd stormed over to him to chastise him for his littering.

And all he'd been trying to do was save a spider. Something he feared would hurt him.

Poor August. He deserved so much better.

He hopped out of his truck and came around to the bench, approaching me with caution, hands in his pockets. I tamped down the almost tangible need to rush toward him, to have his solid, safe arms tight around me. I didn't deserve his kindness. A ride was more than I had a right to even ask.

"Thanks for coming." I couldn't look at him, so afraid he'd see my undeniable failure. So afraid he'd see the real me—the scared little girl fighting to climb out of a slippery ditch of her own making. The woman who hid behind her causes and dreams as a way of making herself feel validated, feel more superior than everyone else.

"I will always come for you, Amie Martin."

A sob escaped and I forced it down, moving past him to open the back door of his truck. I lifted my suitcase to heft it in.

"Here. Let me." August came to my side to assist me. Once he had my suitcase settled inside, I placed my large plastic bag of paints, brushes, and canvases on top. Luke's words pricked my spirit.

You're just a child, playing in fingerpaints . . . You'll never get anywhere.

I slammed the back door of the truck and climbed into the passenger seat, inhaling the familiar scent of August—spice and soap and coffee. More tears pricked my eyes and I ordered them away. Enough. I only had myself to blame, and facing August was the first in a long line of hard confrontations.

As we drove out of downtown Bar Harbor, I stared out the window, thankful for August's silence, grateful to be going home.

And never more frightened to do so.

34

August had driven an hour in silence before finally pulling off Route One into a Hannaford parking lot in Belfast.

In the passenger seat, Amie didn't stir.

"You hungry?" he asked.

She shook her head.

"I'm going to get some coffee. Do you want tea?"

"Yes, thank you."

She didn't offer to come in with him, and he didn't ask. When he returned, he handed her the tea and he sipped his coffee. It burned his tongue and he lowered it to his lap.

"You want to talk?" he asked.

She shook her head, continuing to stare out the window.

He swallowed. "Did he hurt you, Amie? Because if he did, we have to report him. We can't just—"

"He didn't hurt me, August. Not like that, anyway."

She'd slept with him. Don't ask him how he knew, but he knew. And why should that surprise him? She ran away with him. No doubt they stayed in the same fancy hotel, probably the same bed. The guy had deep pockets to stay at Orchard House for days on end. No doubt he'd swept Amie up into a fancy world of money and art. And while he didn't know what had gone wrong, he could tell she'd gotten her heart broken.

"You're not going to tell me."

She pressed her lips together, her face pale. "I'm just not cut out for that kind of life."

He snorted. "That's it, then?"

"Yes, August. That's it."

"So, you're telling me I drove all this way in the middle of the night because you missed your organic foods and yoga sessions?" He felt himself spinning out of control, and he breathed around his emotions, forced control into his system.

"Yes," she said, without an ounce of fight in her voice.

"You're lying." But he couldn't be sure, not with Amie. And did he even have a right to know? She'd left him. Left him high and dry. Besides taking the drive up here, what right did he have over her life? What right did he have to demand she tell him what happened in Bar Harbor with Luke? "Amie, if we don't talk about this now, I'm going to take you back home and we'll live our normal lives again. And you'll push me away and I'll see you around town and it will kill me to never know what went wrong between us."

Her eyes snapped to life. "Is that all you can ever think about? Yourself? What went wrong between us? Well, I have a newsflash for you—this is not about you. I shouldn't have left home. I screwed up. Now I have to go back and have my face rubbed in it, okay?"

His jaw tightened. He returned the keys to the ignition and started the truck. "No one's going to rub your face in anything."

She sighed. "I'm sorry. I shouldn't have—I'm so grateful you came to get me. I'm just sick of men thinking I owe them something. I just want to be left alone."

Her words cut through him. For in them, he saw a part of the hurt Luke had caused her, and he hated him for it. More so,

August hated that she lumped him in the same category as that lowlife. And was she right? Did he believe she owed him an explanation in exchange for the ride? That all he wanted was what she could give him?

But no. He loved her and wanted her happiness. Maybe that hadn't always been true in the past, but he was a changed man. Of course, he wouldn't remind her of that now, on the way home to her family. Now, he would simply give her a ride. Simply offer to be here for her.

He took the truck out of park and left the parking lot. He claimed to love Amie, but it seemed he never could understand the best way to go about showing her. Either he failed at proving he was clean from addiction, or he proposed before she was ready, or he demanded reasons and excuses from her.

Would he ever learn the best way to show Amie Martin how much he really loved her?

☙❧

WHEN AUGUST PULLED INTO THE DRIVEWAY OF ORCHARD House, I couldn't bring myself to feel much of anything except defeat. I stared off at the orchards, beginning to bear small green apples, at the bookshop with its merry lights twinkling from within.

I cleared my throat. "Did you—did you tell anyone you were coming to get me?"

"No. I didn't think it was my place." He put the truck in park.

"Thank you, August. I really do appreciate the ride, and I don't take it lightly. I'll pay you for gas when I have the money."

Delivering pizzas may not be outside the realm of possibility for me, after all.

"You don't owe me anything, Amie. I'm happy to do it."

I forced a smile. I wanted to lean in and give him a kiss on the cheek, but I stopped myself. If I cared for August's feelings, I couldn't afford to perform careless gestures like that.

"Thank you." I pushed open the passenger door and August hopped out to help me with my suitcase.

I took it from him. Slowly, I lugged my bag of art supplies up the back walkway along with my suitcase. But before I could open the door, Mom burst through it, her face wreathed in a smile, tears falling down her cheeks.

And then I was in her arms, soaking in the soft warmth of her, the light flowery scent of her familiar perfume. Her hair brushed against my tears and I breathed deep around my sobs.

Somewhere in the distance, I was aware of August's truck leaving the driveway. A place deep inside me wanted to run after him, to thank him one more time for coming to get me.

But I couldn't manage to lift my head from Mom's embrace. The feel of everything *home*.

⁂

AFTER I'D TAKEN A SHOWER, UNPACKED MY SMALL SUITCASE, and thrown a load of laundry in the washer, I laid on my bed. I breathed deep, trying to plan my next steps, whatever that might look like.

A soft knock came at my door.

"Come in."

Mom appeared, her hair pulled back in a ponytail, jeans and a t-shirt on. She looked good. Her arms toned and tanned; her hair sun-bleached from working in the garden.

"How's my girl?" She sat on the edge of my bed and I scooted over to give her room, turning on my side to face her.

"I'm okay."

Mom wound her fingers in her lap. "Do you want to talk about it?"

I thought about brushing her off as I'd done August in Belfast, but I couldn't bring myself to push her away. I shrugged.

"You don't have to, but it might make you feel better."

I dragged in a giant breath that made my belly rise, then forced it out in one long exhale.

"I didn't sleep with him," I finally said.

She stared at me for a minute, then let out a snort of disbelief. "You think that's what I was worried about?"

Again, I shrugged. "I don't know."

"Amie, when you left, of course I was worried for you. We didn't know Luke, we didn't know where you were going, you weren't answering our calls and texts. But what worried me most was how badly your heart must have been hurting for you to leave how you did. And if I've played any part in hurting you—and I'm sure I'm not blameless—then honey, I am so, so sorry."

More irritating tears pricked my eyes. I was the one who'd run away without saying goodbye, the one who'd ignored Mom's calls, and *she* was apologizing?

I shook my head, swiped my wet cheeks with the back of my hand. "Mom, you didn't do anything. The problem is me. The problem is always me."

She pushed back the hair on my forehead like she used to do when I was a child, crying over a broken piece of pottery or a ruined piece of clothing. "My dear, dear girl." She continued stroking my head, and for once I didn't mind. A smile bent her lips. "Do you remember when you all put on *Matilda*?"

A corner of my mouth curved. "I wanted to be Matilda so badly, but Josie thought Maggie should do it since she was older and more experienced at acting."

Mom nodded. "But you practiced those lines morning, noon, and night. You sang your heart out, and in the end, neither Josie nor Maggie could deny you. And you played the part beautifully, with your heart and soul."

I stared at my ceiling. "Sometimes I wish for things to be simple again."

"My point, honey, is not that life should be simple again, but that you've always had a strong will and a strong mind. There's nothing wrong with you. God made you this way, and it is a gift."

I sighed. "I used to think so," I said quietly. "I'm not so sure anymore. Everything I seem to touch lately withers. I don't know what I want out of life, Mom. But I do know I'm so, so sorry for hurting you."

Her hand stilled from where it lingered at my shoulder. "I forgive you. I'm just glad you're home now. And if you want an adventure, let me be in on the planning next time."

I snorted. "It might go better if you have a say in it." I rolled my head to look at my wall. "I quit my job at Colton. I don't have enough money for art school. Even if I did . . . Mom, I don't think I want to go. I—I might be done with art for now."

She studied me. "Oh?"

I bit my lip. "I'm not sure I have what it takes."

A grin played across her face.

I cocked my head. "What?"

"Dear girl, I'm quite sure you have what it takes to accomplish whatever you set out to do. You had it in you when you played Matilda, and you have it in you now. Maybe the problem is simply not knowing what you want. And that's okay."

I lifted my hands in frustration. "Well, what do I do in the meantime? I can't just sit around and twiddle my thumbs all day."

She patted my leg. "Perhaps, for now, you take a break from art. See how you feel without it in your life. See if it calls to you. Pray about where the Lord would have you go."

Had I ever sought out God's wisdom in my art? In my life, even?

"I will," I said, and found myself meaning it.

Mom's gaze caught on something on my nightstand. She

picked up the small card. I still remembered the name on it. *Abundant Life Church*.

"A lady at the hospital chapel gave it to me. She wanted me to visit," I said.

"Did you?"

I shook my head. "But maybe I will." I met Mom's gaze. "Would you be hurt if I went to another church?"

She shook her head. "Honey, you've always walked your own path, and there's nothing wrong with that. You are a grown woman and if part of you inviting God to be a bigger part of your life means going to another church, then I give you my blessing. Not that you needed it, mind you."

I smiled. "Thanks."

Mom slapped her hands on her thighs and stood. "Okay, if you're up for helping me put together some potato salad or make a cake, you're welcome to come down to the kitchen."

Funny how just a week ago the thought of helping Mom in the kitchen would have caused me to roll my eyes and feign boredom. Now, I couldn't imagine anything better than tucking myself alongside my mother in our spacious kitchen, peeling potatoes while listening to Maggie's kids clamber off the bus.

I sat up. "Sure. What's the occasion?"

"Need you ask? We're having a welcome home cookout celebration tonight in your honor."

Now, it was my turn to roll my eyes. "Mom, I was gone for four days."

Her gaze caught mine. She tilted her head. "No, I think you've been gone much longer. But I think you're coming back for good this time."

I sniffed, nodded, and threw my arms around her in a side hug as we started down the stairs. I hoped she was right, because I wasn't sure I ever wanted to leave again.

🦋 35 🦋

Belonging is a funny thing. Because you might belong somewhere—in a family, or in a group, or in a town, or in a community, but owning a sense *of* belonging is actually quite different. Where I lived had dictated I belonged in Camden, my birth making me a Martin. But I hadn't felt I belonged. I couldn't settle in.

But the night of my homecoming, when Bronson near wrestled me into the grizzly folds of his arms without a word of condemnation, I felt I belonged. When Josie lugged car seats and high chairs and a nursing blanket over to Orchard House and made me promise we'd have a girls' night out one day really soon, I belonged. As Josh asked if I wanted one of the organic hamburgers he and Maggie had bought for me (along with a gluten free bun, of course), I belonged. As Lizzie cried happy tears when she put her small arms around me, and as Aunt Pris let out a feisty *humph*, saying she was glad to have the great-niece back who understood her best, I felt for the first time in maybe forever, that I did actually belong in this family. They loved me, and because of that simple fact, I belonged.

Why hadn't I seen it earlier?

As I dished up a scoop of potato salad alongside my gluten-free organic hamburger, Tripp sidled up next to me. "Hey, Ame. Can I talk to you for a minute?"

I blinked and nodded, following him to a spot off the side of the barn. Beside us, wisteria grew up and around a ladder above the bookshop door, releasing a sweet summer scent.

Tripp shifted from one foot to the other, an uncharacteristic movement for his normally confident form. "I'm glad you're home."

"Thanks. Me, too."

"I know I left you a voicemail, but I wanted to tell you in person . . . I'm sorry for running a short fuse on Monday. I was stressed, and I let it all blow out on you. I'm sorry."

I shook my head. "Tripp, you have nothing to apologize for. I was flighty and irresponsible and—" I cut myself off. I couldn't continue beating myself up for handing a hundred-thousand-dollar check to Dog-Doo man. "I'm sorry for all the trouble I put you through. Did the Hills blow a gasket?"

"August had to do a little sweet-talking, but they're staying with Colton. We're working it out. The check will take a few weeks to get reissued, but we're managing."

"Good. Is Eileen coming back soon?"

Tripp rubbed the back of his neck. "Eileen isn't coming back."

"What? Why?"

"Turns out she's quite attached to her new grandson and is going to babysit full-time when her daughter goes back to work."

"Oh."

"Amie, I'd really like it if you'd come back to Colton Contractors. No pressure, if you don't want to after everything that's happened, but you really are good at the job—"

"Except for losing huge sums of money, which is kind of a big deal when it comes to business."

Tripp cracked a smile. "Except for losing huge sums of money, you are a rockstar. Will you consider it? We're hurting without you. Or at least come back until we can find a suitable replacement?"

I trailed my fork in the potato salad. Did I really want to hop right back in where I'd left off? I inhaled a wobbly breath. "Can you give me the weekend to think about it?"

"Absolutely." He squeezed my shoulder. "No matter where you go, Amie Martin, you will succeed. You're a bright light and I pray you never lose that."

I blinked back tears and hugged Tripp with the arm that wasn't occupied with my plate of food. I squeezed him, noticing that every ounce of attraction I'd ever felt for my sister's husband was blessedly, thankfully gone.

"You're like a big brother to me, Tripp. I hate disappointing you."

He squeezed my arm before letting go. "Amie, you could never be a disappointment."

He jerked his head toward the sound of a truck pulling up behind us. "Hope it's okay. I invited August."

"Of course."

"He loves you like crazy, you know."

Heat crept over my face. "I know."

"See ya." Tripp walked away just as August ambled over.

"Did I scare him away?" he asked.

I smiled. "We were finished. He just offered me my old job back."

"Yeah? You going to take it?"

I looked out at the orchards, to the blanket of trees unrolling themselves neatly up the hill. In the apple tree nearest the barn, Davey and Isaac swung like monkeys from a low branch. Amos toddled toward them.

I met August's gaze and my stomach lurched. I wanted to beg him for another chance, but I was scared. I wanted to tell him how I didn't trust myself, how I wasn't any good at relationships, at trust, or at faith . . . all the important ingredients of a successful romantic bond. Instead, his eyes held mine, prodding me to share my heart.

"I don't know," I finally said. "I told Tripp I'd let him know by Monday."

"That sounds smart."

I raised an eyebrow. "It does?"

He shoved his hands in his pockets. "Sure. You probably have a lot of thinking to do."

"I do." More than I could wrap my head around. "August—"

"Amie—"

He shook his head. "You first."

I bit my lip, staring at my uneaten hamburger. "I'm sorry I was so standoffish with you on the drive home. The truth is, I do want to share everything that happened with you, but I think I have to figure myself out first. Does that make sense?"

"Can I confess something?"

My insides tripped. Had he fallen back into gambling? Was he going to confess now and break any possible reconciliation for us in the future?

And yet, who was I to judge? I thought of Luke's hands on me, of us cuddling in that motel bed together, our passionate kisses, and my skin crawled. Getting involved with a man with a gambling addiction was probably not any better than running away with a wandering artist.

People would always disappoint me. I would disappoint myself at times.

It was the way of life.

"Okay," I said.

"You will *never* make sense to me."

I laughed, and he continued. "But I'm okay with that. In fact, I think it's part of the unique Amie Martin draw."

I shook my head. "Apparently you're a glutton for punishment." If me running away with a starving artist didn't deter August, what would?

236

"Maybe. But I think I'm finally ready to let you go."

"You—you are?" A pitch of disappointment churned my stomach.

"You're like a beautiful bird. And it kills me to think I'm the one trying to put a cage around you."

"What?" I was the one who'd run away. From Orchard House, from my family, from myself even. I hadn't been running away from—my thoughts stalled, for they weren't entirely true. I had been running away, at least in part, from August. And he saw that. And he was letting me go.

Not because he wanted to, but because he loved me.

I blinked back the wetness gathering in the corners of my eyes. "Thank you, August. I—I just need some time."

"I know." He leaned forward and kissed me on the forehead. His lips didn't linger, though I pressed myself into their warmth, wanting him to draw his arms around me, wanting to feel his security and love.

But then he was gone, walking back toward his truck.

"Aren't you going to stay?"

He shook his head. "I told Pops I'd sneak him in some steak tonight. Can't disappoint the old man."

We bid goodbye and I waved as August's truck rolled back down the drive. I glimpsed his dirty blond hair in the sideview mirror, intense affection warming my heart.

He had grown up since we dated. He was proving he knew what real love was by letting me go, by sticking with his grandfather in the difficulties of sickness, by stepping in to handle business matters for Tripp.

Whether we ended up together or not, August would be okay. More than okay.

And that, at least, made my heart happy in a small way.

❧ 36 ❧

August had never seen the old guy quite so happy. Though Grandpop hadn't wanted a big to-do about his coming home from rehab, August had at least ensured Pops had his favorite meal—beef stroganoff with sourdough bread.

Aunt Pris had joined them and she'd raised an eyebrow when she tasted the beef stroganoff. "Who in the world cooked this?"

August tried to suppress the heat in his face. It tasted okay, didn't it? "I know it's not like anything Mrs. Martin cooks, but I tried to follow the recipe—"

Grandpop and Aunt Pris's eyes widened. Aunt Pris stabbed her fork through the air. "Young man, this is the best stroganoff I've ever tasted." She looked to Pops. "Isn't it, Ed?"

Pops nodded. "I can honestly say I've n—never tasted anything b-better." Grandpop's words were slow, but he'd progressed by leaps and bounds in the last two weeks.

August smiled at his grandfather, joy erupting in his chest. Not just over the fact that his grandfather approved of the meal, but that he was home and regaining his health daily, that he was marrying the woman of his dreams the next day.

After they finished dinner, August stood and stretched. "I'm going to take care of the dishes, but if you need help getting to bed, Grandpop, let me know."

"Oh, I think I'll m-manage on my own. B-besides, Priscilla can help me."

August wagged his finger at the elderly couple. "Now, now, marriage vows are tomorrow. No hanky-panky tonight."

Pops drew himself straighter, a bit of his old self in the action. "I'm an eighty-five-year-old m-man. If I want a little hanky-panky the night before my w-wedding, then it's none of your concern, young man."

Aunt Pris's hands flew to her face. "Ed!" She shook her head, turned to August. "Rest assured, there will be no—no, hanky anything."

August chuckled as he cleared the plates, leaving the room as Aunt Pris scolded his grandfather. With the private home help they'd been able to arrange, hopefully Grandpop and Aunt Pris would truly get to enjoy one another's company for however long God saw fit to give.

August filled the sink with soap and stared off at the waning sunlight out the kitchen window. As always, he thought of Amie, of their last conversation the day she'd returned to Camden. Whenever he prayed about his relationship with her, the Lord impressed the notion of patience, of waiting on His timing.

In a culture that prided itself on two-day shipping, store-to-door groceries, and constant cell phone connection, patience was not a commodity abundant in anyone in America, much less himself. But the Lord was teaching him. Slowly, sometimes painfully.

Amie had agreed to help out as secretary at Colton Contractors, but only until Tripp could find a replacement. Seeing her every day again was like medicine for August's heart. The awkwardness had gone and he looked forward to their shared smiles and mindless chatter around the coffee pot. He'd spent a lot of time in the book of Psalms lately, filled with wisdom about waiting in the difficult, about leaning into God for courage.

And that's what August planned to do. If the end result was not as he hoped, he planned to cling to God's plan and wisdom all the more.

THE WEDDING WAS SIMPLE, WITH ONLY PASTOR MARK, AND HIS wife, the Coltons, and the Martins in attendance. Mr. Colton didn't want a big fuss and initially didn't even want an official ceremony, but considering Aunt Pris had spent half of her first wedding—in which she hadn't wished to marry the groom— helping her sister birth our dad, my great-aunt insisted that a backyard wedding at the Colton Estate and simple midday meal would be appropriate.

"A wedding can't pass by with nary a nod, no matter how old the bride and groom," she insisted.

I tended to agree.

There was no long walk up the aisle for Aunt Pris; instead, Mr. Colton and Aunt Pris stood side-by-side, holding hands as Pastor Mark led them through simple vows. After that, we all ate a catered meal on the back patio, the scents of hydrangeas mixing with the faint scent of the sea.

When we neared the end of the meal, I caught August slipping inside the house. Aunt Pris rose and held her hand out to Mr. Colton, who cocked his head at her.

"Don't I at least get a dance, my love?" she asked.

Mr. Colton rose with little effort. "I've b-been waiting for this dance all my life."

I blinked back tears as they held one another, their hands entwined like vines that had been growing together for years. When notes from the piano in the house began playing through the open window, I blocked out everything except for their melody.

Earth Angel.

The only reason I recognized it was from the many times I watched *Back to the Future* during my teenage years. But the way Mr. Colton appeared choked up, I could tell the song meant something to the older couple.

But who was playing? I scanned the crowd, noting everyone was present except for August. Had he hired someone to play the old piano in the dining room for his grandfather?

As the notes wound down, Mr. Colton leaned close and kissed Aunt Pris's cheek. A blush stained her skin. I supposed there was a first time for everything. I shook my head as August emerged from the back door. Mr. Colton waved him over, wrapping his stronger arm around him and squeezing.

I watched the exchange, trying to decipher the embrace all the more when Tripp joined the twosome. Mr. Colton gestured to August, and Tripp called out, "Give it up for my little brother, who takes after our dad more than any of us knew."

August gave a small bow, his grin nothing less than cheeky.

Wait. *August* had played the piano?

After Mom cut the cake, I amused myself watching Amos eat his piece in huge fistfuls. In a whirl of energy and blue maxi dress, Josie carried two large pieces of cake over to me. "Come with me," she said, handing me a plate.

I scrunched my eyebrows.

"Where are we going?"

"Our old hiding spot."

Slipping off my sandals, I hid a giggle and ran across the grass of the side yard with Josie toward the forsythia bushes that bordered the Colton home. The home we'd grown up in sat on the other side.

I turned my body to see if anyone from the wedding celebration saw us. But no one seemed to pay any attention as we crawled into the thick green bushes that turned the color of lemons in the spring. Both the Martin and the Colton children had burrowed in their depths at one time or another.

Josie let out a mild curse as she crawled in.

"What's the matter?"

"I used to be a lot smaller, that's what's the matter."

I giggled. "If you get in, I'll let you have my piece of cake."

She grunted. "No way. You're eating every sugary, gluteny, creamy dairy bit of that piece, and you're enjoying it. We're celebrating today, after all."

I ducked behind the bushes, sitting cross-legged in the pine needles and dirt. My dress would be ruined, but for once, I didn't care.

Josie had sought me out to share this moment and this place with her. She could have asked Lizzie, or even Maggie or Bronson, but for some reason, she'd chosen me.

Just beyond the bushes, I glimpsed our old house.

"It looks different," I said quietly.

"No, it doesn't. It looks exactly the same."

I studied the old paint, the back door we'd clambered in and out of a thousand times.

"Maybe you're right." I shifted to remove a stick from where it poked my backside. "Or maybe it looks different to me because we're not there anymore."

Josie considered this. "I think I get that." She continued studying it from her crunched position. "Yes, actually, you're right. It *does* look different."

Wow. Josie admitting I was right. This should be a celebratory occasion.

We were more alike than I tended to admit.

She elbowed me. "Dig in."

I glanced at the chocolate cake, moist and topped with sweet cream frosting. But Mom made the cake—so not too sweet. I dug my fork into the triangle edge of the slice and slipped it into my mouth.

I groaned. "That is so good," I said, already going for another bite.

"Right?"

I gobbled up the rest of the cake with gusto, and when Josie and I finished, she took our plates and put them off to the side.

"How are you?" she asked.

I studied our old home through the delicate green leaves of the forsythia. "I'm good."

"I mean, are you happy to be home?"

I swallowed, wanting to answer honestly. "I am."

We were both quiet for several long moments before Josie spoke. "You know, for so long I couldn't wait to get out of Camden, live in the city. It wasn't until I came home that I realized how much I missed it."

I put my palms on the soft ground behind me and straightened my back. "I do know what you mean, but I was only gone for four days. And I didn't come home pregnant."

"You don't think you did, anyway."

I glared at my older sister. "I *know* I didn't. Good grief, why does everyone think I had to have slept with the guy?"

Josie shrugged. "I figured if you loved him enough to run away with him, you'd have slept with him, I guess."

"I didn't love him. I loved the idea of a glamorous life as an artist."

Josie smiled. "Can I tell you something?"

"You're going to anyway."

She elbowed me again. "So, you know how I always wanted to be a crazy successful writer?"

"Yeah."

"Well, now that I'm there—you know, now that I kind of made it, I'm not quite sure why I always wanted the crazy successful part. Like, just being a writer should have been enough all along."

"But the crazy successful part helps you pay the bills, doesn't it?"

Josie cracked a smile. "I suppose. But it also means I have to keep up with TikTok and Instagram and sending out newsletters. And don't even get me started on book touring. It was fun to meet readers, but it was also the most single draining experience of my life—and I've gone through labor *twice*."

"So, you're saying I should keep art as my fun thing."

She shook her head, her chestnut ponytail swishing back and forth. "I'm not telling you what you need to do at all. I'm only saying, if you're chasing after validation—like I was—then it's never going to be enough. You know what I've found is enough?"

"What?" I whispered.

"The people I love. Not just Tripp and the boys, but my siblings, my friends. All those beautiful people right out there on that lawn. I'm not saying it'll be the same for you, all I'm saying is don't doubt our love, Amie. Because we *love* you. No matter how many wacko diets you try or how many times you bug me about painting my toenails or how often you lecture us on the dangers of plastic, we love you just as you are, and no matter what. *I* love you, Amie."

A tear slid down my cheek. "Thank you. That means a lot to me right now." What's more, I could tell Josie meant every word.

"Can I just ask one question?"

"Yes, I will give you a pedicure."

She smirked, pinching my arm. "What's with you and August?"

I groaned. "Who knows? I don't understand men at all. If I want to get married, I'll probably to have to marry myself. It's a thing, you know. Sologamy. It's growing in popularity."

Josie gave me a look of pure disgust. "I hope you're joking."

I cracked a smile. "About actually marrying myself? Yes. About it being a thing? No."

Josie rolled her eyes. "I told you I'd love you no matter what, and I mean it. Even if you force me to help you plan a sologimous —is that the word?—wedding. Doesn't mean I won't think you're crazy though." She tugged me out of the bushes. "Come on, my boobs are telling me it's feeding time."

"Did anyone ever tell you that you have such a motherly way with your words?" I grabbed my plate, crawling out of the forsythias behind her.

She slowed and placed her arm around me. "Anytime you need to hear more of my motherly wisdom, I'm here. I appreciate adult conversation these days more than you know."

I smiled, squeezed her waist. "I think I'll actually take you up on that offer."

❧ 37 ❧

After the caterers had cleared out and we'd put chairs and tables away, most of my siblings had left for home. I stayed to help Mom clean up the food. Mr. Colton and Aunt Pris sat in rockers on the front porch, and I thought it the sweetest thing in the whole world to see them holding hands and rocking in a synchronized fashion.

Mom and I were heading out the door to the front porch when heavy footsteps sounded on the stairs behind us.

"Oh, hey, August." Mom shifted the plastic Hannaford bag from one hand to the other. Her cake-cutting utensils clinked inside. "You did a lovely job on the piano today."

His gaze dropped to the carpet, color tinting his cheeks. He was absolutely adorable. "Thanks."

I turned to Mom. "You go ahead, Mom. I'm going to make sure Aunt Pris is settled."

Mom's gaze flicked from me to August. "You have a ride home?"

"I can take her home, Mrs. Martin," August volunteered.

She smiled at the two of us. "Okay. See you kids later."

246

She left through the front door, stopping to talk to Mr. Colton and Aunt Pris.

"It was a good day," I said, turning to August.

"It was."

I pointed at the duffel bag in his hands. "Going somewhere?" It was so strange to know nothing of his plans. He'd been completely professional at the office, smiling and conversing only casually. And even though it's what I asked for, what I thought I even wanted, my heart clenched with want whenever in his presence.

August dropped the bag onto the floor. "Just Tripp and Josie's. Figured I'd give the honeymooners some privacy on their wedding night."

I smiled. "That's considerate of you."

"Yeah, well . . ." He kicked the duffel bag toward the door.

"I didn't know you played piano so well."

"Pops made us take lessons when we were kids. My dad played. I think he wanted us to follow in his footsteps."

"But you didn't."

"Tripp was hopeless at anything musical. I—I just couldn't hold up under the expectation of bringing my father's memory back into my grandfather's life."

"Oh, August," I whispered. I had no idea. Had we ever talked of his parents' death? While I'd spoken often of how Dad's death affected me, had I ever asked August about how his parents' deaths had affected him?

"When I was thinking of a wedding present for Pops and Aunt Pris, the idea of playing came to me. I got it tuned, asked Aunt Pris for a song recommendation, and practiced my heart out while Grandpop was at rehab."

"You sounded beautiful." And here I hadn't thought August had an artistic bone in his body. But I was wrong, once again. Even his career—architecture—required intense creativity. Why had I never acknowledged it?

"Thanks."

"Can you play anything else?"

His humility turned over in a cocky grin. "Can. I. Play. Anything. Else?" he drawled, moving to the piano in the back of the house. "What do you want to hear?"

I laughed as I followed him, trying to hide how impressed I was by tossing my hair over my shoulder. "I don't know. Something. . . classy."

August lifted the piano cover and took a seat at the long bench, raising one eyebrow. "There's enough room for two."

"I think I'll appreciate the show from here." I didn't know if I could trust myself around him. Didn't know if I wanted to be close to him yet. Besides, I was looking forward to observing the entirety of August playing—something I couldn't do if I sat beside him.

He made a show of stretching his arms and his fingers, pulling them over his head and rolling his neck. He shot a dashing grin at me and I crossed my arms, shaking my head.

And then, he started to play. I recognized the tune instantly and a warm heat rose up from the floor to my middle. "Hallelujah." August played with confidence, his fingers roaming over the keys, coaxing life to them, stirring gorgeous, beautiful notes into the air. Notes that my mind sang the words to. Words that I didn't believe August had chosen by accident but with extreme intentionality.

And then, he began to sing. His voice would probably never make it on a reality show, but it was beautiful, carrying the melody, putting strong words to the gentle notes, drawing me to him all the more. I studied his strong back and shoulders, sunlight from the window illuminating his fingers over the ivory keys, his concentration both evident and respectful, as if he refused to give his father's old piano anything but his best.

As if he refused to give me anything but his best.

My insides melted as the music continued, August studying

me as he sang about nothing being on his tongue but hallelujah, and without warning, tears pricked the corners of my eyes. The notes, the words, they all conjured up images of shattered love being mourned, of true love finding victory, of faith being clung to in the midst of it all.

Was it the music, was it everything I'd gone through while leaving Camden with Luke, was it my history with August, or was it simply that I no longer wanted to deny that this man, despite our past—or maybe even because of it—had undeniably wheedled his way into my heart by proving over and over again that he loved me. That he wasn't going anywhere, even when I showed him the worst parts of myself.

As the song wound down, August played the last of the few gentle notes while turning to me.

"Do you have any other requests?"

Was he kidding? I'd be an absolute puddle on the floor if he played anything else. I shook my head, took tentative steps toward him, and lowered myself beside him.

"I'm sorry I never asked you about your parents when we were dating. You know, you were right about me being selfish. I was. I'm—I'm trying to be better."

His fingers dropped into his lap, the room growing silent. "I never wanted to talk about them much."

"You were young. So young. I'm so sorry, August."

He swallowed, his back straight. "I don't remember much about them, honestly. A few things—my mom making cinnamon rolls for Christmas morning, my dad playing this piano."

"What did he play?"

"A lot of things, but I remember Lennon's 'Imagine' the most. That, and Beethoven's 'Moonlight Sonata.'"

"He didn't play light."

A soft smile curved August's mouth. "He didn't live light. Not that we didn't have fun, but I think he inherited my grandfather's serious side." His smile fell. "I hate to think about losing Grandpop."

I slid my hand into August's warm one and squeezed. "Your grandfather is making an amazing recovery, in true Colton fashion. And now that he has Aunt Pris to keep him on his toes full-time, I don't think anything will stop him."

August laughed softly. "I think your aunt may be his best medicine. He started rapidly improving after she proposed."

"You've been good medicine for him too, August. You've done so much these last few weeks—not only for your grandfather, but for the business, for Tripp. For me. In some ways, I hardly recognize you from a year ago."

"Maybe I'm finally growing up," he whispered, looking at me with such hope in his eyes, I couldn't breathe.

His gaze dropped to my mouth, but I knew he wouldn't close the distance. He'd promised to give me time. If one of us were going to bridge this gap between us, it would have to be me.

I hitched in a breath, and my gaze tangled with the deep blue of his own. In it, I saw all of him—the grieving little boy who'd lost his parents, the feisty adolescent who refused to play the piano, the teenager chasing after me at dances, the college freshman who'd lost his way with gambling and girls, the redeemed grandson who earned a rightful place in the family business, and now, the honorable man who poured everything he had into taking care of his ailing grandfather and helping run Colton Contractors, not to mention pursuing a girl who didn't deserve his attentions.

In that second, I saw his whole story. I saw *August*. And I loved him.

Dipping my head closer, August's hushed words feathered my cheek. "You're making it mighty hard for me to keep my distance."

Without another thought, I closed the space between us, and an intense tingling pinged around my insides the moment his lips touched mine. We sank deeper into each other, and I couldn't think straight. A seismic tidal wave washed over us and through us, sweeping away all sense of time and place. Nothing else mattered. Nothing mattered but me and August and the connection we shared in this kiss.

An audible clearing of a throat behind us startled us apart.

"My dear P-Pris. It seems these two are having more fun on our honeymoon than w-we are."

We both stood. I attempted to hide an embarrassed blush.

"Sorry, Pops. I was trying to get out of your hair, but Amie begged me to play for her."

I rolled my eyes.

"M-must have been some p-playing." Mr. Colton's kind gray eyes twinkled beneath his bushy beard.

"It was." I broke away from August's side to give my great-aunt a peck on the cheek. "Do you need anything, Aunt Pris?"

"I think I have everything I need."

"I'll bring Cragen over tomorrow?"

She nodded. "Thank you, dear."

I hugged Mr. Colton. "Congratulations, you two. It was a lovely day." I stood back, taking them both in. "Your story is a beautiful one. That you have gone through so much and still . . ."

Aunt Pris gave me a knowing look. "Sometimes the best stories are the ones with struggle in them. Ed and I have had our share, but I'm so grateful we're together now."

"D-don't wait as long as we did to get your happy ending, though," Mr. Colton piped up.

Aunt Pris playfully slapped Mr. Colton's arm. "Oh, leave them alone, Ed."

We bid them goodbye and headed for August's truck. While I hoped he'd ask me to accompany him to Josie's to play with the boys, or at least take a walk or a drive, he drove me straight home.

Once in the driveway of Orchard House, he gave me an almost bashful smile. "I'll see you on Monday?"

Monday. For work.

I opened my mouth to tell him I didn't want to wait an entire day to see him again. That I didn't want to find ourselves being awkward in the office, that I didn't regret what had happened on that piano bench. But I couldn't force my mouth open because what if August *did* regret it? Was it fair of me to demand his attentions now that I thought I was ready?

So instead, I gave him a small smile. "Thanks for the ride, August. I enjoyed hearing you play."

And then I left. More thoroughly confused than ever before.

Thanks for the ride, August. I enjoyed hearing you play.

Amie's words echoed in August's head as he drove out of the driveway of Orchard House and toward Tripp's home. Why hadn't he said more? Why hadn't he stopped her, kissed her again, asked her to come to Tripp's to hang out with him longer, asked her to be with him for the rest of his life?

But no, they'd already walked that route, and it hadn't gone well.

But man, that kiss. That kiss was enough to leave him speechless in Amie Martin's presence for the rest of his life. It was enough to tie his tongue in knots as much as it had done his heart. In it, he felt how badly Amie wanted him—maybe even needed him.

So, why had he hesitated?

He shook his head. No sense trying to fool himself, he knew exactly why.

He pulled into Tripp's driveway and gazed at the beautiful landscaping, the porch decorated with potted flowers and a spring wreath—courtesy of Lizzie, he'd been told. All of it symbolizing the happiness of the family within. Not always perfectly happy, of course, not kept from the cares of the outside world, but joyful. Because no matter what, they had one another.

"You going to come in, or are you redesigning my house in your head?" Tripp's voice sounded to the left of him, and August snapped out of his reverie.

"Sorry. I was thinking."

Tripp nodded. "Boys just went down for a nap, so Josie might kill us if we go inside and wake them up. You up for a walk?"

August pushed open the door of his truck. "You bet."

They headed to the woods in the back of the yard. Tripp had started a path through it all, eager to give his family a way to experience the peace of the forest in their own back yard.

"You think Pops is okay?"

"With Aunt Pris? Never better. The nurse is coming tomorrow morning after church, along with the physical therapist. But who knows? Marrying the girl of his dreams might be a quicker way to health than any therapy."

Tripp chuckled. "You got that right."

They walked in silence for several long minutes, their steps synchronized, a chorus of birds singing around them.

August scratched his cheek. "Can I ask you a question?"

"Shoot."

"How did you get past Josie . . ." He cleared his throat. This might be harder than he thought.

"Josie . . ." Tripp prodded.

"Josie sleeping with another guy?"

A knowing look came over Tripp's face and he breathed long and deep, then stopped walking. "You're bothered about Amie running away with Luke."

August kicked the toe of his sneaker against a rock that protruded up from the ground. "Yeah, I'm bothered. I mean, I offered her all I had and she ran away with a guy she barely knew. Now . . ."

He remembered that fiery kiss on the piano bench. He

wanted to trust it, wanted to sink deep into all it seemed Amie offered him, but the truth was, on the tail end of that kiss came another thought. Luke's lips on Amie's. Luke close to her in all the ways August had once been. And she'd let him. Now that it hadn't worked out, had she decided to settle?

The thought twisted painfully in his chest.

Tripp started walking again, and August followed. "Our situations aren't exactly alike. I had never dated Josie before she and Finn were together. She came home pregnant."

"But you'd loved her forever." Just like he had loved Amie. How would it have been possible for him to grow up next to the Martins and not fall in love with that lively, golden-haired fairy?

Tripp nodded. "I didn't always handle it great, either, if you remember. When Josie told me she was pregnant, I near flipped my lid. I remember torturing myself, imagining her with Finn over and over again. Remember when he turned up and proposed?"

"Boy, do I ever. You laid him out flat."

"I was stupid and hotheaded. And angry about what I couldn't control. There were much better ways to go about it."

August mulled over his brother's words. "You think that's what's bothering me? That I can't control what Amie did?" Maybe so. If he could control the youngest Martin, he would have made sure she fell in love with him from the get-go.

Tripp shrugged. "I have no idea what's bothering you, but I do know that real love—like how God loves us—can't be forced. Free will is what makes love such an amazing thing."

August let that sink in. His brother was right. As usual. "I kissed Amie today. Well, she kissed me, I guess."

"You don't sound thrilled."

"It was great—what I wanted for so long. And then I went and ruined it by thinking about her and Luke together. It made me doubt . . ."

"Made you doubt . . .?" Tripp rolled his hand, prodding August to finish the sentence.

"Her motive for kissing me, I guess. Like, am I just the safe answer for her? And how can I get past her and that artist together?"

Tripp nodded, contemplating. "It's not easy, that's for sure. But as far as we can tell, Luke is out of her life. What you have to do is forgive Amie, and, if you want any sort of relationship with her, choose to trust her."

August clamped his lips shut. "I can't be the settle-guy."

"The what?"

"You know, the guy she's settling for."

"Right. You're worth more than settling for, little brother. Even with that hair of yours."

August gave his brother a hard punch on the shoulder. He was forever joshing August about the attention he gave his hair.

"You need to talk to her."

"I know."

In many ways, he'd gone after Amie like a lovesick puppy his entire life. Part of him thought he was crazy to even question that kiss, to question Amie at all.

But in the end, he wasn't willing to settle for being second best. To simply be the guy she could depend on to be there when all else failed.

And what would God want for him?

He'd read enough of the Bible to believe that God often advised people against what they desired because He wanted to give them something better. Even though sometimes, that something better wasn't at all what they wanted.

Maybe a happy ending with Amie wasn't what God wanted for him. And although the thought tore at him something awful, maybe he'd simply have to man up and face it.

❧ 39 ❧

The morning after Aunt Pris and Mr. Colton's backyard wedding, the morning after August's kiss that had upended my entire world, I walked into Abundant Life Church with my arms crossed over my chest and my head down, doubting every step but not giving myself the option to turn back.

It was an old church, boasting a square steeple with a simple meeting house attached. I hoped I'd find Kyra soon. I was in one of the hard wooden pews in the very back of the sanctuary by the time I realized that everyone, except for me, boasted dark skin.

I blanched, likely making me the whitest white person who had ever entered this building. My heart beat fast, demanding to be let out from behind my ribcage. I glanced around, my gaze skittish, as I contemplated how to tactfully leave.

I'd never been the most obvious minority in a room, and though I thought it wouldn't matter to me, it did. Is this how so many felt in white neighborhoods every day? And yet, I'd always said it didn't matter. Here though, I wondered if I would make the parishioners uncomfortable by being here. My ancestors had enslaved the ancestors of the people in this room. How could I even begin to show them respect? Perhaps I didn't belong in this place, intruding, making myself at home.

I quietly cleared my throat and, clutching my purse, turned to leave. But I ran into a soft body, and when Kyra set eyes on me, she squealed. "Sugar, you came! I'm so glad you came!"

Her welcome near toppled me into the pew the next row up. I gave her a tentative smile. "Hi, Kyra."

She turned around to usher a heavyset man with soulful brown eyes toward me. "This is my Joe."

He held out his hand and I took it. "Nice to meet you."

Kyra placed a hand on Joe's arm. "Honey, this is the girl I met in the hospital chapel, the one that was praying for you."

Joe's eyes lit up. "Oh! You're the girl. Well, I thank you mightily for praying for me. I'm still this side of the earth, so I guess your prayers worked."

I smiled, wondered if I should take the credit Kyra gave me for my prayers. I mean, sure, I prayed for him in the chapel, and maybe one time after, but I doubted I was the result of any healing from God.

"How's your grandfather?" Kyra asked.

"Much better. Thank you so much."

"I guess we both have lots to be thankful for then, don't we? Now, would you like to sit up front with us or would you like us to sit back here with you?"

I appreciated that she took it as a given that we would sit together. Still . . . "I—um, are you sure it's okay that I'm here?"

"What? Of course, it's okay. You prayed my Joe back to health —anyone who prays for my Joe is a friend of this church, that's what I say. Don't care if you're whiter than chalk, all are welcome here."

I bit my lip. "Okay, if you're sure, but I think I'll stay back here. Don't feel like you have to stay with me, though. I can catch up after."

She *tsked*. "Don't be silly, sugar. There's enough room in this pew for all of us." She pushed her way in, sitting on my right, Joe on her other side.

There was a lot of chatter in the church, and when a familiar-looking couple smiled at me as they sat in the pew directly in front of us, I did a double-take. The young man named Marcus pointed at me, jumping up and down. "Me!" he shouted.

"Hi, Marcus. It's so good to see you," I said as the woman in the pew guided an elderly lady beside her.

Miss Esther. I knew she went to church in this town, but I hadn't made the connection. I smiled at her, feeling almost at home simply by acknowledging her presence. When we first moved into Orchard House, Miss Esther had been a fixture by Aunt Pris's side. As her dementia grew worse, she came around less and less. Even now, it saddened me that her smile was hazy, that she clearly couldn't remember who I was.

"Me!" Marcus said again. He'd called me this when I taught him art at Bronson's Orchard Camp last summer. I was surprised he remembered me.

"Miss Amie," Mrs. Davis gave me a warm hug. "What a lovely surprise to see you here. Marcus hasn't stopped talking about art camp since we started him last month. Thank you so much for the suggestion."

I wasn't sure I'd be able to find an art camp that accommodated kids with special needs, but when I had, I'd made certain to pass the information along to Marcus's mother. "I'm so glad he likes it."

"He loves it." She dug out her phone and scrolled. "Here's his latest. I mean, can you believe my son drew that?"

I looked over her shoulder at the black-and-white sketch of Miss Esther. I shook my head. "That is seriously amazing, Mrs. Davis. Marcus is gifted."

And he was.

"Well, you encouraged us so much last year. Thank you for that."

At the altar, a man in a multi-colored shirt banged lightly on a goblet-shaped drum. The congregation quieted and another man in a black suit walked up to the pulpit, calling for the start of the service. He made some announcements, including the gathering of small groups, an opportunity to give and work with the Black Church Food Security Network, and a new study concerning the environment called, "Celebrating and caring for God's creation."

Aside from Sunday School as a girl, I've never attended a Bible study, but I felt a tug in my spirit at the mention of these projects —things dear to my own heart that I didn't often see people talking about in the church I grew up in. But here were people practicing faith in God through social justice, through environmental studies, and, judging from the man in a colorful shirt preparing to play a drum, with the creative arts.

The man began worship with his drum. No words, just the haunting bass of the drum, reminiscent of African music. That was followed by some old spiritual hymns with plenty of clapping and enthusiasm, and even some jazz music. Then a woman in a beautiful headdress came to the pulpit. She read from the book of Luke.

"To some who were confident of their own righteousness and looked down on everyone else, Jesus told this parable."

I listened to the short parable about two men at the temple, one a Pharisee and one a tax collector. The Pharisee thanked God that he was good—not like robbers and adulterers or even like the tax collector beside him. But the tax collector didn't even look up to heaven. All he said was, "God, have mercy on me, a sinner."

The lady finished the story with Jesus's words. "I tell you that this man, rather than the other, went home justified before God. For all those who exalt themselves will be humbled, and those who humble themselves will be exalted."

The man in the black suit stood as the woman in the headdress sat in one of the chairs behind him. I settled in, finding my mind more open to listening to the sermon than usual. Was it the different vibe and culture that surrounded me, or was it my experience as the prodigal this past week?

As the man spoke of God's heart for the humble sinner, of his faithfulness to those who didn't have their lives together, an overwhelming sense of wonder filled me. It was like my eyes were opened to Jesus for the first time in my life. In this moment, I didn't just glimpse the ugliness of my shortcomings and sin, I glimpsed God's beauty. A beauty that blotted out all of my ugliness.

As the congregation gave enthusiastic amens, I knew the man's eager words were meant for everyone—and yet I felt them directed like an arrow straight at me.

I could see myself in both the judgmental Pharisee, always thinking I knew better than those around me with my strong opinions and beliefs on everything under the sun, and I could see myself in the repentant tax collector—beaten down by life and my own decisions these past couple of weeks. Seeking a place of healing, a God who would dare grant me mercy.

The man in the suit continued. "Remorse can turn to two things—guilt or repentance. While guilt pushes us away from God, repentance draws us to Him. My brothers and sisters, come to Him, draw near to Him! He never misunderstands you. He will never disappoint you. He's always there, waiting for you to fall into His arms."

As he ended his sermon, he went into a passionate prayer, thanking God for his love, mercy, faithfulness, and saving power. The congregation responded with like passion.

The pastor continued. "If you're wondering when God is going to show up, if you're going through challenges but you don't have the Gamechanger in your life, if you don't have Jesus, the One who knows the beginning from the end, and the end from the beginning . . . if you're here today and you want a relationship, come on forward. It's not magical, you just have to ask him to be Lord of your life, to start a new journey to your Promised Land, to the place God has planned for you since before you were born."

The pastor kept talking, but his words faded into the background of my thoughts. In their place, I heard one all-consuming voice.

Come to me.

And suddenly, nothing in the world could stop me from stumbling my way up to that altar, to kneeling down and surrendering my all to a God who not only saw me and knew me but loved me the way I'd always longed to be loved.

❧

I WALKED OUT OF ABUNDANT LIFE FEELING LIKE A NEW woman. I stayed at the church for a long while, talking to the pastor, talking to Kyra and Joe. They all prayed for me and Kyra must have pronounced "Hallelujah, Jesus!" about a hundred times over me before I walked out the door.

I couldn't wait to talk to Mom. And all of my siblings. As I drove out of the church parking lot, a new fear clamped hold of my throat though. Would they write this off as another one of my passionate, but albeit temporary, endeavors? Worse, would how I felt now—like I would do anything and everything to show God how thankful I was for His grace—fade with time? Would I grow bored of Him as I grew bored of my spiritual group last year? As I grew bored of my lamp art?

I shook my head, refusing it to be so. No. I would attend Abundant Life every week. I would get involved. I would join their environmental study. I would get to know the other congregants. I would actually remember to pray for Joe and his diabetes. I would read my Bible. I would prove to God that He hadn't been wrong in showing me His love in that small church building.

I remembered August trying to share something similar that had happened to him the night he proposed to me in the book-

shop. I'd been so quick to write it all off. He'd been excited about
. . . what had he called it? An experience. Now—now I understood. Not that God had told me to propose to August or
anything, but I understood how amazing this feeling of grace was.

I wanted to tell August. Though I almost turned left toward
his house, I couldn't make myself spin the wheel. August had been
distant after our kiss the day before. What if he didn't want to see
me? What if he brushed off what had happened to me this
morning as I'd brushed off his experience?

God, guide me in all this. I'm so new. I know I'll stumble. Help me.

I jerked the wheel right and started for home.

Once parked in the driveway of Orchard House, I ran inside,
more grateful than ever to see Mom at her usual spot in the
kitchen.

"Mom!"

She startled and removed her yellow dish gloves. "What is it?
Is Aunt Pris okay? Is—"

I shook my head, enveloping her in a hard hug before pulling
back. "I—I gave my life to God today."

She blinked, mouth open, before giving a short gasp. "You—
you did?"

I nodded vigorously. "I went to Abundant Life Church this
morning—Miss Esther's church. Remember that card on my
nightstand? Well, it was the strangest thing, but I felt God calling
me, you know? And it's like I get it now. The Pharisee and the
humble tax collector? I'm both, you know? But I want to be
humble. I want to be close to God. I don't want guilt to get in the
way." I was rambling. Rambling, and I couldn't stop.

Mom laughed, shook her head, and squeezed my arms. "Amie,
my dear girl, slow down. This is great news."

"I've never known anything like this. I honestly don't know
what took me so long. But did you know that God actually loves
me? Like, even my crazy ideas and even though I screw up all the
time and—"

"I do know. Amie, I hope I never was an obstacle to you thinking God didn't love you—"

I shook my head emphatically. "No, Mom. I—it was like I had blinders on. I couldn't see, but now I do." I continued rambling, telling her all the things I planned to do now that I understood God's call on my life.

She smiled, shook her head. "Let's go sit, okay?"

She led me to the back patio where the shade of an elm just reached the spot where two chairs sat beside a sturdy table. She clasped my hand.

"Honey, I am thrilled, and I'm going to be praising God for the rest of my days."

I scrunched up my forehead. "Then why do I already feel a *but* coming on?"

She smiled. "I know how you tend to throw yourself behind what you're passionate about, and I can't wait to see what God's going to continue to do in your life." She grabbed for my hands. "But, it's tempting to be so grateful for what He's done that we forge ahead doing great things for God and leave Him behind. Remember, lean into His strength going forward. You don't have to *do* anything—He's already done the hardest work. Any good thing you do for God is simply a way to worship Him with your life, to show gratitude."

Worship with my life.

I liked the sound of that. And best of all, I didn't need to do it on my own.

Mom squeezed my hand. "Honey, you have so many talents and gifts. I'd hate to see you try to fit yourself inside some box of what you think it is to be a Christian. Listen to God, pray, seek His face. He'll tell you where you're meant to be and what He's calling you to do. And it will likely be as unique as you are."

My shoulders relaxed. "Thanks, Mom. That's just what I needed to hear."

She hugged me tight. "Faith is a journey. Please remember, no matter where life takes you, that you always belong—in our family, in this home, and most definitely in the arms of God."

I blinked away the wetness in my eyes. "Will you pray for me, Mom? I'm scared I'm going to mess this up or that God's going to leave me or that I'm still not going to know what to do with my life."

"Amie, I've been praying for you since the moment I found out you were coming into this world. And I'm not going to stop now." She slid her hand over the top of mine and bowed her head, words pouring from her mouth. Beautiful words. Words I'd likely heard her pray before but hadn't given them any mind. I sank into her prayer, peace stirring my spirit along with a sense that, though I may not know all the future held for me, God knew.

My future had always been in His hands, but for the first time, I was actually trusting Him with it.

40

After a breakfast of blueberry pancakes and church with Tripp's family, August drove back to his house. Grandpop and Aunt Pris's house. Not for the first time, he wondered if he should make plans to move out. Then again, with both Pops and Amie's aunt getting along in years, it might be handy to have a young, able-bodied guy around.

Amie hadn't been in church. But he would not let the day go by without making a point to talk to her. About the kiss. About his doubts. About the role faith was beginning to play in his life. About everything.

No more beating around the bush. No more hiding. From here on out, he'd be open about all of it.

He'd just pulled into Grandpop's driveway when his cell rang. His heart skipped a few beats when he saw Amie's name flash on his screen. He put his truck in park before answering.

"Hey, Amie. I was just thinking about you."

"You were?" Just hearing her voice soothed the raw corners of his heart. They'd figure this out. Tripp was right—they simply needed to talk.

He lowered his voice. "Yes. I was thinking about yesterday and —how I really think we should talk. Are you available today?"

"Yes. Actually, that's why I called. I have something I want to tell you."

Why did his pulse speed up at her words, as if anticipating something bad? As if he suffered some sort of PTSD when it came to Amie. Good things, followed by bad. Was that to be the way for them forever?

"Okay, great." He forced surety into his voice. "I just got home. I need to check in with Pops but then I'm all yours."

He wondered if his words made her blush. He hoped so.

"Do you want to meet somewhere?" she asked.

"Sure. Name the place."

"How about Curtis Island Overlook?"

The place of their first date. Well, not first date. First date after he'd returned to Camden at the very beginning of the summer. "Perfect. Can you give me an hour?"

"Absolutely," she said. "See you then."

"Amie?"

"Hmm?"

"I'm really glad you called."

He could only hope and pray they could talk things out this one last time.

They hung up and August grabbed his duffle bag from the passenger seat. He and Tripp had stayed up late the night before around an outdoor fire, talking about everything and anything under the sun. Remembering bits and pieces the other had forgotten about their parents, reminiscing about Pops in their growing up years, reliving school antics, and their time in the Martin home.

When the fire had died down, August had stared into the glowing embers. "Thank you, Tripp."

"For what?"

"For everything. For being hard on me sometimes, for caring about me when no one else did or when Pops was too busy trying to figure out how to raise two boys. I'm not sure I ever thanked you."

Tripp didn't get sentimental often, but there was no doubt his brother choked back emotion. "For a long time when we were young, it felt like you were all I had. August, you've been with me the longest, and I'm so glad we're not only brothers, but friends. You rock, little bro, and in case I haven't told you lately, I'm proud of you."

August had given his brother a bear hug. "You're not so bad yourself," he joked.

Now, August headed toward the house, but again his phone rang out. He glanced at the screen.

Liam Jeffries.

August's blood ran cold, uncertain whether to answer. It had been a good two years since he'd spoken to Liam. Old college buddies, they'd spent more time in the casinos than classrooms. And while he didn't share any hard feelings toward Liam, neither did he want to make a habit of spending time with him.

Not that he needed to be rude.

In one decided motion, August swiped right on his phone and raised it to his ear. "Liam, hey."

"Colton! How's it going, buddy? Where you been, anyway? I miss seeing you around the tables."

August released a nervous laugh. "Yeah, trying to stay away from those, actually."

"You? You're kidding me, right? Tell me you're kidding." Though it was barely noon on a Sunday morning, it sounded as if Liam was two sheets to the wind. August remembered the time in his life when he would have been right beside his friend.

He chose to ignore Liam's question. "Get any sleep last night, Liam?"

"Me? Naw, well, a couple hours maybe, if you want to call what me and Shanaya did sleeping."

Shanaya? Didn't ring a bell.

"So, what's up?" August asked. He really didn't have time for a trip down memory lane or to hear how wonderful the slot machines and roulette wheel had treated Liam. He had to check on Grandpop, make sure the scheduled nurse had come that morning, see if Aunt Pris needed anything. Then, his meeting with Amie.

"I'm over at Hollywood Casino. Hit it big last night, real big. You should have been there. The house had nothing on me. Blackjack, if you can believe it."

August couldn't summon up one word of congratulations for his friend. What was he supposed to say? It wasn't as if he believed all gambling morally wrong, but he refused to get sucked back into it. Liam's biggest win three years ago matched two months of honest work at Colton Contractors for August. Too bad he'd lost it all the next day in the same casino.

August cleared his throat. "Liam, I'm in the middle of something. Did you call for a reason?"

"Oh, man. Sorry, August. What have you been up to?"

"I'm back living with my grandfather, working the business."

"In Camden? Thought you said you'd do anything to get away from that sinkhole."

Yup. He had said that at one time. Even thought he'd meant it. Crazy what some time could do to a person's perspective.

"It's not so bad," August said.

"Man. Well, hopefully you're staying away from that girl who drove you crazy at least. Ali, Andrea . . . what was her name?"

"Amie."

"Amie, that's it. That one had you whipped. Couldn't even have fun with the boys when you were trying to impress her."

"Is there something you needed, Liam?" August repeated through gritted teeth.

"Yeah, yeah, sorry, man. Was wondering if you wanted to come down and have some fun today. Looking for a partner. I've been hitting the poker tables big time, just need a little oomph."

Oomph. Money.

Warning flags went off in August's head.

"No," he said.

"Colton, this is a sure thing. I'm on this crazy streak, man."

Is this what August used to sound like?

"I'm not interested. All the best, Liam."

He was about to hang up when his friend changed his tone. "I'm sorry, man. I shouldn't have asked. I know you're trying to keep your nose clean. I just thought—"

"You thought wrong. Really, I have to go."

August heard Liam swallow thickly over the line. An uncharacteristic gesture for his friend, as far as he could remember.

"August, wait."

August didn't hang up, but neither did he invite Liam to continue.

"I'm in trouble."

There it was. "What kind of trouble?"

"I was winning last night big time. But . . . I ended up losing it all. All of it, August."

"I'm sorry, Liam." And he was. He remembered the desperation behind the unpredictable games, the highs of winning, the lows of losing it all. And then, the desperation at the very bottom of that low. Desperation to steal from your own grandfather, or, in Liam's case, to call a friend he hadn't spoken to in years.

"I just need a little bit to get me through. I know I can get back up. This is my weekend, and poker's my game."

"I'm not giving you any money, Liam. I've worked hard for what I've earned, my grandfather even forgave me the money I took from him. I'm staying miles away from any casino—I can't afford it." Literally and figuratively. Though he thought he'd conquered his temptation, he wasn't stupid enough to put it to the test. "What about Shanaya?"

"She—she left me last night."

"After you lost."

"Yeah, after I lost."

August dragged in a deep sigh, lowered himself to the porch steps, placing his duffel bag on the step beside him. "Aren't you tired of it all yet, man? Sure, winning's fun, but you've been at this for what—three years? What do you have to show for it? A big fat goose egg. Dude, it's all the proof you need that you got to stop."

Silence. Then, "I've tried to get out, but I keep coming back. How'd you do it, man?"

"I was tired of losing." At the tables, at life, at earning his grandfather and Tripp's approval. "I'd had enough. When you've had enough, you'll walk away, too."

Liam inhaled a quivering breath. "I think I've had enough."

"Good."

"Hey, can I ask another favor?"

"You can ask," August said warily.

"Can you give me a ride back to my folks' house? Mom's in New York City with the sister."

Liam's dad had died his senior year of high school, leaving him in a house full of women. But instead of stepping it up, he'd hid his grief in the throes of gambling. Not that August could fault him for it—only by the grace of God had he conquered his own addiction.

But had he conquered it? Was driving to Hollywood Casino to pick up Liam a wise way to ensure he stayed clean? And the casino was more than an hour away. The same casino where he'd wasted his grandfather's twenty thousand dollars. Not to mention driving Liam to his own home west of Bangor and then driving back. So much for his day with Amie.

"I can't, Liam. I'm sorry, I have plans."

"August—please. I have no one else. I'll be sleeping on the street tonight if I can't get a ride."

August groaned, and Liam must have sensed his weakening, for he continued. "I'm going to get help. Maybe you can give me some pointers. A couple months ago I looked into Gamblers Anonymous. Is that something you ever tried?"

His friend was serious, then. What kind of a person would he be to walk away from Liam now, when he was asking for help, when he was willing to try to turn his life around?

Did August deserve the grace his grandfather had shown him? The grace God had shown him? No. Well, this was his opportunity to spread a little help and love to a guy who very much needed it.

He exhaled. "I can be there in a couple hours. I'll call you."

"Man, you're the best. I owe you big time."

"Just get some help."

"Will do, my friend." He said it as if it were the easiest thing since rolling out Play-Doh in kindergarten. He prayed Liam would be able to see the journey through.

They hung up, and before August stood to go inside, he scrolled down to Amie's number.

"Hey," she said, her tone low and sultry.

His insides twisted with want. "Hey, yourself." He cleared his throat. "Listen, something came up. Believe me when I tell you this is the last thing I want to do, but a friend's in a bind. He just called me, and I have to go give him a hand."

"Oh. Okay. Anything I can do to help?"

He could ask her to go for the ride with him, but he could imagine how well that might go over. *Want to ride with me to the casino, Amie, while we talk about our past, present, and future?*

Not going to happen.

"I'm sorry, Amie. There was nothing more I wanted to do than see you today."

"I'm bringing Cragen over to your house later. Maybe you'll be back by then?"

"I hope so. Can I call you?"

"Sure. I hope your friend's okay."

"He will be."

They hung up and August hung his head, praying for Liam, for himself, and for the talk he wouldn't have with Amie as soon as he liked.

41

By the time August pulled into the parking lot of Hollywood Casino, his head throbbed. Unless he counted his cup of coffee that morning, he hadn't eaten anything all day. He'd driven without stopping, eager to get the good deed done and be home. Maybe he'd be back in time to throw a few hamburgers on the grill. Amie could come over. They could play Canasta or Mexican Train or some other old person game with Grandpop and Aunt Pris. The physical therapist said games were good for Grandpop, that they'd help both motor skills and language.

August put his truck in park and searched the recent calls for Liam's number. He dialed. It rang several times before going to voice mail. He hung up, dialed again. This time, a breathless Liam came on the phone.

"Auggie!"

August stifled a rebuke at the hated nickname. "I'm here, Liam."

Loud voices, none distinguishable, and then the unmistakable sound of slot machines. Call him crazy for thinking Liam might wait outside for him.

"Man, just give me a minute." He lowered his voice. "I already got an ace in the hole, there's no losing."

"What? I thought you said you were out of money? Liam, get out of there now. I drove all this way."

"T-ten more minutes," his friend slurred.

August hung up, throwing his cell phone on the passenger's seat and just barely stifling a curse. What had he expected? To come riding in on a white horse to save his stupid friend in distress? He was not waiting another minute. He'd already wasted ninety minutes of his time, not to mention the gas it took to drive here and the headache he earned from the highway miles.

He put the truck in drive and pressed the gas a little too hard. But before he pulled out of the lot, he'd changed his mind. In a burst of fury, he hit his steering wheel and allowed his head to fall back on the headrest, silently cursing Liam up a blue streak.

Would he be able to walk through those doors and resist the tables and slot machines? With his anger toward Liam still stewing, he felt no urge to bet anything. He could go in, search out his friend, drag his sorry backside out of the casino and back home. And then, he'd wash his hands of the matter altogether. If Liam wanted to talk, fine. But this was the last time he was putting himself on the line for his old friend.

Grabbing his keys and phone, August pushed up his sleeves and walked with determined steps into the casino, the bright orange Hollywood sign above both familiar and haunting at once. He walked through the elaborate lobby, the tall ceilings and elegant woodwork and moldings a testament to the gobs of money the casino earned. He headed for the card room, not thinking twice about which direction it was. Muscle memory or something like that.

He walked into the room, hating himself for almost feeling at home. He inhaled the heady scents of musk and orange mixed with something like ginger and clove. It smelled of sophistication and possibilities. In Gambler's Anonymous, he'd read that casinos infuse their ventilation systems with highly aromatic, extremely expensive oils to create the experience they desired for their guests. After all, the scents of sweat, alcohol, cigarettes, and desperation were not exactly selling factors. They needed to hide that somehow.

August zeroed in on one of the poker tables and caught the back of his friend's dark head. He strode up to him, jabbed him on the shoulder. "Come on, time to go."

The other players raised their eyebrows at August.

Liam flicked him an annoyed glance. "I'm in the middle of a hand."

It was poor table etiquette to leave even if Liam had already folded, which he hadn't. August glanced at Liam's cards. A Royal Flush. Man, oh man.

His mouth grew dry as he folded his arms, studying his friend's cards and the generous mound of chips on the table. Liam was right. He *could* win big. For a split second, he wanted to plant his feet and cheer Liam on—maybe even get in on a game himself. But the very next second, reality swooped in. He remembered sitting by the fire, Tripp telling him he was proud of him. He remembered crying in a pathetic mound on the kitchen floor, Grandpop standing over him telling him his debt was paid. He thought of Amie, finding those scratch tickets in his glove box, the hurt in her eyes.

He remembered reading Grandpop's Bible, the words coming alive on the page.

He was not this man. Not anymore. And he refused to go backward—down a path of destruction.

And neither could he be responsible for Liam's choice, either. He tapped his friend again. "I can't be in here. I'm going back to the truck. Ten more minutes, and I'm gone, Liam. I mean it. Ten, and I split for good."

Liam's gaze connected with his. Good. His friend knew he

wasn't joking around. He nodded. "This hand, and I'm out of here."

"Okay." August turned and walked out of the card room, each determined step feeling like a final victory in the battle he fought against his gambling addiction. He sat in his truck and noted the time, ticking off each minute with a prayer for his friend. When ten minutes came and went, he sighed, starting his truck. He'd done what he could, but now that he finally held freedom over this thing, he refused to let his friend's chains bind him.

He drove toward the entrance of the parking lot, but not before he noticed a frantic waving in his rear-view mirror. He let out a short laugh, put on the brakes, and waited for Liam to open the passenger door.

"Had enough?" August asked.

Panting, Liam hopped up in the truck. "I'm not sure, but I'd like to find out."

August held his hand out to Liam, giving him a firm hand-shake. "I'd say you walking out of there is a great starting place."

⚶

I GIGGLED AS BRONSON'S FIANCÉ MORGAN SCRUNCHED HER EYES shut and spread her fingers in front of her face, as if about to witness a gory scene on a big movie screen. "No, no stop!" she said to Josie.

"I'm serious, you guys, I still can't get the vomit smell out of my car. Toddler vomit knows no limits. I've cleaned that thing from top to bottom, scrubbed between the cracks, steam-cleaned, air-freshened, driven on the highway at seventy-miles-per-hour with all the windows down for an hour, and I still smell it."

Maggie shook her head. "You clearly have no choice but to sell the car."

Josie's jaw dropped. "No way. We just finished the payments on that thing. I'm driving it into the ground."

"Puke scent and all?" I asked.

Josie shook her head, a dejected look on her face. "Puke scent and all."

I looked around the back patio at our impromptu girls' gathering. Mom had whipped up two batches of spinach and artichoke dip and we all dipped tortillas into the creamy dip. I'd told my sisters and my future sister-in-law about all that had happened that morning, and they'd hugged me, telling me they supported my decision to attend Abundant Life Church for the foreseeable future. Josie even said she'd like to visit sometime.

Now, I breathed in the scent of Mom's nearby roses, the summer air tinged with a hint of salty breeze off the harbor. A perfect day. If only I'd been able to see August.

"I think maybe you should travel with those vomit bags they carry in airplanes," I said to Josie. "Just in case."

The group laughed and Lizzie shifted in her seat. "Even though you are making having children sound horribly unappealing at the moment, I wanted to let you all know that Asher and I have decided to try to have a baby."

I squealed. Josie lunged at Lizzie, wrapping her arms around our sister. Maggie and Mom hugged each other. Beside me, Morgan squeezed my arm in excitement.

Lizzie held her hands up. "Don't get too excited just yet. We're assuming this is going to be a long road for us, that's why I'm telling you all now. I might need your support—scratch that, I *know* I'll need your support. I've done a lot of research, and while it's possible for Asher to have a baby, we'll likely need some outside help."

Maggie slid her hand over Lizzie's. "We're here for you, Lizzie. You have the best support system on the east coast sitting right in front of you."

Lizzie smiled, looking pretty with a small smattering of freckles the sun had brought out across her nose. "Thanks, guys."

Maggie looked out across the vibrant orchards. "Looks like

this family's growing a lot more than apples these days, huh Mom? Love, babies, faith—all the best things."

Mom smiled at Lizzie, then at me. "I'd say so."

I sat up in my chair. "Mom, did you decide when you're taking your vacation?"

Maggie snapped her fingers. "Good thinking, Amie. I almost forgot we're force-feeding her some time off."

Mom laughed. "Actually, I was talking to Charlotte just yesterday. There's an innkeeper's conference at the Mount Washington Resort in early November. I was thinking about cashing in my time then." She winked at me.

"What are the dates?" Josie asked, taking out her phone.

Mom rattled off the dates, while Josie started delegating tasks on the spot.

"Whoa there, I haven't even registered for the conference. I'll let you know by the end of summer, okay?"

I took out my phone to mark my calendar, just in case. Josie began citing the importance of time off, especially for a small business owner. A ding came from my phone and a notification popped up on my screen. A text from Lacy. Probably a yoga meme —we liked to find the funny ones and send them to each other a couple times a week.

I tapped into it. But it wasn't a meme. It was a picture. A crowded room with bright lights. A casino?

A text came in from Lacy again. *Thought you said your boy was done with gambling?*

My boy? I zoomed into the photo, disbelieving my eyes. August, arms folded in front of him, studying a card table. A card table at a casino.

A dizziness overtook me and I blinked, willing my eyes to see something different in the photo.

"Amie—you okay?" Maggie's voice came from far away, but I couldn't grab onto it, couldn't latch on and drag my gaze up to keep from drowning in that image.

Instead, I shook my head, as if shaking her off, and stumbled away from the patio and my family. I needed shelter, privacy. I walked around the barn and sought an apple tree a few rows into the orchards. I hid beneath its boughs and stared at my phone, hating the image.

It could be a mistake, right? Someone who looked like August who happened to be at Maine's biggest casino?

I enlarged the picture with my fingers, but there was no denying that the man studying the table was August. I tapped into Lacy's name and hit the button to call my friend.

The phone rang and rang. Finally, on the fifth ring, she answered. "Amie? One sec." The sound of people talking and slot machines ringing faded as she must have moved to another room.

A moment later, she came back on. "Hey."

"I can't believe it." I wasn't sure why I called Lacy. Because I wanted her to say something that would confirm this was all one big mistake?

"I came for the afternoon with Missy to play a few slot machines. When I saw him, I did a double-take. That's him, right? August?"

"Sure seems so," I squeaked out. "We were supposed to hang out this afternoon. He said he had to help a friend."

"He's helping someone, all right. I'm so sorry, Amie. I almost didn't send it, but I thought, with everything he's put you through, you had a right to know."

I swallowed. "Actually, I'm coming to realize he put up with way more than I ever did."

Lacy snorted. "You kidding? Well, looks like he's ready to give you some more trouble now."

"Thanks for sending it, Lacy." Was I truly thankful, though? Would a part of me rather not know? Rather continue a relationship with August with blinders on?

But no. Obviously August's struggle wasn't over. I sniffed back tears. It was better I knew. Could I help him? Show him the grace he showed me when he came to pick me up in Bar Harbor?

"You going to call him?" Lacy asked. "Or do you want me to set him straight for you right now?"

"No." I was done being the gambling police. I remembered August's comment about me being president of the litter brigade when we'd reunited in Hannaford's parking lot. I couldn't police his every move, neither did I want to. God had set me free today, not to condemn August, but to give me a new life.

"Thanks, Lacy. I better go. See you tomorrow?"

"Sure thing. I'll call you later, okay? I'll guide you through some deep breathing for this kind of stuff."

I pictured titles on my meditation app. *Relaxing Beach Guided Visualization. Stress Pause. Don't Strangle the Man You Love When He Revisits an Old Addiction Meditation.*

"Thanks, Lacy."

We hung up, but I couldn't stop staring at the picture of August, couldn't reconcile it to who I thought he was, who I thought he was becoming.

But what ended up driving me to my knees wasn't disappointment for myself, it was genuine concern for the man I loved.

I sank to the grass. *God, you've given me so much today. Give me the grace to help August through this. Even if it hurts. Even if we can't be together. Give him freedom, Lord, and help me love him through this. Help me love him like you love me.*

42

When he was about twenty minutes away from Camden, August called Amie. Maybe she hadn't eaten dinner yet. Maybe they could get some takeout and visit the Overlook. Or maybe, if Grandpop and Aunt Pris hadn't made dinner plans, he could still put those burgers on the grill.

He'd seen Liam home. The two had a good talk on the car ride, and although Liam hadn't made any solid commitments to stay away from gambling, he seemed to be willing to give it a try, seemed encouraged by August's story.

For that reason alone, August didn't regret going to pick up his friend, even though he would have much rather spent the afternoon with Amie.

"Hello?" He sank into the sound of Amie's voice, excitement thrumming in his veins. This was it. Their real beginning. He felt it in his blood.

"Hey, sorry I took so long. You still up for some dinner?"

"Can we talk first?"

"Okay. I can come pick you up."

"I'm actually already out. Can we meet at the Overlook in

about twenty minutes?"

"Sure."

Instead of stopping at home, August drove straight to the secluded spot. He parked on Bay View Street behind Amie's jeep and made his way along the short path to the bench.

A cool breeze came off the harbor, sweeping away what could have been uncomfortable heat. Ahead, like a symbol of home, stood the Curtis Island Lighthouse and its Keeper's House. The light shone, readying for dusk.

And there, sitting on the bench, was his golden-haired girl. He'd loved her since they were kids, counted himself beyond blessed to have a second chance with her now—or was it a third chance? He'd lost count.

He came behind her, squeezed her shoulders, leaned close to her ear. "Hey." He released her shoulders and came around to sit beside her on the bench a healthy space away. "I'm sorry about this afternoon. My friend Liam needed some help."

She paused. "Were you able to help him?"

"I think so."

"That's good." She sucked in a long breath, her chest rising and falling beneath her t-shirt. "Something happened to me this morning, something huge. I went to this new church and I asked for forgiveness, August. I gave my life to God."

His insides did a happy jig. "That's awesome, Amie. I've been praying we'd find faith together." He was still so new to it all himself. How in line with God's grace to allow him and Amie to discover this path together. "I'll come to this other church with you, if you want. Anything—"

"Please, let me finish."

Why was she so sad? This was *great* news. If anything could have cemented the beginning of a beautiful relationship, wasn't it a shared faith?

"Okay . . ."

"God's forgiven me a lot. I realize that now. And I don't have a right to hold judgment over you after receiving such grace, but August, I can't have a relationship with you built on anything but honesty."

He scrunched his forehead. "I completely agree. Amie, I want that for us, too."

Her hands dropped to her lap and she stared at the pine needles and worn grass at her feet. "This isn't easy."

He grasped her hands. "You're talking in circles. I know it won't be easy. I admit, I'm still struggling with you running away with Luke. Thinking about you and him together—it sends my blood steaming. But I'm willing to move forward, to forgive our pasts if you are. I—"

"I wanted to move forward too," she whispered.

"Then let's do it." He squeezed her warm fingers.

"Lacy was at the casino today."

Slowly, realization dawned on him. Lacy had seen him at the casino. She'd told Amie and now Amie thought . . .

He shook his head. "Amie, no. You remember my friend from college, Liam?"

"Your gambling buddy. Yeah, I remember him."

"He called me this afternoon, begged me to pick him up. Of course, I doubted the wisdom of it, but I saw myself in him, you know? I wanted to help. I wasn't gambling."

She bit her lip. "Lacy sent me a picture. You were at a card table. August, I care for you, and I can see how hard you've been trying to stay away from gambling. I—I want to help. Go with you to a meeting or counseling or maybe you call me when you feel like going to a casino or buying a scratch ticket . . ."

Was he hearing right? Amie thought he was gambling and she was offering to *help* him?

Warmth bloomed in his chest for the woman before him whom he already loved, who he suddenly found himself loving even more.

But he needed to set things straight. "Amie, I'm clean. I

swear it. Liam wouldn't come out of the casino, so I went in to get him. I admit, I was scared of being sucked back in, and for a half-second, I considered it. But I walked away, Amie. From the card tables, from the slot machines, from all of it. I told Liam he had a decision to make and I went to wait in my truck."

જ⁂ૹ

AUGUST'S WORDS SWIRLED AROUND ME, SENDING OUT SHOOTS of beautiful possibility. Was I understanding right?

"I wasn't in there long enough to even buy tokens, Amie. Please, trust me on this."

It made sense. "I want to believe you . . ."

He scooped up my hands again. "Then do, because I am telling the complete and honest truth."

"What happened with Liam?" I asked.

"I thought he was staying in the casino. I started driving out of the parking lot before he came out. He plans on getting help, and I want to support him how I can. I told him I won't be dragging him out of casinos every weekend, but I'd go to his first Gambler's Anonymous meeting with him."

I had a decision to make: trust August and risk him hurting my heart again if I was wrong. Or give up the thought of "us" and do what was best for him—as a friend.

But something deep inside told me he was telling the truth.

August tapped into his phone. "I'm calling Liam. He'll tell you exactly what happened, play-by-play. He'll—"

I placed my hands on August's fingers. "Don't."

He stilled, glanced up at me. "Don't? But how will you—"

"I believe you," I whispered.

"You do?" Hope lit his eyes, making them bluer than the ocean before us.

I nodded. "Sometimes, believing is more like a knowing,

maybe even without proof. It's faith. I—I have faith in you, August."

His eyes shone. "Thank you." He bit his lip. "But even when you thought I fell back into it all . . . you were going to try and help me?"

My throat threatened to close. "Because I love you," I whispered.

And then his arms were around me, drawing me in with their warmth and security. "Amie, I love you so much. I will do everything I can to make sure I never hurt you again."

"You will hurt me, and I'll probably hurt you, but then we'll forgive and we'll seek grace. Together. I'm sorry I ran away with Luke. I want you to know we didn't—I mean, we did sleep in the same bed and I kissed him, but it never went further than that. I couldn't."

August studied me, those alarming blue eyes soaking me in. "Wow." He ran his tongue over his lips, closed his eyes. "I am so, so thankful to hear that. I mean, I was ready to show you grace, but wow. Amie, I want to show you love and grace for the rest of my days if you'll let me."

"Yes," I breathed, my heart nearly bursting with the promise in his eyes, the knowing in my spirit that I could trust him to make good on his word.

Slowly, he lowered his mouth to mine, pulling me into his arms soft and slow, and then more urgent, drinking me in. And I couldn't imagine anything in the world more wonderful than being in his arms.

This time, for good.

43

Five Months Later

"Make sure it's covered!" I yelled from my spot in the dining room as I worked to hide the corner of the canvas with my body. Around me, my siblings and their significant others, along with their kids and Aunt Pris and a robust-looking Mr. Colton, surrounded the canvas.

August squeezed my hand and leaned over to whisper in my ear. "Stop being so nervous. She's going to love it."

I gave him a quick peck on the cheek, my heart erupting in gratitude for this man, for this family, for all the blessings God had given me. Not to mention the beautiful diamond solitaire that made its home quite comfortably on my ring finger. I couldn't wait to marry August Colton in the spring.

"She's coming!" Davey yelled, hurrying to place his small body in front of the canvas along with the others.

A moment later, Mom bustled through the door, suitcase in hand.

"Welcome home!" we called in somewhat disjointed fashion.

Mom's jaw dropped. "Well, what in the world is all this?"

Josie grinned, bouncing little Eddie on her shoulder. "Just a big ol' Martin family greeting."

Maggie stepped forward. "Mom, we hope you had a great time off, but we are so glad you're back. Seriously, we have no clue how you do it all."

"And I for one miss your food!" Bronson said, earning him an elbow from Morgan. He wrapped his arm around her, and my brother and I shared a smile. Bronson and Morgan would be married New Year's Eve. Right after their wedding, I'd be deep in the planning of my own.

Mom laughed. "Well, I missed you all."

"How was the conference?" Lizzie asked. She looked a little pale today. The hormones she was taking for her and Asher's IVF treatments sometimes made her nauseous, but as always, she remained bright and positive.

"Restful and inspiring. I'm ready to dive back in. And it was great to catch up with Charlotte. Now, what are you all hiding?"

Tripp craned his neck at me. "What do you say, Amie? Can we unveil?"

I nodded and we parted, revealing the oversized canvas to my mother. I watched her carefully, not wanting to miss a second of her reaction.

She took it in, then placed a hand to her mouth, her face crumpling with emotion. "Oh my goodness, it's beautiful. Amie, it's perfect."

I hugged her and turned to study the painting with her. I considered it my best yet. Three months ago, we'd had a professional picture of all the kids and spouses and soon-to-be spouses and grandkids taken and for the last two months, I'd worked on painting it, adding my own unique take and style.

Now, my gaze roamed over Maggie and Josh, Davey, Isaac, and Grace, then Josie and Tripp, toddling Amos, little Eddie. Lizzie sitting in Asher's lap, his wheelchair almost completely hidden, Bronson and Morgan at the end near one of the apple trees, and on the other end, me and August. A snapshot in time. A picture that represented Mom and Dad's legacy.

"I'm going to hang it in the living room, of course. Amie, I had no idea you could do people so well. It's—it's masterful."

August elbowed me. "Working at the art camp is paying off, I guess."

I smiled. It was, though not so much in what I was getting as what I was giving. After spending more time at Abundant Life Church with August, I'd talked often with Marcus's mother about how well Marcus was doing at the art center. I'd been inspired to pay them a visit, and the director had hired me on the spot.

It wasn't an ordinary art camp. It was a nonprofit with a mission to provide education and community to those with autism and those who processed information differently. Their goal was inclusion, acceptance, and kindness, and they were open to all ideas when it came to art.

Art, like faith, had the power to heal. And slowly, I was beginning to accept my place in the world—a place I might not have expected, a place that didn't make me revered and well-known, but a place that was just as important as I strove to help others realize their true potential.

I'd never been happier.

As the family traveled to the living room to see how the picture would look positioned above the couch, August tugged my hand, holding me back in the kitchen. He kissed me soundly on the lips.

"I'm proud of you."

I didn't bother to hide my glow. How could I contain it when I had so much to be thankful for?

"And I'm proud of you."

In helping Liam, August had taken on a bigger role in Gambler's Anonymous. Not to mention stepping it up in the family business as his grandfather made the difficult decision to move back from the company in part-time retirement.

"What are you proud of me for?" he asked.

"For everything you do. But mostly, for keeping that cell phone out of your front pocket."

He nuzzled my neck. "No chance am I doing anything to ruin the chances of having babies with you, Amie Martin."

I giggled and snuggled deep into his arms, sighing with contentment. I couldn't wait to marry this man, couldn't wait to spend the rest of our lives creating love and family and a legacy that, if I were half as blessed, could be like the one Mom and Dad had built.

I leaned my head against his shoulder. "Thanks for always making me feel like I belong."

He squeezed me tight. "Amie, you will always belong in these arms. Forever and ever, for as long as God gives us."

Now that was something I could definitely place my faith in.

Read on for a glimpse of the final book in
The Orchard House Bed and Breakfast Series,
Where Promises Remain!

CHAPTER ONE

After running The Orchard House Bed and Breakfast for nearly four years, not much throws me off-kilter anymore.

Sure, there have been surprising—even challenging—moments. The time Aunt Pris's friend, Esther, tried to steal our antique dining room candlestick holders by hiding them in her pants during one of her bouts with dementia. The time the Duchess of Tonga demanded we bow upon entering a room in her presence, though we had our reasons to doubt her claim of royalty.

I could go on, but the point is, we've had our fair share of adventures. And now, with the last of my five children about to leave home for good, the adventures would be mine alone.

I swallowed down the thought, turning to my laptop screen. Then again, there was nothing like a new project to distract from self-pitying thoughts, and the email before me might be just the ticket to accomplish the task.

I got up from my seat at the kitchen bar and walked with hurried steps through the butler's pantry into the guest living quarters where my oldest daughter Maggie worked at the bed and breakfast's front desk.

"Maggie, did you see—" I stopped short. My daughter wasn't behind the desk, or anywhere in sight, for that matter. Rather, a burly man with a close-cropped beard and hair graying at the temples stood, finger hovering over the bell on the desk. He wore a button-down flannel shirt with the sleeves rolled up, revealing forearms covered in tattoos. I glimpsed the intricate ink of a compass and a rope on the arm closest to me.

I blinked. "I'm sorry. I thought my daughter was here. Welcome to Orchard House. Can I help you?"

He smiled, and it was a nice smile. A little worn and rugged around the edges, but warm and genuine, spreading all the way up to his eyes, which crinkled at the corners. He held his hand out to me. "Hello. My name's Kevin. Kevin Williams. I just moved in next door."

"Oh!" I placed my hand in his, the large warm fingers enveloping mine. "I'm Hannah. It's nice to meet you." The Perry home had sold only a few weeks ago. If I'd known our new neighbors were moving in so quickly, I would have planned to reach out —at least bring over a coffee cake. Then again, with Amie and August's wedding fast approaching, I'd been a bit out of sorts. Not at the top of my planning game.

He squeezed my hand and a flush worked over my body. Huh. Now *that* was new. Unless it was simply a hot flash. Those certainly were becoming more and more commonplace.

I released his hand. "How are you enjoying Camden?"

"Great town. I'm looking forward to the fishing."

"Be sure to try Penobscot River. It's famous for its landlocked salmon. The best I've ever had."

His eyebrows raised. "You a fisherwoman?"

I laughed. "Good grief, no. But I try to know a little bit about everything to help our guests find their adventures."

He nodded, stroking his beard thoughtfully. "A woman who knows a little bit about everything. I'll keep that in mind."

His gaze didn't leave me, and although I'd received my fair share of admiring glances from the opposite sex in my fifty-two years, this one served to rattle me in an altogether different way. Not an entirely unpleasant way. Was it my hormones or the fact that the last of my children was about to fly the nest? I'd never been alone—not in my entire life. For goodness sakes, even Aunt Pris had up and left Orchard House—the only home she'd ever known—last year when she married her longtime love and our old neighbor, Ed Colton.

And I was happy. Happy for Aunt Pris and for Amie. Happy that Maggie and Josie built families with the men they loved. Happy Lizzie had found Asher, that they were trying to have a baby with the help of IVF. Happy that my only son, Bronson, had also married the love of his life this past New Year's Eve.

Yes, my children were all finding their way. In love, in their careers, and in faith. Nothing could bring me more joy. Why then, did this impending dread fill me when I woke each morning? Why was I, a grown middle-aged woman, afraid of being on my own?

I blinked, breaking the connection, and walked behind the desk, shuffling papers in an attempt to hide my blush—ahem, hot flash. I glanced at his left hand. No ring. What was I doing? Why did it matter?

I cleared my throat. "It's wonderful to meet you, Kevin. If you ever need anything—a cup of sugar, restaurant recommendations, a book to borrow, please don't hesitate to call on us."

There. I was being neighborly, but I was also signaling the end of the conversation.

"Actually, I was hoping to talk to you about a shed I'm building."

"Okay . . ."

"I'm considering cutting down a tree to make room for it. An old elm. It shows signs of rot, but still has plenty of foliage. I wanted to ask your thoughts on it."

"My thoughts?" Was he concerned I'd think the shed ugly? A distasteful addition to the neighborhood?

"Well, I'm a tree-guy myself. Can't live without my trees. I tend to get attached to them, particularly if they've been around for a while. I didn't want to go cutting it down without your approval."

I squinted at him. "Is the tree on my property?" If so, why were we even having this conversation—the tree was not his to cut down. Then again, why would he plan to build a shed on our property? And if so, we had bigger problems to discuss.

"No, ma'am."

I shook my head, bristling at the "ma'am." "Hannah."

He nodded, smiled. His eyes were the color of pine trees in midwinter. "Hannah."

"I'm sorry, Kevin, but if the tree is on your property, I don't see as to how I have a say in the matter."

"Well, like I said, trees are a big deal in my estimation, and you can see this tree from your back patio, maybe even get a little shade from it in late summer. If you're attached to it . . ."

Oh. Well, that was considerate. I moved to place my hand on his arm, but stopped myself. "That is extremely thoughtful, but it's your tree. If you want to cut it down, you should. I promise not to take any offense whatsoever."

He shifted from one foot to the other. "I might sleep better tonight knowing you took a look at it with me."

This burly, tattoo-covered man would lose sleep over what a near stranger thought about him cutting down a tree on his own property? I was more concerned about the aesthetics of his shed.

I smiled and started toward the door. "Far be it from me to mess with a good night's sleep."

He chuckled, scooting ahead to hold the door open for me. We walked around the back of the Victorian, toward the book-shop and the back patio, side-by-side. Kevin gestured to the orchards. "Beautiful property."

"I never get sick of it. It was my late husband's great-aunt's. We renovated the home and moved in four years ago." Aunt Pris had gifted the home and property to me for Christmas last year. I still found myself choking up at the gesture. Yes, I knew she intended to hand it over to me in her will, but the fact she was willing to do so while she was still alive meant even more.

"Ed's home is my home now," Aunt Pris had told me. "The Orchard House is thriving under your caring touch, Hannah. I want you to have it in every sense of the word."

Kevin's voice broke into my remembrances. "And you run the orchard and the bed and breakfast?"

"My son, Bronson, is in charge of the orchards. He and his wife run a summer camp here, too. They've done a wonderful job."

"Busy place, then."

"We are, but we try not to bother the neighbors." I gave him a sidelong glance.

"No bother on my end. I love kids."

We strode past my herb gardens, the faint scent of basil reaching my nostrils. That reminded me, I needed to make pesto for the pasta tonight. Bronson wouldn't eat pasta without . . . too late, I caught myself.

Bronson wouldn't be coming to dinner. Neither would any of my other children. Even Amie, the last of my children still living at home, would likely be off with August planning last-minute wedding details.

It was fine, of course. More than fine. I had the entire bunch over every Saturday night for dinner, and I was grateful for that blessing. Grateful I was able to still live close to my five children.

I shook my head, focusing on the man beside me. "How many do you have? Kids, I mean?"

He raked a hand through his hair. "No kids, unfortunately. My wife had some medical issues in her teens that prevented her from having children. It was the one thing she regretted not being able to give me, but if I could do everything all over again, I wouldn't change a thing."

We came to the edge of the property and stopped walking, the ancient stone wall before us, ragged and fallen from years of New England weather. I loved the character and imperfection of it, how each stone told a chapter in the story of the stone wall. "You lost her?"

He nodded. "Six years back, to cancer."

I couldn't deny the sudden kinship I felt to this near stranger. I'd never gone to a grief support group, but perhaps I could have benefited from one. "I'm sorry."

"I'm sorry about your husband."

"Thank you." I still missed Amos, the way his passion for life kept him immersed in new projects, the way he would come out of his study with an open book to discuss a new theory or thought with me, the tender way he treated each of our children—teaching them to love deeply, to think wisely, to be curious about everything under the sun.

Strange how five years had, in some ways, flown by without him. Though I'd give anything for one more day with my husband, time had eased the sting of his absence. I'd grown a business, watched each of our children find their way. And while I still sometimes shed tears at night when I found the other side of the bed cold and empty, I also could honestly say Amos would be pleased with how I'd led our family these last five years. How the trials, in a miraculous way, had grown my own faith.

Kevin pointed to the tree growing up from his side of the property about three feet from the stone wall. Tall and stately, it reached long arms over the wall and into Orchard House property, sending shade into a generous portion of our yard.

"It is beautiful," I said. "But Bronson complains every autumn about the leaves he has to rake up. You said there's signs of rot?"

He pointed to a hanging branch about halfway up. "Lots of missing leaves. Also, the bark is gray in spots instead of brown and it's splitting from the main part of the tree." He pointed again. "See there?"

I nodded. "If it falls, it could do some damage."

"Normally, I'm not one for cutting down trees at the first sign of a little rot, but you're right—it could hit your patio and your house the way it's leaning. Not to mention, this seems to be the best place for my woodshed."

I turned to him. "I heartily agree. I hope you can sleep better knowing we've discussed this."

He grinned, his green eyes sparkling. "Thanks, Hannah. It was nice to meet you."

"You too. And if you need a tree guy, I can ask my son-in-law for a recommendation. He's in the construction business and knows some good people."

"That's mighty thoughtful, but there's no need. I'm the tree guy."

"Oh. Well, be careful." I shook my head. "Sorry, mother of five kids speaking here. I'm sure you're always careful."

"I am."

I waved, turning to go. "See you around, then."

"I might be low on sugar soon. Could come knocking."

I smiled before another hot flash could be seen on my face. It had been a while, but was he . . . flirting with me? More so, how did I feel about that? While I'd grown used to rebuffing the advances of Stuart Stanley, the unsavory owner of Stanley Construction, who made it a habit to race up to me when I passed his home on my walks, I wasn't used to welcoming a flirtation.

If that's what this even was. Had Amos and I ever even flirted? He'd been so sincere and direct with his affection, I couldn't remember any flirting. Huh. Too bad. Maybe we'd missed out.

As I ducked back into the Orchard House, this time through our back living quarters, I tamped down the need to call my best friend Charlotte, and instead focused my attentions on the email I received.

An email that had the potential to bring new life—and profits—to The Orchard House Bed and Breakfast. The attempt would at least keep me busy—so busy I wouldn't have time to dwell on the fact that very soon, I would be completely and utterly on my own.

CHAPTER TWO

Kevin watched his new neighbor walk toward the big Victorian home, half kicking himself for flirting so easily with her. He didn't want her to think less of him. Truth be told, he didn't make a habit of flirting with women, or even dating, since his Katherine died.

He sighed, looking down the hill through a small grove of pines and maples and out toward Camden harbor. His wife would have loved this place. They'd talked about retiring here one day. Once he sold the logging business, once she felt ready to retire from teaching.

But God had other plans for them. Plans Kevin couldn't quite get on board with, even after six long years.

He peered up at the elm, looking forward to getting back in a tree. It'd been too long. But not anymore. He was ready to take it easy. Fish, climb all the trees he wanted, take some hikes, check out that little church down the hill, maybe do some camping . . . who knows, maybe he would end up borrowing some sugar from his pretty new neighbor.

His phone rang and he dug it out of his pocket, his heart speeding up at the sight of the Portland number. "Hello?"

"Mr. Williams? This is Rita Bridges."

He swallowed around the grapevine-sized knot in his throat. The social worker had only conducted the home inspection yesterday.

"Ms. Bridges. I didn't expect to hear from you so soon."

She cleared her throat and he could imagine the stout middle-aged woman adjusting her thick glasses with the gesture. "We've already conducted the home study and the background check. We only needed the inspection to complete your application."

One of the reasons he'd made a quick job of unpacking. He'd tidied the dickens out of his new home—a simple cape. He'd made up the guest bedroom to be as welcoming as possible. Considering he never had any kids, much less a teenager, he wasn't sure he had passed the social worker's sharp eye.

"I've just signed off on the last of the paperwork, Mr. Williams. I'd love to bring Owen by this afternoon if that works for you."

His chest felt like it had been struck by the force of a falling oak. "This afternoon?"

Ms. Bridges tone softened. "Owen's been here in our office. There's nowhere for him to go, as is often the case with teenagers. We've rushed your application, Mr. Williams. As I stated before, our hope is to reunite Owen with your sister, that this will be a temporary placement."

His sister. Deidra. His insides twisted. How had his little sister fallen so deep into drugs and prostitution? And how had he allowed their separation to go on for this long—so long that he hadn't even known a sixteen-year-old nephew existed until Ms. Bridges had tracked him down two months ago?

He released a long sigh. "Of course. I'll be home this afternoon. What time did you say you'd be by?"

"Three o'clock okay?"

"See you then." He hung up, shoving his phone deep in the

pocket of his loose-fitting jeans. He glanced up at the elm, imagined the woodshed he'd build in the future. But not today. Today, he needed to go to the market and stock up on food fitting for a growing teenage boy. Not that he knew exactly what that was—none of the many kinship or foster care books he'd read covered what to feed a sixteen-year-old boy. But he'd been one himself forty years ago. He'd figure it out, wouldn't he?

He gave one last glance over to the bed and breakfast, where his pretty neighbor lived and worked. He'd thought he would have some time to settle in before Owen's arrival. Cut down his tree, do some fishing, start his shed . . . he hadn't even had time to run out of sugar yet.

But all that would have to wait. As soon as he'd submitted the kinship care application, he'd vowed to make Owen a priority. In some ways, he credited God with the timing of it all. He'd just sold his business and, for the first time in his life, had spare time on his hands. Not that he'd planned to spend it taking care of his sister's son, but turning the boy away was an option he refused to entertain.

No matter how far Deidra had fallen, she was family. Somewhere in her troubled spirit was the little girl who he'd given piggyback rides to and sneaked extra marshmallows in her hot chocolate during Christmas. Maybe Owen was the key to finding his way back into her life.

Kevin opened the door to his new home and grabbed his car keys and wallet off the counter, deciding on grilling hamburgers that night. What kid didn't like hamburgers? He'd grab some chips and pickles and maybe some of those sugar cookies from the bakery. They'd eat outside on the picnic bench. Maybe they'd talk fishing. Or maybe Owen would want to help him build his shed.

As he drove to the market, Kevin's spirits lifted. Surely, this wouldn't be so bad. Yes, some people had a hard time of foster and kinship care, but his sister's kid would probably be a walk in the park, grateful to be out of the DCYF office and in a real home with his uncle. What else did a teenage boy need besides good food, a warm bed, and some honest work to keep him occupied and out of trouble?

❧

"Hey, Mom." Amie breezed in the back door of the Orchard House.

I looked up from where I loaded the last of the breakfast dishes into the dishwasher from that morning's meal service. Fruit, coffee cake, avocado toast with cashew cream, yogurt with my homemade granola, and our guests' choice of Strawberry Shortcake Pancakes or Lobster Eggs Benedict with Lemon-Herb Butter—my personal favorite—both served with crispy bacon. Though I wasn't one to boast, I took special pride in preparing the five-course breakfasts. The quaint location and the old Victorian, complete with author-themed guest rooms that included Louisa May Alcott, Henry David Thoreau, Emily Dickinson, Ralph Waldo Emerson, Nathaniel Hawthorne, and Robert Frost drew the first-timers, but my breakfast was what kept our regulars coming back. Not to mention the regular referrals we enjoyed. I couldn't imagine a more fulfilling job. Sure, it was sometimes exhausting, but that was a small price to pay for doing satisfying work.

"Hey, honey. You're home early."

Amie opened the fridge. A splatter of yellow paint marred her otherwise flawless cheek. She scrunched her nose. That's right— I'd bought the sparkling waters in the plastic again instead of the glass bottles. She hated that. She grabbed an orange. "Half day today. We have a class coming in for a field trip tomorrow, so I might have to stay later."

Amie worked at a nonprofit art camp that held a mission to provide community to those with autism and to their families. She thoroughly enjoyed the work and had started painting again on the side, selling several on consignment at the shops downtown. Josie, my second oldest daughter, had even mentioned we'd sold one of Amie's paintings in the gift shop yesterday.

Amie sat at the kitchen bar and peeled the orange over a napkin. "Just caught the new neighbor pulling into his driveway. He's kind of cute."

My head snapped up, seemingly of its own volition. "Is he now?"

She narrowed her eyes at me, the yellow paint on her cheek crinkling. "You've noticed!"

To my horror, my face heated yet again. Pretty sure this one wasn't a hot flash. Quickly, I averted my eyes to squirt dishwashing liquid into the soap compartment. Good grief. Was I a schoolgirl?

"He actually stopped by earlier in the day." My tone was breezy. Definitely breezy.

Amie wiggled in her seat. "And?"

"And nothing. He wanted to ask me about a tree that's close to our property line. He seems very nice."

"Married?"

I gave her the same look I used to give her when she asked me to buy more sculpting clay after I'd just bought some the day before. "Are you in the market for a new groom?"

She slapped her hand on the counter. "Ew, gross, Mom. He's, like . . . *old*. For me, anyway. I'm talking about for you."

I sighed. "Amie, if you think I'm chasing after our new neighbor—"

"Not chasing. More like, open to possibilities."

I crossed my arms at my waist and leaned against the counter. "Even if I were open to possibilities, I simply don't have time to date." I walked to the adjoining breakfast nook where my laptop sat and opened up the email I'd read earlier. I turned the computer toward my youngest daughter. "And look at this. You think Orchard House would stand a chance?"

Amie slid off the bar stool and bent to read the email. She flung her blonde hair over one shoulder, her ocean-blue eyes lighting up. "Camden's Hospitality Grant?" She kept reading. "Twenty thousand dollars? Mom, that would be great, and no one deserves it more than you, but what would you use it for?"

I bit my lip. "A few things. I need to update our booking engine. We should really be cloud-based. I'd also love to create some sort of loyalty program for our returning guests. I need new linens—bed and bath, which I plan to order regardless of the grant. I could use more help—with you moving out and Lizzie not feeling well so often with the IVF treatments, not to mention Bronson's trouble keeping up with the yardwork—I could benefit from hiring from the outside. Maybe even from Dad's mission."

Amos's mission was his legacy. I loved to support the men and women trying to get back on their feet however I could, paying them for doing odd jobs and yardwork as I was able. Perhaps it was time to establish more permanent positions.

"That all sounds great."

"And . . ." I hiked in a big breath, as I hadn't yet voiced my newest idea. "I want to add more guest rooms."

Amie's mouth fell open. "What? Where?"

"In the back of the barn. Bronson only uses part of it for the camp and we have more than enough room for our events. I'd like to create a carriage suite, something a bit bigger than we have upstairs. Perhaps transform the apartment above the bookshop into another suite as well. Guests who want a more private experience might really enjoy it, and two more rooms—suites—would create an incredible potential for profit."

"And a lot more work for you. More cleaning, more laundry,

more breakfasts." She narrowed her eyes at the running dishwasher. "More dishes."

"Hence hiring the outside help."

Amie tapped her perfectly polished nails on the table. "I don't know, it all sounds great, and you know me, I'm all for women-owned businesses and you're doing a kick-butt job, but don't you think you might want to slow down a little?"

I shut my laptop. "Amie, you make it sound like I have one foot in the grave. The Lord is not anywhere near done with me and I refuse to sit back and twiddle my thumbs just because all my kids are—are . . ." My bottom lip trembled. *Leaving*, is what I intended to say, but I couldn't push out the words.

Amie stood and wrapped her arms around me. "Mom, none of us are going far. And you know me—I can't cook for anything. You'll probably be so sick of me and August begging you for a decent dinner, you'll be wishing for some alone time."

I blinked away impending tears and forced a smile as she released me. "Don't you dare be planning to stop by out of pity. I'll be perfectly fine. And if I get this grant, I'll be busier than ever."

"That's just it. There's more to life than work. You and Dad are the ones who taught us that. All I'm saying is you could be open to certain"—she jerked her head in the direction of our neighbor's property—"possibilities."

"I'm open to possibilities, dear. I'm just not chasing them down."

She tapped her chin. "So, you're open to them, huh?"

"Amie Martin, don't you dare start meddling in the affairs of our neighbor."

She shrugged. "No worries. You know me, I'm always on my best behavior." She winked and flounced up the stairs to her bedroom.

I groaned. My youngest daughter had matured by leaps and bounds the last few years. Surely, she wouldn't be so bold as to approach our neighbor on my behalf. *That* would be downright humiliating.

I blew my hair out of my face and opened my laptop again, intending to begin the application for the grant. But as I downloaded the form and began filling out the lines, my thoughts kept snagging on the handsome face of a certain new neighbor and wondering how soon it might be before he ran out of sugar.

CHAPTER THREE

"What's a guy gotta do to get some chips around here?" My son Bronson craned his neck over the picnic table, where his sisters chatted with paper plates filled with hamburgers, hotdogs, and potato salad.

One of my favorite nights of the week was Saturday, when all of my kids and their families—including my biggest loves, the grandkids—came over for dinner. This being the first warm night of the year, we'd taken our get-together outside, my growing family spilling over from the back patio into the yard. Maggie and Josh's nine-year-old twins Davey and Isaac conducted a swordfight with sticks while Josie's three-year-old Amos looked on with wide eyes.

"Hold your horses, haven't you ever heard of ladies first?" Amie said, dumping a generous portion of potato chips onto her plate.

Bronson scoffed. "Ladies, huh?"

His wife Morgan elbowed him playfully. "Be nice, Bronson, or Amie might change her mind about you walking her down the aisle."

August, Amie's fiancé, shoved in, dumping a few chips onto

his own plate. "No risk of that happening, Bronson. She needs you." He thrust the chips at Bronson. "Take 'em while you can."

Bronson made a show of putting the chips under his arm like a football and squeezing through the press of bodies to his chair on the corner of the patio. Josie's husband, Tripp, caught the action. "That reminds me. We need some flag football around here. It's been too long."

Josie bounced eleven-month-old Eddie in her arms. "Only if we take turns handing off this one so I can play."

"I'll watch the grands after dinner so you can all get in on the fun," I said, taking a seat beside Aunt Pris and her husband Ed.

Amie shook her head. "Count me out. I refuse to walk up the aisle with broken bones if I can help it."

"I'll help Mom watch the kids." Lizzie moved her potato salad around with her fork and my stomach lurched as Asher squeezed her arm, mouthing, "Are you okay?" to her. She nodded and gave him a small smile.

I tried not to worry about my sweet, quiet daughter. She'd conquered thyroid cancer as a teen and had overcome a lot of anxiety as she matured, including conquering her stage fright. She and her husband Asher wrote and recorded songs, many that hit national top forty lists. But her latest struggle—trying to get pregnant—may be her toughest challenge yet. With Asher being paralyzed from the waist down, they knew they'd likely need help conceiving. But the hormones had been tough on Lizzie, as well as a failed attempt at one round. She seemed more fragile these days, and every morning and night I prayed that God would grant her a child of her own and strengthen her body and her spirit.

We ate with the usual loud, boisterous tumult that ruled our family gatherings. Josh and Tripp broke off into a serious conversation about the Red Sox's chance at the World Series that year, Amie and Maggie debated the necessity of a wedding guestbook, and the rest of us laughed at Josie admonishing Amos not to put Cheetos up his nose.

As dinner wound down, I began clearing the table. I'd just come out of the house a second time to grab the condiments from the outside table when I spotted my youngest child jogging lightly toward our property line. Amie waved her hand and shouted a greeting into . . . a tree?

Wait. The elm tree. I craned my neck, squinting at . . . yes, a man up in the tree, attached with some sort of harness.

"Hello, neighbor!" Amie was shouting. My family quieted at her greeting, even the kids.

Amie Martin, do not embarrass me, I scolded in my head as I remembered her words to me a few days ago. Was this her way of "opening me up to possibilities?"

"Hello," Kevin called back. It was hard to see, but was he grinning?

"My name's Amie. I think you met my mother the other day?"

He answered more quietly this time, and I pretended disinterest as I continued to clear the table. By the time I had gone in the house and back outside again, however, Amie was approaching the patio with a smug grin on her face. "Turns out he loves football." Amie shrugged.

I hid a smile and shook my head. Could I fault her for being neighborly?

A few minutes later Kevin came over, an obviously reluctant teenage boy at his side. Amie took the lead in introducing him to everyone, assuring him there wouldn't be a quiz on names later. When she got to me, she paused. "My beautiful and available mother, Hannah, but you've already met her, haven't you?"

"Amie," Maggie hissed.

I wanted to crawl under the table. But no. I was a mature, grown woman. I refused to allow my daughter to embarrass me. "Hello, Kevin. Wonderful to see you again. And who's this?" I looked at the boy, long dark hair falling in front of one eye, pale skin, and large circular holes in each of his ears.

Kevin put a hand on the boy's shoulder. I didn't miss how the teenager pulled away at the touch, nor how Kevin's mouth turned downward. "This is my nephew, Owen. He's staying with me for a bit."

"How lovely. Do you like football, Owen?"

He shook his head.

"Well, no pressure to play. I was just about to take out ice cream sandwiches if you'd like one."

The poor kid looked ten kinds of out of place. But he nodded. The group split into teams and I ducked inside to get the ice cream treats for the grandkids. Aunt Pris and Ed bid their good-byes. Amie, Lizzie, Owen, and I watched the group toss the foot-ball. To my surprise, Kevin kept up with Tripp and Josh, throwing an expert pass to Asher, who caught the ball in the makeshift endzone. A flutter of something foreign moved in my chest as I watched my neighbor reach out muscled, tattooed arms to punt the ball.

"Single, huh?" Lizzie asked.

"Yup." Amie hadn't lost her smug look.

I rolled my eyes just as a beat-up Honda pulled into the driveway and parked. Huh. All our guests for the night had already checked in and none of them drove a Honda. I asked for the make and model of our guests' vehicles upon checking-in, so I could keep an eye on whose room was empty and free to be cleaned. If a guest's car was in the drive, they were likely in their room and I tried not to bother them.

A skinny young woman in tight jeans and a midriff top spilled out of the car. She closed the door and straightened, smiling at the group of us. The football crowd had just called a break and was swigging waters and digging into ice cream sandwiches. Little Eddie whined in my arms and I stood, bouncing him as I started toward the young woman—a girl, really. Something about her looked familiar, but I couldn't place her. Had she stayed here before? Or maybe she was a friend of one of my children? But none of them were running up to greet her.

"Hello. Welcome to Orchard House." I smiled.

She pushed brown hair behind one ear. "Hello. I—I'm not sure I have the right place."

"Oh, that's not a problem. This is the Orchard House Bed and Breakfast. Were you looking for another inn? There's quite a few in this town."

"I'm not looking for an inn. I'm actually looking for a person."

"Perhaps I can help. It's a small town." Eddie whined again and I readjusted the pacifier in his mouth and bounced him a bit more.

"I'm looking for a man named Amos Martin."

I stilled, my mouth suddenly dry. Was this woman a former student, then? Or perhaps someone my late husband had counseled? I hated to be the one to tell her the news that he'd passed.

I bit my lip before answering. "I'm sorry, but Amos passed. Five years ago, actually. I'm so sorry."

The woman's mouth fell open. She blinked, shook her head. "No . . . no, he couldn't have . . ."

I led the woman to a nearby chair and Lizzie handed her a bottled water.

"I'm so sorry." I placed a hand on her thin shoulder. "He touched many lives. Were you a student of his?"

She looked up at me and piercing brown eyes stared back. All at once, I knew why they were so familiar. But no . . . that was impossible, of course. Amos didn't have a younger sister, especially not this young. Perhaps she was a distant cousin? I bounced Eddie and Josie came to my side, sliding him from my arms.

"How did you know Amos?" I lowered myself to the chair closest to the young woman.

"I didn't know him, actually, although I was hoping to. You see, Amos Martin is—was—my father."

ACKNOWLEDGMENTS

Thank you once again to my amazing editor Melissa Jagears for her wonderful insight and sharp eye. A huge thanks to critique partner Sandra Ardoin for her writing wisdom and listening ear. Thank you to Donna Anuszczyk, Erin Laramore and Priscilla Nix for their proofreading help! Any remaining mistakes are mine alone.

Thank you to Pastor Mike from Journey Christian Church for giving beautiful sermons and inspiring the sermon Amie hears at Abundant Life Church. Thank you to Flying Starlings Farm in Southeast Massachusetts for inspiring the idea for the art camp in this story.

Thank you to my ever-supportive family—my husband, Daniel, and my sons, James and Noah, who always cheer me on. Lastly, to the Author of life. You write the best stories. Thank you for allowing me the privilege to join in for a scene or two.

ABOUT THE AUTHOR

Heidi Chiavaroli (pronounced shev-uh-roli...sort of like *Chevrolet* and *ravioli* mushed together!) wrote her first story in third grade, titled *I'd Cross the Desert for Milk*. Years later, she revisited writing, using her two small boys' nap times to pursue what she thought at the time was a foolish dream.

Heidi's debut novel, *Freedom's Ring*, was a Carol Award winner and a Christy Award finalist, a *Romantic Times* Top Pick and a *Booklist* Top Ten Romance Debut. Her latest Carol Award-winning dual timeline novel, *The Orchard House*, is inspired by the lesser-known events in Louisa May Alcott's life and compelled her to create The Orchard House Bed and Breakfast series. Heidi makes her home in Massachusetts with her husband and two sons. Visit her online at heidichiavaroli.com

Made in the USA
Middletown, DE
24 January 2023

22737397R00194